# When I Was Yours

# SAMANTHA TOWLE

# OTHER CONTEMPORARY NOVELS
# BY SAMANTHA TOWLE

*Revved*
*Revived*

*Trouble*

## THE STORM SERIES

*The Mighty Storm*
*Wethering the Storm*
*Taming the Storm*

# PARANORMAL ROMANCES
# BY SAMANTHA TOWLE

*The Bringer*

## THE ALEXANDRA JONES SERIES

*First Bitten*
*Original Sin*

*Craig, you saved my ass on this one.*
*You are always saving my ass.*
*I honestly couldn't live without you.*
*I love you.*

# Adam
## BEVERLY HILLS · JULY 2015

The shower's running.

Not a good sign when you live alone. It can mean only one thing. I brought a hook-up back to the bungalow.

*Fuck.*

Fighting my eyes open against the morning light streaming into my bedroom, snapshot memories of last night begin to dance around my pounding head.

Max turned up at my office. Talked me into going out and drinking with him.

Shots. Way too many shots.

Then, two women came over to join us.

One was blonde, a natural, with long wavy hair. Petite body. She even had hazel eyes. Her face was pretty, not beautiful like Evie's but pretty enough. Because of that, I couldn't help myself. I had to have her. Not because she was hot—which, of course, she was—and not because I just wanted to get laid. No, it was none of those things.

I fucked the blonde because she looked exactly like Evie, my ex-wife.

*I can't believe I did it again. Jesus, I really am a sick fuck.*

Trust me, what I've done is like an alcoholic falling off the wagon.

I don't have a sex addiction—even though I do like sex *a lot.* No, I have an addiction to fucking women who look like my ex-wife.

Sick, right?

Well, I *had* an addiction, which apparently has kicked back into play.

*Fuck!*

I haven't pulled this crap in a really long time. Up until last night, for five years—barring a slip-up three years ago—I'd successfully avoided having sex with any women who reminded me of Evie.

*Three fucking years down the drain.*

I'd actually thought I was cured. Guess not.

For a long time, after Evie had left me, all I did was screw random Evies. All they had to be was petite with long blonde hair, and I would let my imagination do the rest.

According to my therapist, screwing Evie's look-alikes was my way of dealing with her abandoning me. Supposedly, I was trying to re-create the one time in my fucked-up life when I had felt truly happy—before it all went to shit.

Funny because, even though my life had sucked before Evie, ultimately, she was the sole reason it went down the path straight to hell.

I should've known from the moment I met her that, eventually, she'd be my downfall. I mean, I am Adam, and she's my fucking Eve. It had been written in the cards.

My therapist said I was mourning the loss of her, like she'd died or something. Maybe if she had, it would have been easier. At least I'd have known why she'd left me.

But no, all I got—after a year together and one week of marriage—was Evie disappearing without a word.

I mean, we had been fine, happy even. Or so I'd thought. I had gone out on my one-week-late bachelor party, kissing her good-bye before leaving, and when I got home, waiting on the coffee table for me were annulment papers with her signature on the dotted line, a note beside it saying, *Sorry*, and her wedding ring sitting on top of it.

And that was it.

I haven't seen or spoken to her since. That wasn't for my lack of trying. Of course, I repeatedly rang her cell. I left her panicked, then angry, and then just plain old desperate voice mails. And I kept calling until her mailbox was full.

A few days later, her number was disconnected.

Even then, I still refused to believe she'd just left me.

So, like the sad fuck I was, I tried to find her. I hired the best PI in California to look for her.

But after a few weeks of trying, he came up dry. It was like she'd fallen off the face of the planet.

I didn't want him to give up though. I offered him a shitload more money to keep trying, but he told me there was no point. He said the reason he couldn't find Evie was because she didn't want to be found.

And there it was. I had my answer.

She'd really left me.

She was gone, and I was never going to see her again.

Up until that point, I'd held things together with the hope that he'd find her, and I could bring her back home.

But that was never going to happen.

That was when I fell apart. I couldn't breathe, like I was suffocating from the pain. It was the worst kind of agony.

I just needed to forget—forget everything, forget *her*.

So, the first thing I did after leaving the PI's office was go and score some coke, which was easy enough to do in my world. I had used coke in the past, pre-Evie, for recreational use. That was the norm in my so-called privileged world.

I snorted that fucker on the spot, and a small sense of relief washed over me, but it wasn't anywhere near enough. I was looking for total oblivion. So, I took another hit, and then I left the dealer with an eight ball in my hand to get me through the rest of the night. Next up, I went to a bar, and I started drinking with the intention of never stopping until, at the very least, I was comatose.

Unfortunately, I woke up the next morning with that same agonizing, suffocating desolate feeling.

I just wanted death to come and fucking take me.

As I came around, my skull pounding from the drugs and alcohol, I discovered that I was in bed with an unfamiliar girl beside me. But as I looked at this girl's face, I realized she didn't look so unfamiliar. Actually, she looked a hell of a lot like Evie. They could have been sisters, given the right lighting. Then, the girl woke up while I was staring at her. She smiled as she put her hand on my cock, and I felt a strange sense of relief.

Without another thought, I fucked her again. And it was in those first few seconds of pushing my cock inside the nameless Evie look-alike that I didn't feel like I was going to die.

There was nothing. I was numb, free of the pain.

And that was when I realized that screwing someone who looked like Evie would free me from the pain more than coke ever would, not that it'd stop me from snorting it in tandem with sex. They just kind of went hand in hand.

But from that moment on, I'd search out that nothingness like a sniffer dog tracking drugs.

I never slept with the same girl twice. No, because in my fucked-up brain, it felt like a betrayal against the only woman I'd ever loved—you know, the one who had left me in this fucking mess.

So, screwing these women once was fine. Twice would be a betrayal that I apparently couldn't do.

I know. It's fucked up.

But this was my life for the next five years.

When the pain was unbearable, which was pretty regularly, I would take some coke and go out to a bar alone. I'd stay out until I found someone who looked enough like Evie to get me through the night. I'd chat her up with sweet words and empty promises—not that it was ever hard for me to get laid. Then, I'd take her back to her place or a hotel, a pub restroom, or an alleyway—I wasn't fussy, so long as I could fuck myself into oblivion—and I'd feel that comforting numbness that would get me through a few more days.

It was an addiction I couldn't seem to break, not until my father died. Trust me, it wasn't the grief that made me want to sort out my life. No, it was the glaring fact that I didn't want to die in some shitty hotel room with coke up my nose and a faceless lay next to me in bed—like he had.

Although my lay would have been female, unlike his.

My father was men all the way, much to my mother's dismay. That was only because she was worried about his preference for men getting out and ruining her public image.

So, when my father died, after five years of living with my coke and sex addiction, I put myself into rehab. I found out from my counselor that I didn't actually have a sex addiction. I was addicted to having sex with women who looked like my ex-wife.

Tragic, right? Yeah, well, tragic is my middle fucking name.

Two years after rehab, I did fall off the wagon once when I thought I saw Evie.

I was in San Francisco. My studio was shooting a movie there, and they were having problems on the set. Basically, the director was threatening to walk out on the movie because the lead actress was being a mega bitch. That mega-bitch actress was my mother. So, I had to go there to handle her because no one else could.

When I was driving through the city, heading to the set, I swore to God, I saw Evie walking down the street.

By the time I pulled over and went to look for her, I saw no sign of her.

I was sure it was her.

Looking back, it was probably just another look-alike. I was always good at finding them.

Even still, I was so convinced that it was Evie that I got back in touch with my PI and had him look into it.

Yet again, he came to me a few days later with nothing.

That night, I got drunk off my ass and fucked an extra from the set who had long blonde hair and a tight ass. She looked like Evie from behind. And, yes, I kept her faced away from me the whole time I was screwing her.

Pathetic, I know.

That was when I figured it was time to get myself another therapist.

And I got a damn good one, and he helped me stay Evie-look-alike free.

Until last night.

What triggered last night's occurrence, I have no clue.

A few days ago would have been my and Evie's wedding anniversary, if we had made it that far. But these last three years, I'd gotten through those missed anniversaries without slipping.

So, aside from that, nothing else happened to set me off—except for a lot of alcohol, which wasn't a rare occurrence when I went out drinking with Max. We usually got drunk and then got laid.

I'm not celibate. I did abstain for a time as part of my therapy. But that was a while ago.

Now, my goal is to just avoid having sex with Evie look-alikes.

I have tried to date in the past, but I could never get it to work. Trust is a big issue for me. Basically, I don't trust anyone with a vagina. I think that, essentially, all women are untrustworthy cold bitches.

My therapist is still working on that one.

Apparently, that comes from mommy issues as well as my ex-wife issues.

As you can see, I'm not a good candidate for a relationship.

But I am a guy, one who works hard and likes to fuck harder. So, I still have one-night stands but just in a healthier manner. I have sex with brunettes or those with black, pink, blue, purple, or red hair. Any color goes, except for blonde. Taller chicks are better, as Evie was tiny. I avoid any temptation I can. Skin color doesn't matter. I don't discriminate. I screw anyone I find attractive, but for my own sanity's sake, I avoid small blondes who remotely resemble my ex-wife.

Or should I say, I did until last night when my drunken self thought it would be a good time to fall off the wagon.

My therapist will be so proud. Guess I'm going to have to call him.

I scrub my hands over my face, letting out a long tired breath.

I'm really not looking forward to facing the look-alike, and I need to get to work. I have back-to-back meetings all day.

Grabbing my cell, I check the time. Seven thirty. Among the emails and messages filling my screen, I see a couple of texts from Max from late last night.

*Just for the record, I tried to talk you out of taking the Evie look-alike home. I all but threw my brunette at you. THAT is how good of a friend I am. And it had nothing to do with the fact that the blonde told us she was a gymnast, and I wanted to screw her.*

*So, tell me, was she as bendy as she looked?*

*Fucker.* Laughing, I shake my head.

Max is my oldest and best friend. We've known each other since high school and come from the same background. We both have crappy parents, so we jelled immediately. He knows all about my problem. Max went through the whole Evie thing with me from start to finish. There are only two people I trust in this shitty world, and Max is one of them.

I hear the shower turn off, so I quickly text him back.

*Good to know that you wanted to screw someone who looked like my ex-wife, fuckface.*

I get an instant response.

*Hey, fucker! Good morning to you, too. And I never said I wanted to screw her because she looked like Evie. I said I wanted to screw her because she was a fucking GYMNAST!*

I let out another laugh as I type a reply.

*You're a sick man, Max.*

Then, I finish off the message.

*And, yes, she was as bendy as she looked.*

Dropping my cell on the bed, I glance longingly at the swimming pool right outside my door. I don't even have time for my morning swim. My mornings always feel off if I haven't been in the water. And this morning definitely feels off. Surfing would be my ideal way to start the day, but that will have to wait until the weekend, like always, when I can get to my beach house.

*God, I fucking hate the corporate life.*

On a sigh, I get up and pull on last night's boxer shorts. I don't want to have the uncomfortable morning-after conversation with the look-alike with my junk hanging out.

I've just covered my goods when the look-alike, whose name has evaded me, comes wandering into the bedroom, wrapped in a towel.

I inhale sharply as I see the reason why I fell off the wagon.

*Fuck. She really does look like Evie.*

A hell of a lot more than I expected. That, combined with last night's consumption of alcohol, explains my current predicament.

I really went all out last night.

The look-alike smiles at me, biting the corner of her lip. Her hand is gripping the top of the towel, holding it in place.

I can't do anything but stare at her. I feel like my insides are twisting in all the wrong directions, and I have the sick urge to fuck her again.

*Jesus Christ.*

I close my eyes to break the connection.

"Is this as awkward for you as it is for me?" she asks softly.

I open my eyes and stare over her shoulder. "Yeah." *More than you'll ever know.*

She lets out a laugh, squeaky and high-pitched. It's nothing like Evie's soul-touching soft laugh.

*Fuck.*

She needs to go—now.

"Look"—I scratch the back of my neck as I take a step toward my bathroom—"I've gotta jump in the shower and get ready for work. I'm running late already. You okay to let yourself out?"

"Oh…yeah, sure."

I hear the disappointment in her voice loud and clear.

Instead of feeling like shit, I just feel relieved that she'll be getting the hell out of here, and I can pretend that last night didn't happen.

"Cool." I tap a hand on the doorframe and disappear into the bathroom before she can say anything more.

Pulling my boxer shorts off, I turn the shower on hot and step inside. I put my head under the spray and close my eyes. But all I can see behind my lids is Evie's face.

"Fuck!" I hiss, punching my fist against the tiled wall.

After ten years, I'm not over her, and I'm still pulling this same shit.

*What the fuck is wrong with me?*

*God, I hate myself. And I hate Evie.*

I hate her for living her life without me.

And I hate that I haven't been able to live without her.

Because, really, all I have done for the last decade is exist inside the haze of my memories of her.

Half an hour later, I'm showered and dressed for work in a suit and tie. I hate ties, but as the head of Gunner Entertainment, I have to look the part.

I head into the living room of the bungalow I call home five days a week. There's no sign of the blonde, except for the lingering strong scent of perfume.

*Thank God.*

I live in a rented bungalow at The Beverly Hills Hotel. I could get an apartment, but I can't bring myself to put down roots here. Even though I grew up in Beverly Hills, it's never felt like home.

Home is in Malibu where my beach house is. It's the house that Max and I rented for our year off before we headed to college. It's the place where I met Evie and where I spent the best year of my life with her—before she left me, and my world came crashing down.

The minute I graduated from Harvard and started working for my father, I was granted access to my trust fund. The first thing I did with that money was go straight to Malibu, and I offered a stupid amount of money to the owner of the beach house. He sold it to me on the spot.

For the three years that I had been away at college, I had kept up with the rent on the beach house. I didn't go back there in all that time, but I couldn't let it go either. I couldn't bear the thought of anyone else being in the place that was hers and mine.

The first time I went back inside the house was torture. She was everywhere, in every room.

But no matter how much it hurt, I needed to be there. I needed to be close to her in the only way I could be.

I probably should sell it now, and buy a new house, as I know it isn't healthy to hang on to the place. But it's the only thing I have left of her, and I just can't bring myself to let it go.

During the week, I'm forced to be in Beverly Hills because Gunner Entertainment is here. It's my family's studio that my great-grandfather started in the early days of making movies. When my grandfather took it over after his father had passed, he turned it into one of the biggest movie studios in Hollywood. After my grandfather passed, my piece-of-shit father, Eric, took over, and during his last few years, he almost ran the studio into the ground. He was too busy screwing any guy he could, pretending to me and the rest of the world that he wasn't gay. All the while, taking the drugs, which eventually killed him.

And wasn't I just my father's son? Aside from fucking dudes, that is. I took on his form down to the letter.

It was always set that I would take over the family business. Didn't matter that I didn't want to. I never wanted anything to do with it. I hate the movie business.

My mother, Ava, is a self-righteous bitch of an actress. My father married her to get his heir to the business. And she was a beautiful up-and-coming actress, ruthless enough to marry a gay man and give him the son he needed.

In return, she got to star in every big blockbuster he could give her. He made her famous, just as he'd promised. She's one of the biggest names in Hollywood.

I was just the transaction which gave them both what they wanted.

Ava was never around when I was growing up. She was usually filming on set somewhere, and even when she was home, I rarely saw her.

She didn't give a shit about me. Still doesn't.

My life was lonely back then. The only person I had in the world was Max.

Until I met Evie. And for the first time in my life, I felt wanted and loved by someone.

And, God, did I love her. Evie was everything to me.

She gave me the reason and strength to tell Ava and Eric to shove the studio up their asses. I walked away from it all to be with her.

I married her, and then a week later, she was gone.

I haven't seen her since.

After she left, I was adrift. So, I grabbed ahold of the only thing I knew. I went back to the family business. I fell right back in with the sharks, and I've been swimming with them ever since.

Grabbing my keys off the side table, I let myself out and start the short walk to the hotel's coffee shop to get my morning coffee.

Making my way through the hotel, I exchange pleasantries with the staff on duty. When I reach the coffee shop, I push open the door and step straight into the past.

*Evie.*

She's standing behind the counter. Her face is turned slightly to the right, her attention on the TV mounted on the wall, and her hair is pulled back into a ponytail.

But it's her.

I feel like a speeding train has hit me, and I'm pretty sure my heart has stopped beating.

It's really her.

*She's here.*

"Evie?" I breathe out her name, like I'm taking my first real breath in a very long time.

Her body stiffens at the sound of my voice. And I watch as her face turns my way. Those big whiskey-colored eyes that I fell in love with all those years ago meet mine, and my world stands still.

She looks exactly the same.

*How is that even possible?*

Maybe it's not. Maybe I'm hallucinating. I mean, falling off the wagon with that chick might have tipped me over the edge, and now, I've finally boarded my very own train to crazy town.

I don't know how much time has passed while we've been standing here, staring at one another. My hand is still holding the door open, my foot a step into the past, and my fingers are gripping the wood so tightly that I'm surprised I haven't ripped a chunk out.

Then, her eyes shut down on me, and she looks away. It feels like she's ripping my heart out all over again, and a rage I didn't know possible floods my body and mind. And it's all channeled in one direction—*her.*

I need to get out of here before I tear her and this place apart.

Turning, I step back and pull the door with me, slamming it so hard that the shop front rattles. I'm surprised I didn't smash the windows.

I get about ten steps away before my blinding anger takes over and turns me back around, marching me straight back there.

The lobby is empty, which is a good thing because I probably look like an insane person right now—not that I actually give a fuck about what people think of me.

I yank the door open and stride through, banging it shut with as much force as I did the first time.

Evie's big brown eyes are straight on me, wide and afraid.

Seeing her afraid like this should pull me back a step, but it doesn't. At this moment, I don't think a fucking dump truck could stop me.

I reach the counter and slam my hands down on the metal surface. Leaning forward, I stare at her with cold eyes.

"Why?" I say low, my voice hard.

"Wh-why, what?" Her tentative voice shakes, almost like she's afraid to ask the question.

She should be afraid.

I stare down at the counter and take several deep breaths in and out, trying to control my rage. I can barely hear with the blood pounding in my ears.

One of my hands curls into a fist as I lift my eyes back to hers. "Why. Did. You. Fucking. Leave. Me?" I harshly bite each word out.

I want her to feel the pain in my words. I want her to feel every second of agony I've felt since she tore my heart out and shredded it to pieces.

Her lower lip trembles. She wraps her arm over her stomach and takes a small step back, away from my anger.

In all the time I knew Evie, I never really yelled at her—well, not like this anyway. And I never wanted to have to, but this is what she has reduced me to…reduced *us* to.

We're two almost strangers with a world of hurt sitting between us.

Her eyes sweep the floor. "I-I can't…"

She lifts them back to mine. I can see anguish and indecision in them.

"I…don't know what to say."

My chest is pounding so heavily that air is gusting out of me. "You don't know what to say?" I yell, punching my fist on the counter. "How about the truth? How about telling me why you upped and disappeared on me a fucking week after we got married?"

Her eyes go to the wall over my shoulder. I see a shine of tears in them. It makes me ache for her, and that just pisses me off further. *What right does she have to cry?*

"I-I'm sorry," she whispers.

I erupt again. "I don't want your fucking apologies!" Well, I kind of do, but I want an explanation more. I want to know why she destroyed us…destroyed me.

I take a deep breath and try to even out my voice as I say, "I just want the truth, Evie. I just want to know why you left."

Her eyes flicker to the window, looking at the people passing by. "Please, Adam," she beseeches. "It's my first day here, and I need this job. Can we talk later?"

My head nearly explodes. I half-expect to see my brain splattered all over this counter. "Are you fucking kidding me? No, we can't fucking talk later! Ten years, Evie! Ten fucking years! You owe me an explanation, and I'm going nowhere until I get it."

The door to the café opens, the sound yanking my eyes away from Evie. I don't want any interruptions right now.

A seriously overweight middle-aged guy stands just in the doorway. I don't recognize him. Must be a guest at the hotel.

He looks between Evie and me as the door shuts behind him. His brow furrows, and concern flitters over his face.

We can't look like a picture of heaven right now. More like the very definition of hell.

Evie looks like she's about to burst into tears, and I'm pretty sure my face is bright red from the rage burning up my skin. My hands are now curled around the edge of the counter, and I'm leaning forward over it, invading Evie's space.

Ignoring the guy, I stare back at Evie. "Answers, Evie. Now."

"Is…everything okay here?" Fatty asks.

Letting out a pissed off sigh, I swing murderous eyes his way. "Things are just fucking peachy."

Then, out of nowhere, I feel her hand on my arm.

The touch sends me reeling, searing into my skin, heating me right through to my bones. I haven't felt this way since…since the last time I felt her touch.

"Adam, I know I owe you my time. But, *please*, can we talk later?" Her voice is soft.

And I'm reminded of all the times when we used to lie in bed after making love, and we'd talk about nothing for hours. Her voice was always so soft, so sweet, in the darkness.

"I have my lunch break at one, or I get off at five. Whichever works best for you, I can do. But just not right now. *Please*."

My eyes move down to her hand. I need her skin off of mine, yet I need her to never let go again.

She removes her hand from my arm.

The instant her touch is gone, I feel cold. And the iciness seeps straight back into my ruined black heart.

I watch as her fingers curl into her palm, like I just burned her skin.

I lift my eyes, boring straight into hers.

"Five. I'll come back here." Releasing my grip on the counter, I step back and stride toward the door, passing Fatty as I go.

I yank the door open and then stop before passing through. I turn back to Evie to find Fatty already at the counter. *Guy sure can move fast.*

My eyes meet with hers, and I pin her with my stare. "Five o'clock, Evie, and you'd better be here. Otherwise, I will come looking for you, and you can bet your fucking ass that, this time, I will find you."

Then, I get the hell out of there and slam the door on my past.

# Adam
## MALIBU · JULY 2004

She's here again—rock girl. She's sitting up on that same big rock, a hundred yards away from my beach house, where she sits every day. Hence, the nickname, Rock Girl.

*God, I'm lame.*

With her sketchpad resting against her bent knees, her eyes are fixed on the paper like her life depends on it while her hand freely moves the pencil over the paper, drawing...I have no clue.

I wish I did.

I mean, I could take a wild guess and say she's drawing the scenery—the pier, beach, sand, sky. There's plenty of shit like that here in Malibu. But still, I want to know *exactly* what she's drawing that has her so enraptured.

Like, I *really* want to know.

I've been watching Rock Girl for a week now.

I saw her on the first day when Max and I arrived at the beach house, which will be my home for the next year. This will be my year of freedom before I have to go to Harvard, and then once I graduate, it is on to work for my father to learn the family business.

*Can't wait.* I have to stop myself from rolling my eyes.

Until then, I'm here to surf my ass off—and apparently stalk cute blonde artists.

Every day, at least for the last seven days, at just a little after five p.m., Rock Girl walks along the beach, passing by my house, with a bag on her shoulder, usually wearing a pair of ass-hugging jean shorts and a red tank, which shows off her perfectly formed tits. They're not too big or too small, just the right size to fit my hands, I imagine. And from what I've seen, they look to be real—meaning, when I watch her climbing up the rock, they jiggle about.

I can't remember the last time I saw a hot girl with a real pair of tits, not in the silicone world I've been raised in. Everything in my world is fake, even the people, especially the people.

On Rock Girl's shirt is a logo, covering the left breast, that I can't quite make out. And trust me, I've tried. I've nearly gone blind, staring at that fucker, trying to work it out—not that staring at her tits is exactly a hardship.

I'm assuming her clothing is her work outfit. Either that, or she has a really limited wardrobe, not that I'm complaining because her body looks smoking hot in those threads.

She keeps her long blonde hair, which I would really like to get my hands all tangled up in, tied back into a ponytail.

When she reaches the top of the rock, she sits down and pulls a sketchpad and pencil out of her bag. Then, she spends the next hour drawing. At just a little after six, she packs her things back into her bag, climbs down the rock, and leaves the way she came.

And I watch her.

Every day.

It's not creepy at all.

Okay, maybe it's a little creepy.

But I just can't help myself. There's something about her, something that has captured my attention in a way no one ever has before. And it isn't just her sexy tan legs, great rack, or tight ass—even though those are amazing.

There's just something…captivating about her.

I don't know if it's the way she seems to put all of herself into her art the moment she presses that pencil to the paper or the way she looks so totally free while sitting up on that rock with the wind blowing through her hair, like nothing or no one can touch her.

For that hour, she's free.

But when she steps down off that rock, I can see a heaviness falling down on her, like a cloud of responsibility.

And I know what that feels like.

When I'm out on my board, riding the waves, nothing can touch me.

But the minute I'm back on shore, that momentary freedom I felt is gone.

Sure, I have freedom in the sense that my parents haven't given a fuck about me since the second I was born. So long as I don't bring disrepute to the Gunner name, tarnishing their smoke-and-mirrors lifestyle, then I can pretty much do whatever the hell I want.

But there has always been an expectation of me.

I'm the heir to Gunner Entertainment, the oldest and largest movie studio in Hollywood.

After this year off—that my parents graciously granted me after I'd threatened to do some seriously crazy stuff if they didn't give it to me—I'm expected to go to Harvard and graduate with honors. Then, I'm to take my place at my father's side until the day I take over and become the King of Hollywood.

Sounds like a dream to most. To me, it's a fucking nightmare.

I despise everything about it and what it represents.

The glitz and glamour cover the lies and deceit. My world is filled with frauds, each one with a dirty little secret to hide.

Soon, I have to become one of them, and when I do, I fear that I'll turn into someone I've never wanted to become—my father…or worse, my mother. She's a fame-hungry, soul-sucking bitch who cares about no one, except for herself.

I paint a nice picture, right?

Well, call me a cynic, but growing up with the parents I have, you'd be one, too.

I don't want any part of the life they're forcing me to have.

All I want is to become a pro surfer. It's all I've ever wanted. I just want to be in the ocean, chasing that never-ending wave.

When I was fourteen, I tried telling Ava that I didn't want to take over the family business, that I wanted to become a professional surfer. She laughed in my face and then reminded me exactly what would happen if I did.

They'd cut me off cold. I would have nothing.

And believe me when I say, they would leave me penniless, living on the streets, and they would do it without losing a second of sleep.

Especially Ava. She is as hard as the Botox filling her face.

I wish I were brave enough to go it alone. The problem with being brought up with unlimited funds would be to have to live without it. And I don't know if I could do that.

So, for now, I'm my parents' bitch.

Although I might be their bitch and screwed up in more ways than I can begin to explain, I'm not a fucking weirdo. I don't usually hang out on my balcony, watching chicks, like some creeper.

I'm not exactly the shy type. I'm confident—probably too confident sometimes—and when I want a girl, I tell her. I don't hide in my house, afraid to approach her.

And I'm not an asshole—well, not all the time—but I am aware of how I look. When your mother is one of the most beautiful women in the world—even if she is a demon from hell—you stand a damn good chance of scoring lucky in the gene pool.

And I scored well.

At six-three, with an athletic body that I've gained from all my years of surfing and swimming, I keep the scruff on my face overgrown and my sun-bleached hair longer.

I have no problem at all with getting chicks. It's getting rid of them that is usually the issue.

But for some reason, I can't seem to get my ass off this balcony to go over there and talk to Rock Girl.

I'm seriously starting to worry about myself.

*For fuck's sake, Gunner. Just go down there and talk to her. What have you got to lose?*

"Hey, fuckface. You still watching that chick?"

Releasing a sigh, I turn to look over my shoulder at Max. "I'm not watching her. I'm…looking at the scenery." I gesture weakly with my hand.

Max snorts out a laugh. "Sure you are, limp dick."

I see Darcy, the girl Max has been banging for the last few days, sidle up beside him. She shoots me a sexy smile.

"Hey, Adam." She lifts her hand in greeting, wiggling her fingers at me.

I lift my chin at her, not bothering to say hi.

Darcy might be hot, but she's an idiot.

And she must think I'm fucking stupid.

She tried to play it off as an accident when she walked into my bathroom yesterday while I was in there showering. My private bathroom, the one you have to walk through my bedroom to get into. Yeah, sure it was an accident, Darcy.

Max laughed his ass off when I told him.

He doesn't give a fuck. And if Darcy weren't screwing Max, I probably would have banged her, as I'm guessing that was what she was there for. I've never been one to turn down a hot girl, even if she is an idiot. But Max is banging her, and we have one golden rule in our friendship. We never sleep with the same chick.

Bros before hos, and all that.

Max is the only real thing I have in this shitty world, and I wouldn't do anything to risk losing him. He's the same with me.

Max's background is pretty similar to mine, fucked-up parents and all, but sadly, between us, I score the highest on the screwed-up-worst card.

We look out for each other. We're brothers in the true sense of the word. Aside from his poor taste in women, he's the best person I know.

Thankfully, Darcy will be gone in a few days. That's Max's MO. He hooks up with a girl and keeps her around for a few days—longest I've seen is a week—and then she's replaced. Me? I don't keep them around. I screw them for one night, and they're gone the next morning.

No repeats. No relationships.

That's exactly how I like it.

And if I sort my shit out, then Rock Girl can be my next no-repeater.

*Actually, something feels very wrong with that statement. Again, what the hell is wrong with me?*

Maybe that's why I can't get off my pussy ass and go introduce myself to her. Sitting up there on that rock, she's perfect to me. If I go over there, I'll only end up tainting that perfection, ruining it.

Spoiling pretty things is a gift of mine. It's a Gunner family trait.

"We're just going to grab some dinner," Max says. "You wanna come?"

I turn around, pressing my back against the sun-warmed railing. "Nah, I'll pass. I'm gonna go for a run."

*Am I? I guess I could go for a run. I could go for a jog along the beach. Maybe speak to a little hottie seated up on a rock…*

"And would that run take you past a certain blonde over there?" Max jerks his chin in Rock Girl's direction.

I lift my shoulders, shrugging at him.

He shakes his head at me. "What the hell is going on with you, Gunner? Why haven't you just talked to her already? It's been a fucking week."

I flicker a glance at Darcy, who has this sudden sour look on her face, and now, she's staring out past me in Rock Girl's direction.

*Yeah, not going to happen, Darcy.*

I strike a glance at Max. I love the guy like a brother, but I wish he hadn't said that shit in front of Darcy. She has a big mouth, and I don't want to get a rep here in Malibu for being a pussy who can't even talk to a girl.

"Nothing's wrong with me. Maybe I just don't want to talk to her.*"*

*I really do. I want to talk her straight into my bed.*

"Yeah, sure you don't want to talk to the super hot girl, Gunner." Max rolls his eyes at me.

"How do you know she's super hot?" The words are out before I can stop them.

As far as I know, Max hasn't seen her up close, not that I have actually seen her up close. Just the quick glimpses of her as she's walked past here. But the glimpses I have gotten, I've liked—a lot.

A shit-eating grin spreads across Max's face. "Because I talked to her yesterday."

"You talked to her?" My voice has suddenly gotten weirdly higher.

*Why the hell did Max talk to Rock Girl? And why is he only just now telling me this?*

He lets out a prolonged deep chuckle. "Yeah, I did. When you went in to shower after your little hour-long hot-girl gazing session, I decided to go for a swim. And your little hottie came back, as she'd left something up on that rock she sits on. A fucking pencil or something. Seemed important to her." He shrugs. "Anyway, after she found this pencil and was climbing back down off the rock, she dropped her bag, spilling her stuff everywhere. Being the gentleman that I am, I helped her pick things up—tampons, lipstick. You know, girl things." He grins.

I lift my eyes to the sky.

*Gentleman, my ass.*

Max wouldn't know a gentleman if one actually came up and smacked him across the face. Not that I would either, but that's not the point. The point is, Max talked to my Rock Girl.

*My Rock Girl? When did she become mine?*

"She seems nice. And she's really hot, bro," he goes on. "I did consider asking her out myself, but I didn't want to break your little stalker heart."

"Hey!" Darcy screeches, swatting him on the arm.

"Only kidding, babe." He gives her that smooth grin of his that all the chicks fall for. "I mean, why would I ask her out when I've got you?"

He pats her on the arm, pacifying her, and the second she looks away, he smirks at me.

*Bastard.*

He'd have asked Rock Girl out even if Darcy was riding cowgirl on his cock at the time.

Nothing stops Max when it comes to a woman he wants. He's like me, in that respect—well, apart from

Rock Girl. Because, out of the two of us, I'm apparently the one without the balls to go speak to her.

"You're a bastard, you know," I say, fighting a smile.

"Takes a bastard to know a bastard." His grin gets bigger.

"True." I can't argue with that.

Now, I'm feeling really twitchy, and I want to ask him more about his conversation with Rock Girl, but with Darcy standing there, I can't. That, and it'd only give Max more ammo to torture me with.

"Anyway, I'm bailing 'cause I'm fucking starving. All the sex works up an appetite, which you would know, if you'd gotten laid lately."

I flip him off.

I got laid a few days ago, and he knows it. Hot lifeguard who works on Zuma Beach. We were down there, surfing, and she was cute. After I finished surfing, I fucked her in her tower in the middle of her shift. Fortunately, no one needed saving at the time.

"You want me to bring you any food back?" Max asks, taking a step back inside the house.

"Nah, I'm good. I'll get something later."

"Bye, Adam," Darcy says in an annoying singsong voice.

*God, I hope he doesn't bring her back with him.*

"Later." I lift my chin at her before turning back to Rock Girl.

She's still sitting there, sketching away. I watch as she puts her pencil down on the pad and tilts her head back toward the sky, soaking the last of the sun up.

She looks so peaceful and so damn pretty.

"Gunner?"

I turn back to the sound of Max's voice. "Yeah?"

"Do me a favor. Just go ask Evie out before you totally lose your man card and quite possibly get arrested for stalking. I really don't wanna have to come bail your ass out of jail."

"Fuck you." I laugh as I grab an empty beer can from the patio table, left out from our drinking session last night, and throw it at him.

Max ducks, the can just missing him.

Then, I realize what he just said. "Evie?"

His lips lift into a knowing smile. "Yeah. That's her name, which you would already know if you'd manned the fuck up and talked to her the first time you saw her." He jerks his chin in her direction. "Just put us both out of our misery and go talk to her." He raps his knuckles on the doorframe before disappearing.

*Why is he so keen on me talking to Evie?*

*Evie.*

I let her name roll around my mind. It's pretty, really pretty.

Adam and Evie. Like Adam and Eve. In the Garden of Eden—or the Bed of Adam—fucking like animals.

*Seriously, what is wrong with me? I'm imagining having sex with this girl, and I haven't even spoken to her.*

*I can't believe Max spoke to her first, and he got her name.*

*Fucker.*

*Okay, this is just stupid. I need to just go over there and speak to her.*

*That's it. I'm going to do it.*

I'll go for a run on the beach, and while I'm there, I'll strike up a conversation with her. If I don't, Max will only torment me about it. And then, he might possibly ask her out himself.

*She's just a girl, Gunner. You've talked to plenty of pretty girls before.*

But the difference is, I never wanted to know anything about those other girls. Each conversation was for one reason only—the end game.

But this one, I think I might actually want to get to know her—and not just know the color of her panties.

I make a quick change into a pair of running shorts and a tank, and then I pull on my running shoes. I tie my hair back, so it's out of the way while I'm running. Then, I grab my water bottle and fill it up.

Before leaving, I make a quick check out back to make sure she's still there.

*Yep, she's there—and yep, I'm still as lame as ever.*

Heading out the front door, I jog along the path on the highway, so I can come onto the beach via the walkway.

I don't want to come out from the back of the house, as it's not far enough away from where she's sitting. This way, I'll be coming toward her for a good period of time, so if I stop to take a break, it won't look so weird.

*When did I start overthinking things? And just exactly when did I lose my balls?*

Apparently, on the day I saw a pretty blonde girl sitting up on a rock.

I jog up the street for a few minutes and then take the path off to the walkway to take me to the beach. It brings me out about three hundred yards away from Evie.

*Game time, Gunner.*

Feet hitting the sand, I begin jogging toward her.

The closer I get, the faster my heart starts to beat. And it has nothing to do with the exercise because I've barely even begun running.

It's because of her.

*What is it about this girl that has me in all kinds of knots? How can I feel so nervous over a girl I've never even spoken to?*

She hasn't noticed me yet. I keep my eyes on her throughout my approach.

She has the tip of the pencil pressed to her lower lip as she stares down at her sketchpad, a frown marring her forehead.

Not that far from her now, I slow my pace, coming to a stop a few feet away from her, under the pretense that I need to stop to catch my breath.

Facing the ocean, I take a drink of water from my bottle.

I slide a glance in her direction.

*She still isn't looking at me.*

And just as I think it, she looks straight at me, her eyes meeting mine. I freeze.

*Holy fuck, she's stunning.*

Way prettier than I first thought. My initial take on her did not do her justice because, up close, she's beautiful. And I know beauty. I've been surrounded by it my whole life.

But her face…nothing compares.

She has the most amazing eyes. Captivating. They're the color of whiskey, huge and shaped like almonds, and they are set in the most perfect face I have ever seen. Heart-shaped with a cute button nose and full lips.

In this moment, her face has literally become the center of my universe. I can't stop staring at her.

And that's probably why she says to me, "Um…are you okay?"

I blink myself free, realizing what a fucking idiot I must look like.

*Way to make a first impression, dickface.*

"Are you an artist?" I point a finger up at her sketchpad.

Then, I have to stop my own hand from punching me in the face at my lameness. *That's my opener? Wow, I just keep getting better and better.*

*Thy name is Adam, and I am a fucking loser.*

A smile tips up her lips, and she pushes her pencil into the top of her ponytail. "Do you think you have to actually sell a drawing to be able to call yourself an artist?"

"I'm not sure." I shrug, my eyes going straight back to her face. It's kind of hard not to stare. She's *that* beautiful.

"Well, if you do, then no, I'm not an artist."

"Do you want to be one?"

She ponders this for a moment, her teeth biting down on that plump lower lip of hers, and I imagine my own teeth doing the exact same thing.

Her eyes come back to mine with an unexpected and surprising intensity in them. "Yes."

For a second there, I feel like she's saying yes to something else. Maybe she's agreeing to the movie reel of dirty thoughts going through my mind right now—me and her, naked and sweaty and tangled up in my bedsheets.

No, that's just *my* wishful thinking.

The thought of sex with her has my confidence finally making his late appearance.

I don't know why, but thinking about sex while talking to a girl always lifts my game. I'm weird like that.

I tip my head to the side, folding my arms over my chest. "Maybe I could buy one of your drawings, and then you could officially call yourself an artist."

She arches a perfectly formed brow. "You'd buy a drawing from me when you haven't even seen any of my work?"

"I would."

"And why would you do that?"

I give a lazy shrug. "Because I can."

That seems to get her attention. She closes her sketchpad, places it on the rock beside her, and moves forward, letting her legs dangle over the side. She curls her fingers around the edge of the rock and stares down at me. "I might be really crappy at drawing, and then you would have wasted your money."

Technically, I wouldn't be wasting my money. It'd be my parents', but I don't want to tell her that I'm a rich kid. It might put her off. Evie clearly works for her money. I'm getting that from the logo on her shirt, which I can now see that it says Grady's Surf Shack. I don't want her to think that I'm a self-entitled brat.

"I highly doubt that you're crappy."

"And how would you know that? Aside from assuming, of course." She gives me a teasing smile.

"Because you seem far too smart to spend your time on something that you know you're not any good at."

"Oh, so now you know I'm smart as well as good at drawing?" She laughs, the sound so sweet.

It makes my cock stand to attention.

"Well, for all you know, as well as being a crappy artist, I could also be as dumb as bricks."

That makes me laugh. "Well, are you?" I ask, my hands coming to rest on my hips.

"What? Dumb as bricks?"

I nod, smiling.

"Quite possibly." She gives me a lasting grin that I feel all the way deep down in my gut. Then, she grabs her sketchpad and shoves it in her bag. "Shit," she mutters, looking around, running her hand over the surface of the rock.

"Something wrong?"

"I've lost my pencil. It's just…it wasn't cheap—well, for a pencil, and—"

"It's in your hair."

"Oh." She touches a hand to the top of her ponytail, her cheeks turning pink. "Thanks."

She pulls the pencil from her hair and drops it into her bag. Hooking the bag onto her shoulder, she starts to climb down the rock.

*She's leaving?*

Her feet hit the sand. "Well, it was nice talking to you," she says, turning to me.

She starts to move past me, and I'm just standing here, like a limp fucking noodle. I watch her go, desperately trying to think of anything to keep her here for just a few minutes longer.

Aside from blurting out that I want to take her out, I'm at a fucking loss.

Then, out of nowhere, she stops abruptly and turns back to me. "Did you change your mind?"

"Change my mind? About what?" My mouth is so dry it's like I'm talking through cotton wool. I've seriously never had this kind of reaction to a girl before. "Do you mean about buying a drawing from you? Because—"

"No. I meant, did you change your mind about asking me out?"

My mouth literally drops open. "I-I—" That's honestly all I've got. I can't seem to get my brain to compute to my mouth, not that it would have much to send.

"I mean, it doesn't matter to me if you have. I was just wondering." Her head tilts to the side, and then a light blush starts to creep over her face as her eyes spark with something that looks an awful lot like realization. "Oh God. Have I gotten the wrong guy?" She presses her palms to her cheeks.

"The wrong guy?" I feel like I've just had a brick dropped on my head.

*Was she supposed to be meeting some other guy here, like a blind date or something?* I sincerely fucking hope not.

"You don't live at that house there?" She points in the direction of my house. "Standing out on the balcony every day for the last week, watching me sketch?"

Then, it hits me.

*Max.*

*Motherfucker.*

Ask me if I've ever been embarrassed.

Never. Not once in my whole life.

Not even when the maid at my parents' house walked in and caught me jacking off to Hentai porn in my bedroom when I was sixteen. Hey, don't judge. I'd pretty much worn out all other kinds of porn by that point, so it was either cartoon porn or old-lady porn. So, Hentai it was. And the fact that I ended up fucking the maid the next day has nothing to do with it.

But the fact is, nothing has ever embarrassed me—until now.

Max told her that I'd been watching her—like a stalker.

I'm going to kill him.

I'm actually going to kill him and dump his body in the middle of the Pacific Ocean, and I won't feel an ounce of remorse.

"Max," I grunt out, practically choking on the heat burning up my throat. "The guy you met yesterday, the one who helped you when you dropped your bag, did he tell you all of that, about me…watching—" I can't even finish that sentence.

Her face clears, and she smiles sweetly, giving a light shrug, as she hitches her bag up her shoulder. "Can't say I've met a Max." Her lips innocently purse together.

She's so met him. And she so knows I've been watching her. I should want to die from the horror of the embarrassment.

But I've realized one glaring fact. Even while knowing all about me stalker-watching her, she still wanted me to ask her out.

I want to marry her on the spot—or at the very least, get her naked and fuck her.

"Anyway, I have to run—"

"Wait, what?"

"I have to go," she says on a smile, taking a small step away.

"No, wait. Go out with me. Right now. I'm not a serial killer, and I'm really not a stalker, honestly. I just liked watching you sketch—in the non-weirdest way possible."

I give her my best smile, and she giggles.

"You know where I live. You're safe with me. And I'll take you anywhere you want to go. You name the place. Just…just say yes. You won't regret it. I swear."

And there's the Adam Gunner I know. About fucking time he showed up.

A big smile pushes up her lips, and if I thought she was stunning before, she's fucking resplendent now.

Heat starts in the center of my chest and quickly spreads throughout the rest of my body. Like hot air filling a balloon and rising up to the sky, she has me floating.

"I'll let you know," she says, taking another step away.

*What?*

That takes me back a step. I didn't expect that response. It's either yes or no usually. Well, actually, it's never no.

A girl has never turned me down before.

"You'll let me know?" I practically choke out the words.

"Yeah." She smiles. "I'll let you know." Then, she turns and starts to walk away again.

But I'm not giving up that easily.

"And why can't you say yes now?" I can feel my confidence starting to waver.

This never happens to me. She's like my very own brand of kryptonite, and oddly, I like it—a lot.

Evie turns to face me but continues walking backward, that stunning smile still on her face. "Well, I figured one more day to wait wouldn't hurt you, considering it's taken you a week to ask me out."

I'm pretty sure I just fell in love.

Well, it's probably more like lust—big lust—but whatever. I have to have her—now.

I take a step toward her, following her. "I think you're fucking amazing."

Her smile gets wider, and she laughs, biting down on her bottom lip. "And I think you might be a little crazy. Oh, I forgot to give you this."

Jogging back to me, she pulls her sketchpad from her bag. She opens it up and tears a page out. She shoves the sketchpad back in her bag and hands me the piece of paper. "I've been working on it all week. I think it's finished." She meets my stare, blinking those stunning whiskey-colored eyes of hers up at me.

My breath catches.

I have never wanted to kiss a girl more than I do her in this moment.

Taking a step back, she breaks the connection. She lifts a hand, her perfect fingers wiggling good-bye to me. "I'll see you tomorrow. And it was nice to finally meet you, Adam."

"Wait…I never told you my name."

"I know." She grins. "Max told me." And on a cheeky wink, she turns and jogs up the beach, leaving me standing here.

I watch her for a long moment, unable to look away. Then, I finally tear my eyes off her, remembering the paper in my hand.

I turn it over and look at it.

It's a drawing of my beach house from her vantage point on the rock. The sun is setting in the background, and I'm standing on the balcony, watching the artist who's sketching me.

*She was watching me, too.*

A stupid grin lifts my face, and my heart starts to beat out of my chest.

I think I've just met the girl of my dreams, the girl who I didn't even know I was dreaming of.

*Evie*
# BEVERLY HILLS · JULY 2015

My hands are shaking. They've been shaking pretty much all day. Every time I think about Adam, the shakes start. How I haven't managed to break a cup, I'm not sure.

He looks the same yet different. He looks hardened to the world. The light that used to live in his eyes has dulled. But he's still as handsome as ever, if not even more so with age.

Adam never looked like a boy. He was always very much a man, even at eighteen. But now, he's reached his full potential. He seems even bigger somehow.

Or maybe it was just his anger that made him seem bigger, more imposing.

All that anger, and it was reserved solely for me.

The guy I left behind all those years ago was not the man I saw today.

I have to wonder if I'm to blame for that.

I glance at the clock. Five minutes until the end of my shift. Five minutes until Adam is here, and he wants his answers.

Answers I can't give him.

So, I'm going to have to lie, something I never wanted to do.

I thought there was a slim possibility that I might see Adam in Beverly Hills, as his studio is here. I wasn't hoping to see him—well, maybe I had a little bit of hope. But I also knew what kind of complications would come from seeing Adam.

It's not like Adam and I run in the same circles. I basically come into Beverly Hills for work, and then I go home to my apartment in Culver City. So, I thought the chances of seeing him were minimal. I mean, I work in a coffee shop that's inside a hotel, for God's sake. Never did I expect for him to come in here.

*Why is he staying at the hotel anyway? Surely, he has a house in Beverly Hills.*

I only got this job through a friend who I worked with back in San Francisco. She'd left there and moved here to be with her boyfriend, taking the manager's job.

When I knew I would be moving here, I got in touch with her, and lucky for me, her assistant manager was pregnant and would be taking maternity leave soon. She couldn't guarantee me that there would be a permanent job at the end of the six months. So, I'm going to look for another job while I'm working this one.

I had to move back up this way because Casey, my kid sister, announced that she was going to the University of California, Los Angeles.

When Casey had told my dad and me that she wanted to study nursing at college, we knew she'd apply to the

University of California, San Francisco, but we didn't know she'd also apply to UCLA. She applied and was accepted to both, and she chose UCLA. She told me she missed home. And UCLA was as close to Malibu as we could get.

I can't say that I wasn't terrified at the thought of moving back up this way, being close to Adam again. But I also can't deny that the thought of being closer to Adam, although terrifying, didn't excite me a little, too.

But that's the thing about us Taylors. We're a package deal. Where one goes, so do the other two. So, there was no choice.

We rented an apartment in Culver City. It's not too pricey for Los Angeles, and it's close to UCLA. For Casey, it's only a twenty-minute drive to school, and for me, it's a twenty-minute drive to work.

We didn't want to wait to move until September as Casey had enrolled in some summer classes. She'd said she wanted to be ready for her courses this fall. Casey has always loved school, loved learning. It's probably because she missed so much school when she was younger. Me? I couldn't wait to get out of school. That probably explains why I still work in a coffee shop.

I glance at the clock again. It's one minute before five.

"I'm gonna head out," I say to Angie, one of the girls I work with.

We don't close until nine p.m. I opened up, so Angie will close.

Getting ready to meet up with Adam, I head into the back and grab my thin jacket and my bag.

When I step back out behind the counter, Adam is standing there.

My eyes meet with his, and nerves ripple through me.

He looks as pissed as he did this morning.

He has every right to that anger, and I have to remind myself of that.

"Hi," I say to him.

"Are you ready to go?"

Well, at least he's asking me this time instead of telling me.

"Sure." I come out from behind the counter, aware of Angie's wide eyes on Adam.

I can understand why. Adam is a *beautiful* man, in every sense of the word—tall with eyes like a turquoise stone and a swimmer's body. Add that in with his natural confidence and alpha stance, and women can't help but stare.

Women ogling Adam was something I had to get used to when we were together, not that it ever really bothered me. Back then, I knew he loved me, and his eyes were only on me.

They're still on me now, just not the way they used to be, and that hurts more than I can begin to explain.

"I'll see you tomorrow," I say to Angie.

"Yeah, see you," she says.

I follow Adam over to the door in silence. He holds it open for me, letting me through first. It might seem like the gentleman is still in him, but I don't think it is—well, not for me anyway. He's probably just making sure I go through the door and don't bolt behind the counter to make a run for it out the back door, which I'm now considering.

I can feel the rage emanating from him, and it's smacking straight into me, like hail hitting a windowpane.

"Where do you want to go to…talk?"

Knowing Adam, he already knows where we're going. He always was a take-charge person.

But I thought I should ask just so I know where I'm going to be killed before he dumps my body.

Just kidding. Kind of.

He cuts me a look. "I have a place here. We can talk there."

Then, he stalks off through the lobby. I have to work my legs to keep up with his long strides.

Then, we're out of the main hotel building, and I follow him through the gardens and toward the bungalows.

I haven't been out here yet. I haven't really had a chance to check out the hotel at all. It's really pretty out here, and these bungalows must be expensive to rent.

"You live here all the time?" I ask from behind him, knowing that his studio is in Beverly Hills.

*I wonder why he hasn't gotten a house.*

"During the week. I'm gone on weekends."

*Okay…I guess that's all I'm getting.*

We reach one of the larger bungalows. He seems to hesitate outside the door, almost as if he's changed his mind about going inside with me.

Then, he seems to make his decision, and he unlocks the door, swinging it open.

Adam walks inside without a word or a look at me, leaving me standing outside.

*All right then.*

I take a deep breath and step inside, closing the door behind me.

He's already taken his jacket off, and he is on the other side of the living space. By the looks of it, he's pouring himself a drink.

Clasping my hands together, I edge a little farther into the room, not really sure what to do.

He throws back the whiskey he poured and then pours another. "You want one?" he asks.

"No, thank you."

He turns to me, glass in hand. His index finger goes to his tie, and he loosens it before pulling it off and tossing it on the table. He undoes the top button on his shirt.

Eyes still on me, he takes another sip of his drink.

I move across a little and press my back to the wall, needing the support.

And we just stand here for a long time, saying nothing, with a world of pain seated right between us.

I know, in this moment, the years I've spent missing him feel like nothing in comparison to having him here before me yet so far away. I miss him now more than I have in all that time combined, and it hurts. *Fuck, it hurts.*

I look away, unable to look at him for a second longer, knowing if I do I'm going to break into pieces.

"You look exactly the same as you did." His low words move across the room, touching my skin. "I hate that." And those words pierce right in, burrowing deep.

I press a hand to my chest, trying to push the pain away. It doesn't work.

"Why, Evie?" His words are soft but filled with pain.

I feel every ounce of his pain, and mixed with my own, it's pure agony.

I part my dry lips, lifting my eyes to his face. But I can't look him directly in the eyes. Looking at Adam is like staring into the sun.

"I…" I shake my head.

"Don't say you don't know because we both know you do."

I feel like curling in on myself and dying.

I don't want to have to lie to him. I've never been a good liar. And I'm afraid he'll see through my lies now.

But I have to do this. I have no choice. I can't tell him the truth. If I tell him that, he'll hate me forever.

*He already does hate you.*

Taking a fortifying breath, I force my eyes to his. Shielding the truth behind them, I shut down. "It wasn't working for me. You and me. I wasn't happy, so I left."

"Bullshit!" He slams his glass down on the table so hard that I'm surprised it doesn't break. "Don't fucking lie to me, Evie. You owe me the truth. The least you owe me is that."

The truth is a hard thing. He might think he wants the truth, but honestly, if he has it, I think he'd realize he never wanted it.

The truth can hurt, and this one would hurt him like a motherfucker.

Adam is well aware, more than most, at how low some people will go to get what they want, but this truth would show him an all new depth to that low. And it will also show him what others will do in the face of desperation.

"I'm not lying." *I'm going straight to hell.*

I can't even explain the level of anger I see crossing his face. It's a rage I didn't know existed in him.

I know Adam would never hurt me, but the way he's looking at me right now makes me want to step back. Far back.

"You were happy." His hard words come out through clenched teeth. "I saw it for myself. You married me, for fuck's sake! So, don't stand there and tell me that you weren't happy. Just tell me the fucking truth!"

He's not going to accept anything that I tell him, so maybe I have to be a bitch to give him the peace he needs on this.

"Was it Ava? Did she do something to make you leave?"

"No."

"So what?" he yells, his hand pulling on his hair. "Was there—" He pauses, like a realization has just come to him. "Was there someone else?"

His words slap me across the face. But a second later, I realize they've given me the out I need. He'll hate me for this, but if he thinks I left him for someone else, then he'll have his reason, and I can go home and cry myself to sleep.

"Yes."

He moves so quickly that I don't get a chance to move away. In seconds, he's in front of me, his hands pressing on the wall on either side of my head.

My heart starts to pound with stress and fear—and yes, desire. Having Adam this close to me after ten years is a lot to take. After spending as long as I have missing him, it's hard to control my body's natural reaction to him.

"You're lying," he hisses.

I swallow. I need him to get away from me, yet I also need him to never leave.

"What do you want from me?" My voice shakes betraying me.

His eyes narrow to slits. "The truth."

"I gave it to you."

"Yeah, but which is it, Evie? You weren't happy, or you were cheating on me?"

*Crap.*

My chin wobbles. "Bo-both."

Disgust covers his face. It makes me feel like shit.

He pushes off the wall, stepping away from me. I sag with relief, but part of my body screams for him to come back.

He leans against the sofa, eyes on the floor. "Who was he?" There's no emotion in his quiet voice.

"No one you knew."

He lifts his eyes to me. They're laced with pain, and it nearly kills me. I have to press my lips together to hold it all in—the truth, and my tears.

"Are you still with him?"

I shake my head.

"Why did you leave Malibu?"

I take a breath. "I left with him because I knew you wouldn't take it well." *Another lie.*

He lets out a sardonic laugh. "What did you think I was going to do when you told me?"

I lift my shoulders. "I just…I didn't want to hurt you." It's scaring me how easily these lies are falling from my mouth.

His eyes are fixed on mine. "Well, you failed. Because you did hurt me. You hurt me a fuck of a lot."

*I know, and I'm so sorry.*

I look away, unable to hold his stare any longer.

"Why did your dad and Casey leave with you?"

My eyes flash back to his. "What?"

"It's a simple question, Evie. Why did they leave with you? I get that you left with your lover boy, but why did they go? That makes no sense. Why would they have uprooted their lives to leave with you? Especially considering how things were with Casey, how sick she was."

"They-they—I needed to get away, and they came with me. They're my family."

He rubs his fingers over his forehead.

Then, dropping his hand, he takes two big steps toward me. Leaning in, he says into my ear, "You're a fucking liar."

I don't know what comes over me. Maybe it's his proximity or the fact that I can't get him to believe my lies—yes, I'm well aware of how laughable that sounds—but I push my hands against his chest, shoving him away.

He doesn't go far.

"Fuck you!" I yell. "I don't know what the fuck you want from me, Adam, but clearly, I can't give it to you!"

I turn to leave.

But he grabs my wrist, yanking me back. "The only thing I ever wanted was the truth, but you seem incapable of telling it to me."

"I've told you the truth!" I scream. "I was young, and I made a mistake! I left you, and I can't change that now! So, just"—I'm panting now—"let it go."

He drops my arm like I've just burned him.

"Let it go." His face is incredulous. Then, he does the strangest thing. He laughs. And I don't mean a small laugh. I mean, a full-on belly laugh.

"Adam?" I say confused.

He looks at me. He's laughing, but anger is still firmly fixed in his eyes. "Trust me, if I could have let it go, I would have fucking years ago."

I don't know what to say to that, but truthfully, I'm in the same position as him. I couldn't let go either. I know, for him, it was for a different reason. He couldn't let go of not knowing the truth, why I left him, whereas I couldn't let go because I never could find a way to stop loving him. Our reasons may have differed, but ultimately, we were in the same position.

He rubs the laughter from his eyes and moves across the room. Picking his drink back up, he takes a long pull.

"Where have you been all this time?" He holds the glass to his chest.

"San Francisco."

Shock flickers over his face. "I was in San Francisco three years ago. I thought I saw you."

*He was there? He saw me?*

"But you were gone so quickly. I called my PI, but he couldn't find any trace of you there. I thought I'd imagined it...*you.*"

"Your PI?"

Hard eyes lift to mine. "I looked for you, Evie, for a long time. I hired a PI, but he could never find you. It was like you'd dropped off the face of the earth. Did you change your name?"

His eyes go to the badge on my uniform that reads *Evie*.

"No, I didn't change my name."

"Your surname?"

"No. It stayed the same—Taylor. Evie Taylor."

"That doesn't make sense." Accusatory eyes flick up to mine. "So, why couldn't my PI find you?"

"I don't know." I shake my head, swallowing down.

*Well, I can think of maybe one reason why he couldn't find me, but I can't share that with him.*

He stares at me, before looking away. "It doesn't make any sense," he mutters to himself. "He even checked for Casey, and Casey would have had to register, at the very least, with a doctor."

"He checked for Casey?" The words whoosh out of me, and my heart starts to pound.

"Of course he did. I was desperate to find you. I would have done anything back then to know where you were."

His impassioned words are like a punch to the stomach.

Deep down I always thought he would try to look for me. But thinking and knowing are two very different things.

My eyes lower to the floor. "I'm sorry."

"For what, Evie? For cheating on me, for leaving me, for the PI not being able to find you?"

"All of it." I force my eyes back to him. "I should have handled it better. I didn't, and I'm sorry."

His eyes search my face, and then he turns away, staring out the window.

"Casey? Is she…?" He leaves the question opened ended, and I understand why. He doesn't know that she's fine. Healthy. Alive.

"She's fine. Good. Better. She's starting UCLA in the fall. She wants to be a nurse. That's why we're here."

"So, she got better?" He turns slightly to look at me.

"Yes."

"She was dying, Evie. And now she's well. Is that why you left? To get some life-saving treatment for her?"

I press my lips together and shake my head.

"Then, why? It doesn't make any sense. None of this makes sense." His voice implores, begging to me.

I look away. "Casey was dying. We got her some treatment, and we were beyond lucky that the treatment saved her life. But that had nothing to do with why I left."

He looks back out the window.

He doesn't say anything for a long time. I'm wondering if I should just leave when he does speak again.

"Do you still draw?" he asks in a soft voice.

"No." I look down at my hands, entwining my fingers together.

"Why not?"

*How do I tell him that leaving him was the hardest thing I ever had to do, and it broke me?*

It broke everything inside of me, and I haven't been able to draw since then. Every time I put the pencil to the paper, all I could see was his face, and I couldn't bear the reminder of what I'd lost.

I don't tell him. That's the thing. I can't ever tell him.

I let go of my hands and wrap my arms around my stomach, trying to hold in all the pain that's threatening to spill out of me, and I just shake my head. "Do you still surf?" I ask him.

I look up to find he's facing me, back against the window, eyes on me.

"Only on weekends."

I guess things have changed so much for both of us. The dreams we had together never made it to fruition with us being apart.

We each became a slave to the choice I had to make.

My eyes rake over him as I remember the Adam I knew ten years ago and compare him to the Adam I see before me. The long hair is gone, replaced with cropped locks. The unshaven scruff on his face is still very much there though. At least some things haven't changed.

"You cut your hair."

"It has been ten years."

"I know. I just…I remember a time when you said you'd never cut your hair." A small smile touches my lips at the memory.

"Yeah, and I remember when you promised to love me till death do us part. Shit changes."

My smile drops from my face. My cheeks sting like he's just slapped me.

I deserved that. Doesn't stop it from hurting like a bitch though.

I turn my cheek, forcing a blank expression onto my face. I don't want him to see how injured I am by his words.

"How long was it going on for?" he asks me in a quiet voice.

I look back to him. "What?"

"With this other guy. How long were you seeing him behind my back?"

I can see how much it's hurting him, thinking I cheated on him, and I hate hurting him. I don't want him to think so very badly of me even though, in some ways, what I actually did was worse.

I blow out a breath. "There wasn't any other guy, Adam. I'm sorry I lied about that. I guess I just said that because…I don't know." I shake my head. "You wanted a valid reason, and I didn't have one to give you, other than…getting married…it was just too much too soon. I panicked, and I ran. I'm sorry. You wanted the truth. That's it."

And I guess, in a way, the truth is in some of those words. It was a lot, us getting married so young. But I never regretted it, not for one second, and I would still be married to him now, if I could be. And I did panic when faced with the decision I had to make. And I did run. So, what I said…it's the best of the truth that I can give to him.

He stares at me for a long moment, so long that I don't know what to do.

Then, he blinks his eyes free, blows out a breath as he runs a hand through his hair and says, "Okay."

*Okay? That's it?*

He isn't questioning why I lied about cheating, and he seems to have accepted my reasoning. It makes me wonder why he's taken it so easily.

Then, I realize that maybe he's just tired of it all. Maybe he just sees that it's time to let go of the past.

And I guess it's time for me to leave.

"Okay," I say, pushing off the wall. Gathering myself together, I turn to the door.

I reach for the handle and pause to look back at him.

I just want one more look before I leave.

He's staring at me, too, a mixture of confusing emotions on his face.

"Good-bye, Adam."

He holds my eyes for a moment, then, looks away. "Good-bye, Evie."

There's a power in his words. He's saying the good-bye he didn't get to say ten years ago.

Taking a deep breath, I hold in the tears fighting to break free, and I walk out and finally close the door on my past.

# Evie
## MALIBU · JULY 2004

My alarm is going off with an annoying insistence. On a groan, I reach over and slam my hand on it, turning it off.

*Time for work.*

*Ugh.*

Summer has only just begun, and I've worked the last seven days straight as a favor for Grady. I can't wait for tomorrow when I can sleep in.

I'm only doing the overtime because Grady is the best boss ever—a retired pro surfer, and the Shack is his life—and he asked me because we're short-staffed at the moment. I'm also doing it because I need the money.

Paige, who works part-time in the shop with Base and me, has been on vacation. And Tad, who does the surf lessons with Grady, has been out sick with the flu. So,

Grady has been pulling Base out of the shop to help with the surf lessons. So, I've been manning the shop alone. But Tad and Paige will be back tomorrow, so I'll get the day off. *Yay!*

For tomorrow, I was thinking, once I drag my ass out of bed, that I might actually spend the day at the beach and lie out in the sun, read a book, swim, and maybe do some surfing.

I can't remember the last time I just spent the day at the beach chilling and having fun. Aside from the hour I get there every day, sketching after work to kill the time I have to wait for my bus.

I can get some real sketching time in tomorrow as well. The beach is my favorite place to go to draw, especially on my spot on the rock. I love that view. I've gotten some great sketches done from up there. I can see right out over the ocean, and it gives me a great view of the pier as well as all the surfers—along with one particular hot guy in a beach house.

*Adam.*

I knew I had to draw him the moment I saw him standing up there on his balcony. I captured the image of him there in my mind and started drawing. What I didn't expect was for him to be standing there every day, watching me.

But knowing his eyes were on my back while I drew the image I had pressed into my memory of him standing there, so tall and so handsome, made me not only want to draw him…it made me want to know him.

He looked so lonely.

The kind of loneliness where he could be surrounded in a roomful of people, and he'd still feel alone.

The kind of loneliness that comes from within, deeply embedded inside of him.

And I wanted to capture that and pull the loneliness out, bringing him to life on paper.

I can't believe I gave him the drawing I'd done of him. It was so ballsy of me, and I'm not usually ballsy.

Actually, the whole thing was pretty ballsy of me, especially when I asked him if he'd changed his mind about asking me out.

God, I'm cringing from just thinking about it.

For all my bravado with Adam, I actually don't really date.

It's not because I don't want to. I just don't really have the time, and I haven't met a guy who I really want to go out with.

I tend not to get dazzled by cute guys anymore. They're in such abundance here, and I see them daily while working at the Shack.

That was up until yesterday when I was dazzled by the super tall and super hot guy who lives on the beach and watches me draw.

I literally couldn't stop looking at him.

With a body like a god, he's stupidly handsome. And when I say stupidly handsome, I mean, he's the kind of handsome that would make a smart girl go stupid and also make that smart girl do stupid things.

I could imagine doing a lot of stupid things with Adam.

A guy like him could make a girl like me lose my damn mind.

He's so intriguing, and his eyes are amazing. They are the most intense blue-green color that I have ever seen. They're practically turquoise. His eyes are like an infinite pool of water, a place you could easily get lost in and never once get bored.

And a girl like me could easily get lost in a guy like him.

Aside from all his physical attributes, there is just something about him.

I've been finding myself thinking about him more and more since we spoke yesterday.

Throughout the last week, every day, when I went down to the beach, I wondered if he'd be there, watching. As the week went on, I started to feel a little sad when my hour was up, and I had to leave to catch my bus.

Now, Adam has asked me out, and I really want to go out with him even though I won't actually have time to date him, especially when school starts back up. In my last year of high school, I'll still be working evenings and weekends at the Shack on top of the schoolwork I'll have to do, so that won't leave any time to date.

But Adam has got me wanting things I shouldn't, like doing hot naked things with him.

*Oh my God!* I can't believe I just thought that!

I cover my face with my hands, a blush creeping over my body at the thought.

It's all just so crazy! Adam watching me from his balcony, while I pretended not to know, and was secretly drawing his picture.

Then, his friend Max told me that Adam was going to ask me out. Honestly, when he said that, I nearly burst out laughing. I thought I'd skipped back to kindergarten. I didn't really take Max that seriously—until Adam showed up on the beach and started talking to me.

He didn't seem shy, like I had expected. In fact, he wasn't shy at all. He was the total opposite. If anything, he was overly confident but not in that annoying cocky way that some guys could be.

And I just felt strangely comfortable around him, talking to him. It was like I'd known him for a long time already, which was crazy. I felt like I could say anything to him, and it wouldn't matter.

And I did.

*"I'll let you know."*

I almost laugh out loud at myself.

Listen to me, being evasive. I was dying to say yes.

Honestly, I would have gone out with him then and there if I hadn't had to get home to look after Casey while Dad went out.

Dad goes out one night a week to play darts with his friend Terry. Aside from that, he doesn't go out, so I didn't want to let him down.

But I'm thinking, when I go to the beach later today after I finish work, I might just accept Adam's invitation to go out. It might not turn into anything anyway, but it's a date with a hot guy, and I haven't had one of those in…well, never.

Dragging my tired butt out of bed, I head to the bathroom.

The house is quiet. Casey and Dad must still be sleeping.

Showered, teeth brushed, hair tied into a ponytail, and dressed in my work uniform, I'm ready to go half an hour later.

I head out into our tiny kitchen, which overlooks our tiny living room.

Dad's in there with Casey.

She's watching cartoons while eating breakfast. Typical seven-year-old. You wouldn't know, aside from her short hair, that she only finished having radiotherapy six months ago. She only lost hair in a patch on the part of her brain they were treating. But she said she looked stupid with long hair and a bald patch, so she had me take her to the hair salon to cut it all off.

Casey had an ependymoma, grade II, brain tumor. And she's the bravest kid I have the privilege to know and love.

The tumor was discovered ten months ago, only two years after we'd lost Mom.

Out shopping for my birthday presents, my parents had gotten into a car accident while I was in school and Casey was in preschool. A truck driver had a heart attack behind the wheel, lost control, and careened through the midsection, straight into my parents' car.

Mom was killed instantly. Dad survived, barely.

Casey and I had to go into foster care while Dad recovered in the hospital, as we had no other family to take care of us. Our grandparents on both sides had died before we were born.

Dad had taken some pretty severe trauma to the head, which affected his short-term memory, and he lost use of his right arm.

He can never work again.

My dad had been an accountant. We'd had a great life. We weren't rich, but we weren't poor either.

When Dad had to quit work, it was tough. Fortunately, his old job covered his medical bills. But we still had a mortgage to pay, and the compensation he'd received from the accident wasn't going to last forever.

Then, Casey got sick, and things got worse, substantially worse.

Casey had been having headaches. Our doctor checked her over, and had referred her to see an ophthalmologist. Before she even went to the appointment, she collapsed at school. They rushed her to the hospital, and that was when they discovered the tumor on her brain.

She had surgery where they removed as much of the tumor as they could. Then, she began radiotherapy four weeks later. What was left of the tumor after surgery shrank to nothing with the radiation therapy. The cancer was gone, and the doctor said her physical signs were well. So, she was going to be fine.

But we were left with big medical bills. After Dad had left his job, he didn't take out private healthcare. And surgery and radiation therapy didn't come cheap. So, we had to sell the house and downsize to a three-bedroom rent-controlled apartment on Carbon Canyon Road. The money from the sale of our old house and the compensation that Dad received from the car accident paid off Casey's hospital bills.

Dad's disability checks as well as the money I bring in from working at Grady's are what keeps us afloat. But it's not enough. I work as much as I can at Grady's, taking on extra shifts when they come up, like what I've been doing this week. But I will have to go to part-time hours once school starts back up, and when I graduate, I'll work for Grady full-time until I can find something that pays more.

I would quit school now and work full-time, but Dad won't let me. It kills him that I go out to work now. He wants me to be a normal teenager, enjoying summers at the beach with friends. But I told him that's just not the way it's supposed to be for me at the moment. So, he's given up fighting me on it.

I get a Pop-Tart and warm it in the toaster.

Grabbing my bag, I check to make sure my sketchpad and pen are in there.

I go into the living room.

"I'm going to work." I lean over and kiss Dad on the top of his head.

"You got a hug for me, Case?"

She gets up with a beautiful big smile on her face. "Have a good day at work."

"I'll try to. Love you, Case." I give her a big squeeze before letting go.

I head out the door and do the ten-minute walk to the bus stop. I'm only waiting a few minutes before it pulls up, and I jump on to take a seat.

I pull my sketchpad out of my bag and continue working on a new sketch I've had stuck in my head since yesterday.

Before I know it, the bus is pulling up to my stop. I get off and make my way to the store. Grady is just opening up as I arrive.

"Morning, Evie Girl," he says. Opening the door, he lets me through first.

"Hey, Grady. You want some coffee?"

"You see? This is why I hired you. Because you know just what people want at the exact right time."

"It's a gift." I smile at him.

"Damn good gift to have." He chuckles. "It'll take you far in this world."

I let out a laugh. "If only that was the truth. I'll make us that coffee."

The day is dragging like hell, and my days never drag here. There's always something to do. We're always busy with customers, or we have new stock coming in. The place is always buzzing.

Today hasn't been any different. I've been nonstop busy, but that hasn't stopped the clock from slowing down.

I can only put it down to one thing. I want it to be five p.m.

At five p.m., I'll get to go to the beach, and I'll get to see Adam.

I've turned into one of those girls who go all dreamy-eyed over a boy.

*Do I walk up to his beach house or just go straight to my rock?*

*I mean, he's usually out there when I'm walking along the beach.*

*I guess if he's there, I can go over and say hi.*

*And if he's not, I'll just go to my rock and wait for him to come over.*

*What if he doesn't come over?*

Oh God, I've turned into one of those annoying overanalytical girls.

To stop myself from going insane, I go into the stockroom and grab a box of T-shirts that's just been delivered, intending to get them out on the shelves. I hear the shop bell ring as I've just lugged the box down from the shelf.

Grady's out back with Base, cleaning the boards from the lesson they've just done, so I'd better get back out on the shop floor.

Armed with my box, I walk back into the store and then freeze on the spot.

*Adam.*

He's here in the Shack.

He looks so much more imposing here in the shop than he did yesterday. I mean, I knew he was tall, but I feel doll-sized compared to him.

And he looks even more gorgeous, if that's possible. He's wearing a pair of black board shorts, a red T-shirt, and flip-flops.

He even has nice feet. And I don't like feet, especially men's feet. They're usually all hairy and gross.

But Adam? Well, he has nice feet. They're all tan and sexy and not too hairy.

*Oh God.*

I lift my eyes back up his body to his face, my eyes meeting with his.

There's a sexy smile on his lips.

He totally knows I was checking him out. And you know what? I don't even care that I got caught.

He's hot. It should be illegal not to stare at the man.

I grin at him, and that smile of his deepens.

And I melt into a puddle of goo.

"You need a hand with that?" He nods at the box weighing my arms down.

"Um, sure."

He comes over, and I get a whiff of him. He smells like the ocean and sunscreen.

His hand brushes my arm as he takes the box from me, and I have to control the shiver it elicits in me.

"Where do you want it?"

"On the counter is fine. Thanks."

I watch him walk over to the counter before putting the box down.

*He's here. I can't believe he's here.*

*Did he come here to see me?*

*I doubt it. I never told him I worked here.*

*But then he would have seen the logo on my shirt, if he were paying attention. And I get the impression that not much escapes Adam.*

*But I can't see why he'd come here to see me, as he would have known I would be going to the beach later.*

"So, what brings you to Grady's?" I ask as he walks back over to me.

"You."

*Me? Me!* My insides do a little happy dance.

"Me?" My voice has gone slightly high-pitched.

"Yeah." He moves closer. So close, I have to tilt my head back to look up at him. "Also, I was out, getting a frame."

"A frame?"

"Mmhmm. For the picture you drew for me."

A swarm of butterflies start having a disco party in my stomach.

"You know, you should really let me pay you for it."

"You like it?"

He stares at me for a long moment, so long that my mouth dries, and those butterflies flitter up my throat.

"Yeah, I do. I like it a lot."

*Holy God. I'm so done for.*

The sound of Grady's and Base's voices coming from the back room snaps me out of it.

They both come to a stop when they see Adam and me. Maybe we're standing closer than a customer and shop assistant should be.

No maybe about it, we are.

I take a small step back.

"Hey, man," Grady says to him.

"Hey." Adam gives him a nod.

"Our Evie Girl taking care of you?"

"Oh, yeah." Adam's eyes come back to me. "She's looking after me just fine."

I'm pretty sure my whole body is on fire. With lust. For him.

*Dear God…*

"So…" I clear my cluttered throat. "What are you looking for today?"

"An answer to my question."

"Which question?"

He bridges that gap I just put between us and lowers his voice slightly as he says, "I asked you out yesterday, and you said you'd let me know today. I'm here to get my yes, so I can finally take you out on that date."

*Sweet baby Jesus.*

I'm well aware that Grady and Base are still here, probably being a pair of nosy parkers and listening in.

"And what if I was going to say no?"

"Then, I'd keep asking until you changed your mind."

That makes me smile. "Okay," I say.

"Okay?"

"Yes." I smile. "I'll go out with you."

"Now?"

I let out a laugh. "I can't go out with you now. I'm working. But I get off at five—"

"She's finished for the day." Grady comes over, handing my bag to me.

"What?" I turn to him, taking the bag being pushed at me.

He has this huge grin on his face. "I think you deserve some time off."

"But, Grady, the money. I need—"

"It's covered, Evie. Just go out and be seventeen. Have some fun."

I stare at him for a moment. "Okay. Thank you," I say tentatively. "But I will make up the hours."

He chuckles at me, shaking his head, as I start to move away, Adam with me.

"See ya, Base." I wave at him.

"Later, Evie."

I follow Adam through the store and out the door he holds open for me.

"So, you're seventeen?" Adam says the second we're outside.

"I am. Is that a problem?" I never considered how old he was. I mean, he's clearly older than me. Well, he looks older.

"Not at all."

"How old are you?" I ask him.

"Eighteen. I turn nineteen in September."

"I'm a March baby."

"I'll have to remember that."

He smiles at me, and I feel a fluttering in my chest.

He comes to a stop by a really fancy-looking Mercedes. It's a really nice car.

"Is this yours?" I ask, impressed.

"Mmhmm."

He unlocks the car and pulls the handle on the door. And it opens up. And when I say up, I mean, it literally lifts up, not opening like a conventional car door.

"Wow," I say, my eyes wide.

"Yeah. It's kinda cool, I guess."

It's more than cool. "So, you like cars?"

He shrugs. "I guess. Yeah, they're okay. My parents bought it for me on my eighteenth birthday."

"Well, they must really like you—a lot." I give a teasing smile.

"Not really." He looks away, not before giving me a tight smile.

His body language screams tense, and I really wish I hadn't said anything.

But, now, I think I see the reason for that loneliness I first saw in him.

*Absent rich parents maybe?*

But that car must have cost a fortune. That's some serious money. I got that he was wealthy. Most people in Malibu are. And the beach house he's staying in wouldn't have been cheap. But the kind of money this sort of car would go for is so beyond out of my league that I wouldn't know what to do with it even if I had it.

And it serves to remind me of just how poor I am.

Maybe he won't want to date me when he finds out that we are polar opposites. Or maybe that's just a really shitty thing for me to think. I'm guessing he knows I don't swim in his end of the pool, considering I'm spending my summer working at the Shack.

But poor girl and rich boy? You know what people always think in these scenarios. And I don't want to be that girl ever. Or quite possibly I'm seriously overthinking this. I mean, we haven't even been on a date yet.

"So, you're kind of rich, huh?" I say quietly.

He shifts, like he's uncomfortable, his eyes still not on me, but off in the distance.

I'm starting to get that being rich isn't necessarily a good thing for him.

His hands find the pockets of his shorts. Then, his eyes finally come back to mine. The color in them is so vibrant that it momentarily takes my breath away.

"I am. Is that a problem?" he asks, taking my words from before and giving them back to me.

"No." I shake my head, letting a smile on my lips. "So long as you don't try to buy me a car or anything," I joke, trying to lighten the air.

He chuckles, the tension in him visibly easing. "I'll try to refrain from doing so."

"Good," I say, slipping into the leather seat. "Because I can't drive."

He shuts my door, and I buckle in. He gets in the driver's side a few seconds later.

"So, where are we going?" I ask.

He puts his seat belt on. "You hungry?" he asks me.

"Sure. I could eat."

He turns the engine on, and the radio comes on in the middle of Don Henley's "The Boys of Summer."

"I love this song," I tell him. "It reminds me of…summer."

He glances at me, and I snort out a laugh, causing him to smile so wide that it's dazzling.

"You want the top down?" he asks.

It takes me a minute to realize that he's talking about the car. At first, I thought he was asking if I wanted his top down…to which I would have said, *Yes, please.*

*God, I'm such a pervert.*

Adam must know the direction my brain has taken as he lets out a low chuckle that I feel everywhere. My cheeks start to redden. He presses a button on the dash, and the top goes down, letting the sun in. Then, he pulls out into the street.

We drive for a while, the conversation flowing freely. We've just gotten on the interstate when we get on the subject of surfing. Adam tells me that's why he's in Malibu, to surf. Which isn't surprising. It's why most people come here.

"Do you like to surf?" he asks me.

"I work at a surf shop. It's the law. I think Grady would sack me if I didn't like surfing."

He laughs. "We should go surfing together."

"Today?" I squeak. "It's a bit late in the day to catch any good waves, and I don't have my board or any swimwear."

"No. I meant, another day." He looks over at me.

Heat erupts deep inside me. "Are you asking me out on another date?"

"Maybe." His eyes go to the road ahead, but there's a definite smile touching his lips.

"Isn't that a dangerous thing to do?"

"Dangerous?" His eyes flicker back to mine.

"Well, we haven't even had this date. By the end of it, you might decide that you never want to see me again."

Another look. "I highly doubt it."

"You never know though," I say. "And you can't be sure until this date is over. So, at the end of this date, if you decide you want to see me again, then ask me again."

His eyes come to mine, holding a second longer this time. "I will."

His eyes release me, and I let out the breath I was holding.

Glancing out the window, I see that we're getting close to Point Dume.

Adam indicates a turn and then pulls onto the street, and parks the car. "Do you like pizza?" he asks.

"I do."

"Good." He climbs out of the car. "Any toppings you don't like?"

"Olives and anchovies. But I'm cool with anything else."

Stopping, he leans back into the car. "I swear, you are the girl of my dreams." He gives me a cheeky grin. "Wait here. I'll be back in five, ten max."

*The girl of his dreams…holy wow.*

It's more like twenty minutes before Adam comes back to the car. I would have started to get worried, thinking he'd ditched me, if I hadn't been sitting in his fancy car.

"Sorry about that," he says, sounding a little out of breath, as he gets back into the car, pizza box in hand. "Took longer than I thought."

"You want me to hold that?" I refer to the pizza box.

"That'd be good. It'd be pretty awkward to drive with." He smiles.

I take the box from him, placing it on my lap.

*So, he's not taking me out for dinner. We're having take-out pizza.*

I am so down with that.

He is doing the exact opposite of what I thought he would. And it makes me like him even more.

"Oh, and I got you this." He holds out a rose in his left hand, which he was apparently hiding at his side.

"There was a flower shop next door to the pizzeria," he explains.

I can't speak. I'm staring at it, surprised and overawed. And it is crazy because it's a damn flower. But it's a flower…from him.

"Too cheesy?" He gives me a lopsided grin as he bites the inside of his lower lip, making him look even handsomer.

Way too handsome for my good.

I shake my head, staring into his eyes. My heart is going a mile a minute. "Not cheesy at all." My voice sounds breathless.

Something ignites in his eyes and it makes my stomach flip.

I take the rose from him. Pressing it to my nose, I inhale.

It smells amazing. He's amazing.

Adam turns the engine on. We're back on the road, and a few minutes later, he pulls up into the car park at Point Dume.

"We're here." He turns the engine off and gets out of the car.

I follow suit. Keeping ahold of my rose, I hook my bag on my shoulder and get out of the car, carrying the pizza box in my hand.

Adam is opening the trunk. He gets out a blanket and a bag.

"Here, let me take that." He takes the pizza from my hand. "You're not afraid of heights, are you?"

Smiling, I shake my head. "I spend an hour a day sitting up on a high rock while I sketch."

"Good point."

We walk up the trail for a short distance, and I follow Adam along until we're on a grassy cliff edge, overlooking the Pacific Ocean.

I can hear the waves washing up against the rocks below.

Stopping, he puts the blanket down and then the pizza box. Kneeling on the blanket, he opens his bag and pulls out two wine glasses and a bottle of sparkling water.

"Dinner is served." He grins up at me.

And I feel that smile in all parts of my body, my heart especially.

I kneel down across from him on the blanket. "Do you always carry wine glasses and sparkling water in your car?"

"Only when I know I'm going on a date with a beautiful girl, and I want to impress her."

*Beautiful girl.*

Okay, I might have swooned a little.

"And do you go on dates with beautiful girls often?"

"First time for me."

"Dates or beautiful girls?"

"A date with a beautiful girl."

I let out a little laugh. "Smooth."

He winks at me. On any other guy, it would look cheesy. On him, it works.

"Anyway, how did you know I'd say yes? I could have said no."

"But you didn't."

"No, I didn't." I smile at him. Then I say, "Why did you wait so long to come over and talk to me?"

"Honestly, I'm not sure." His shoulders lift. "I guess, you were so concentrated on your drawing, and I didn't want to interrupt."

"And what changed yesterday?"

"Max."

"Ah, Max. How is he, by the way?"

"Dead. I killed him for telling you that I'd been watching you sketch."

"You need help burying the body?" I say with a straight face.

"Bonnie and Clyde style?" His eyes smile at me.

"Totally." I laugh.

"Well, thanks for the offer—and good to know that you have my back if I need to dispose of a body—but lucky for Max, I love him like a brother, so he's still currently breathing."

We lapse into silence.

"It didn't matter, you know, that Max told me that you were watching," I say softly. "I already knew. I was...well, I was kind of watching you, too." Biting my lip, I slide my eyes to him, gauging his response. "Maybe not as much, but I was watching."

His eyes lock with mine. "The drawing?"

"Yeah." I blush.

"It's really beautiful."

For a second, I wonder if he's talking about me again or the picture.

"I'm glad you like it." I look away, the moment almost too much for me.

I'm feeling too much, too soon.

"Do you have your sketchpad with you?" he asks.

"Yeah. I carry it everywhere with me. Kind of sad really."

"Not at all. If I could carry my surfboard everywhere with me, I would."

"You really love surfing."

"Yeah," he breathes the word out. Then, his eyes meet back with mine.

"I thought maybe you might want to sketch out here after dinner, which we should eat before it gets cold." He opens the pizza box.

"Are you going to watch me sketch?"

His lips tug up at the corners.

"I can look away while you do it, if you want?"

"No." I smile. "I kind of like it when you watch me draw."

Our eyes meet again.

"Me, too."

Adam pulls up outside my apartment building and turns the engine off, plunging us into darkness, except for the low light of the streetlamps.

We were out for hours up at Point Dume. After we ate, I drew for a while, doing a sketch of the view, and Adam watched, asking me questions as I drew.

It was perfect.

Then, we went for a walk until darkness forced us back to the car.

Now that he's driven me home, our date is over. I'm just reluctant to leave him. I've never had such a great time as I've had with him.

I turn in my seat to face him. "Thanks for a wonderful afternoon slash evening. And for the ride home."

"Thank you for saying yes to going out with me."

"I was always going to." I smile, resting my head against the seat.

"Oh, I know."

"Cocky." I laugh.

"Nah. I'm just irresistible."

That he is.

"Are you going to let me pay you for this drawing?"

He's referring to the sketch I did of the view from Point Dume.

"No, because that would be beyond weird—you giving me money while we're out on a date."

"Good point." He chuckles. "Well, thank you for the drawing. It'll look great next to my other one."

I get my bag from the car floor, my rose in my hand. I've hardly put it down all night. "I should get inside." I reach for the door handle.

"I'll walk you to your apartment."

I almost sigh a breath of relief because my time with him isn't quite over yet.

We climb out of his car at the same time, and he meets me at my side.

We start the walk to my apartment, side by side, and I feel his hand brush against mine. Then, his little finger hooks onto mine until he has worked his fingers into mine, and he's holding my hand.

The sizzling sensation from his touch on my skin is indescribable.

My heart is going nuts, and my breathing is out of control.

"Well, this is me," I say as we reach my front door.

Reluctantly I let go of his hand. I get my key out of my bag and turn to face him.

He's a lot closer than I expected. We're literally standing an inch apart.

I can feel the heat of his body, and he smells so good, like the ocean and something so uniquely him.

I look up into his face. He's already staring down at me. And the way he's looking at me…it's like need and desire and a whole other bunch of stuff I can't even begin to explain. It makes my toes curl, and my own need unfurls inside of me.

His hand comes to my face. His thumb brushes over my skin and grazes the edge of my lips, making me shiver.

I have never felt anything like this before, the way I feel with him right now.

I'm pretty sure he's going to kiss me. *God, I hope so.*

"You said if I wanted to see you again, I should ask you at the end of our date." His voice is rough and deep in the silence. "It's the end of our date, so I'm asking. Spend the day with me tomorrow. Go surfing with me."

"Yes."

A smile lifts the corner of his lips. "Yes?"

"Yes." I grin.

His eyes flicker down to my mouth. Something hot and dark enters his gaze, making my mouth go dry.

I swallow. Then, I lick my lips.

His eyes flare and lift to mine. Desire is burning wildly in his eyes, in the heated silence.

Need shoots down the length of my spine.

I have never wanted a guy to kiss me as much as I want Adam to.

"I'm going to kiss you now," he whispers.

*Thank God.*

All I can do is nod. I'm struggling to breathe, so speaking isn't even an option.

He lowers his head to mine, and then his mouth is on mine...and—

*Oh my God.*

It's not that I've kissed a lot of guys because I haven't, but the feel of Adam's lips on mine...is perfection.

He tastes like pizza and mints. It's a weird combination when you think about it, but it works on him. But then again, anything works on him.

His other hand comes up, holding the nape of my neck his fingers push up into my hair.

I can't think or breathe. I can only feel his mouth on mine, and I never want it to end.

I part my lips on a sound of need, my hands sliding up his chest. His tongue gently sweeps over mine. Then, he sucks on my lower lip, and he's pulling back, far too quickly for my liking.

"Tomorrow," he says, sounding way too composed.

Our faces are only millimeters apart, his eyes staring into mine.

I'm so not composed. My breaths are coming out in quick short pants. I'm a mess of emotions, and hormones.

*I really want to kiss him again.*

"Mmhmm."

He chuckles softly. Then, removing his hands from me, he steps away.

My body cries out in distress for him to come back.

"I'll pick you up at seven a.m., so we can get there early and catch some good waves."

"Mmhmm."

"Evie?"

"Yeah?" I'm still gazing at him—well, gazing at his mouth to be exact. He has really nice lips.

"What time am I picking you up?"

I come to a little, focusing on his eyes. Realizing that I'm behaving like a total girl, my face heats. I clear my throat, gathering my wits. "Seven."

He smiles at me, and I feel it deep inside.

"I'll see you then."

I watch as he turns and leaves down the steps.

I fall back against my door, touching my fingers to my lips, the feel and taste of him still there. The kiss was short, but I feel like he's been touching me for hours.

My legs are like jelly while my heart threatens to burst out of my ribcage.

I stay there until I hear his car pulling away, awakening me to move.

I unlock the front door and let myself in.

My dad is in the living room. He never goes to bed until I'm home, not that I'm ever usually out late. I'd text him earlier while I was waiting for Adam to come back with the pizza, to let him know I was out with a friend.

"You have a good time?"

"Yeah. I did." I can't contain my giddy smile.

Dad gives me a curious look, so I tell him a quick goodnight, and I head to my bedroom, looking in on Casey as I pass her room. She's fast asleep.

I drop down onto my bed, pressing the rose to my nose again.

I feel giddy with excitement.

I place the rose on my bedside table, and then I set my alarm for six in the morning. So much for my sleep in. I'm getting up even earlier than I normally do for work.

But ask me if I care.

Not at all because I'll be spending the day with Adam.

*Oh God, am I in trouble.* After having this time with him today, I'm feeling all kinds of crazy about him. So, what will I be like after a full day with him tomorrow?

I'll be done for, that's what I'll be.

So, freaking done for.

## Adam
## MALIBU · JULY 2015

Entering the water, I paddle out on my board, pushing through the waves. Paddling out farther, I need big waves.

I need to surf Evie out of my head.

I need the peace that only being out here can give me.

It's been five days since our talk. I haven't spoken to her since. I have caught glimpses of her on my way back in and out of the hotel as I pass by the coffee shop, but I've avoided going in there.

I've had to go to Starbucks. So, now, I've lost my decent fucking coffee as well.

I've been staying away from her for many reasons, and it's not just the fact that she broke my heart. Seeing her again has screwed me up so much.

I knew I wasn't over her—I'd have to be stupid to ever think I was—but I didn't realize how badly I'd want her again. The urge to touch her and taste her was overwhelming. Just breathing the same air as her was fucking killing me.

Standing there, staring at her, I was eighteen all over again.

From the moment I'd seen Evie sitting up on that rock eleven years ago, I'd been obsessed.

I lusted her, then loved her, and then hated her. I've mentally chased her for the last ten years, never giving her up.

My obsession has always been there.

I never could get enough of Evie. And no matter what she's done to me, whether I love her or hate her, I will always want her.

I fucking hate that.

I hate that she's my weakness. She controls my life, and she's not even a part of it.

Seeing her after all that time…it felt like it should have been more explosive, bigger somehow, epic—not just me yelling at her in a hotel room.

I'd spent that whole day pretending to listen at my shitty meetings when what I was actually doing was preparing in my head what I would say to Evie when I saw her, while also watching the clock like a fucking hawk.

Then, when the moment came, it didn't go how I'd expected it to, and really, I still don't have any answers.

I expected closure, needed it, but all I've got is a truckload of more fucking questions and the incessant urge to fuck her.

No matter what was happening between Evie and me, I always wanted her—even when she was pissing me off, which was not that often.

But wanting her now, after what she did to me…I'm not really sure what that says about me. Probably that I'm fucked up.

The woman shreds my heart and screws up my life, and all I can think about is getting her naked and fucking her.

That's one of the reasons I'm avoiding her—because fucking Evie is the last thing I should do.

Also, I have something to tell her.

In my hypocrisy, I was fighting her for answers when I had a pretty big thing to tell her myself.

I fucked up in the worst way, and I've pretended for a long time that she deserved it. That it didn't matter because I couldn't find her, but now, she's here, and it matters.

In my own pathetic way, I was punishing her by not telling her.

But now, it's time. I have to tell her.

I just have to find the strength to see her again.

I see a big beautiful wave approaching, and I get that familiar feeling of adrenaline pumping through my veins. I'm so ready to ride Evie out of my head, even if only for a few precious seconds. I get up on my board. Then, I'm on the wave, riding it, but my thoughts are still scattered, and the peace I crave is nowhere to be seen.

Instead, I see is Evie's perfect fucking face and I hear her voice in my head with way more clarity than I need right now.

I just need her gone.

*Do I really?*

Yes. I just need to tell her what I have to tell her, and then we're done. And doing this will finally close the door on her.

I won't ever truly be over her. I'll always love her. But I have to let her go now.

It's on that thought that I hit the wave like a novice, and I'm flying off my board. Following in my rookie mistake, I don't protect my head with my arms, and the board smacks me right in the face.

"Fuck!" My voice is gargled up with water, the shock of it momentarily stunning me, and then I'm kicking back up, breaking the surface.

"Jesus Christ," I growl. I touch my hand to my face to make sure I'm not bleeding, but my eye is throbbing like a bitch.

*Fan-fucking-tastic.*

I reel my board in and get back up on it. I ride the whitewash back to shore.

I walk up the sand, dump my board on it, and drop down, lying on my back. I cover my face with my hands and let out a groan of frustration.

"Want to tell me why you just wiped out like a rookie?"

I move my hand away to see Grady standing over me, his overgrown gray hair dripping water on me.

"Not particularly."

He leans in for a close inspection. "Gonna need some ice on that eye."

"It's fine." I sit up. Knees bent, I link my hands over them and stare out at the surf. I envy the other surfers out there, enjoying their solitary freedom, while I'm trapped in my head.

Grady drops down to the sand beside me. "You wanna talk about what's bugging the fuck out of you?"

Grady's been a good friend to me over the years. Probably more like the father I never had.

After Evie left and things went to shit, I moved to Boston and went to Harvard like Ava and Eric wanted, but I always kept in touch with Grady. Part of it was that he was a link to Malibu, my link to Evie, even though he didn't know where she was. She hadn't only abandoned me back then. Somewhere along the way, Grady became my friend.

We surf together every weekend. Max usually comes with us when he's not stuck in the office. He's got a big case at the moment though, and it's eating up his time. He's an entertainment lawyer at his family's company. Hates it just like I hate my job. Max and I were screwed from the second we both were born.

Letting out a sigh, I dig my toes into the sand. Staring ahead, I say, "Evie's back."

I haven't said those words to anyone, not even Max, yet.

"Ah," Grady says.

"Yeah." I exhale. "She's in Beverly Hills, working at the coffee shop in the fucking hotel I call home five days a week."

"You talk to her?"

"For all the good it did me."

"How is she?"

Of course he would want to know that. He cared about Evie, thought of her as one of his own, because that's just how Grady is.

"She's okay, I guess." I shrug. "We didn't really get around to the pleasantries."

He nods. "She tell you where she's been all these years?"

"San Francisco."

"Not that far away," he muses. "Did you get the answers you wanted? Why she left?"

I let out a humorless laugh. "Not really. I got a lot of bullshit reasons but not the truth."

"What was the bullshit?"

"That us getting married was too much too soon, and she panicked and ran." My hand slips into the sand, and I curl a fist around the grains.

"Sounds plausible."

I give him a look. "Sure, if she hadn't upped and left with her whole family. Her panicking and leaving is one thing. Uprooting and moving when her sister was as sick as

79

she was? It's bullshit, Grady. It doesn't make sense. It never did."

"So, what could it be?"

I shrug. "You know, back then, I used to think that maybe it was…"

"Ava?"

"Mmhmm. I just…I don't know anymore." I blow out a breath.

Back when Evie first left, I did think that it could have been Ava's doing. Of course, when I asked her, she denied all knowledge.

*But, then, what could Ava have done or given to Evie to make her leave? To make them all leave?*

*Money?*

It's hard to believe that because Evie was never about money. If it were money, then I'm glad she left because she wouldn't have been the person I thought I loved.

But, then, it's not like she has money now. If she had money, then, she wouldn't be working in a coffee shop.

Sometimes though, I feel like there's a voice whispering the answer in the back of my mind, just slightly out of my reach.

Grady stares out over the water. "You know, you might never get the answers you want."

I huff out a breath. Opening my fist, I let the grains run through my fingers. "Yeah, I know."

"And did you…tell Evie?"

Grady is the only person who knows my secret. And the only reason he knows is because it was not long after I got back from Boston. I just bought the house. It was what would have been my and Evie's third wedding anniversary. I got drunk off my ass, and I broke down and told him the truth.

Meeting his eyes, I shake my head.

"Fucking hell, Adam." He sighs.

"Don't give me shit, Grady. She turned up out of the blue after ten years. I wasn't exactly thinking straight."

"That might be, but you're thinking straight now. She might have left you, but this isn't something you can keep to yourself. She has a right to know."

Bowing my head, I run a hand through my hair. "I know."

I'm just not sure how to tell her.

# Adam
## MALIBU · JULY 2004

"You're actually ditching me to go surfing with this chick?" Max complains from the living room.

"Stop being a whiny bitch. It's just today. And we'll probably see you down there anyway." I get the orange juice out of the fridge and pour myself a glass.

"Yeah? When? In between you both sucking face?"

I let out a laugh. Walking over to the breakfast bar, I lean my stomach against it. "Jealous much? And you were the one who told me to ask her out."

He rolls his eyes at me from his spot on the sofa. "Yeah, but I thought you'd just bang her and move on. That's what you normally do."

"Not this time."

Max sits up, a look of shock on his face. "Holy shit. You haven't fucked her, have you?"

I shake my head before taking a drink of my orange juice. "She's only seventeen. And anyway, it's not like that."

"Not like what exactly?" He gives me a suspicious look.

I lift a shoulder, unable to explain it or anything about what I'm feeling for Evie. "I don't know. She's just...different." I turn from him, putting my glass in the sink.

"Holy fuck. You like her. You want to play boyfriend and girlfriend with her."

"Shut the fuck up. What are you? Five?" I walk from the kitchen to the living room, grabbing a hair tie off the coffee table, and I tie my hair back.

Ignoring me, he laughs. "I get that she's hot—really hot, in fact—but I never thought I'd see the day when Adam Gunner got pussy-whipped."

"Yeah, and if you want to see another day, then you won't call her hot again, assface."

"Touch a nerve, did I?"

*Bastard's winding me up, and I'm totally biting.*

*Why am I biting? He does this all the time, and I never bite.*

"No. She's just not hot to you." I narrow my gaze on him.

"Don't worry, pussy boy. I don't want to go near her if she's managed to voodoo you into breaking your cardinal rule of one night only. I don't want any of that relationship shit." He flicks a hand at me.

"She hasn't voodooed me, you idiot. And we're not in a relationship. We've been on one date."

"About to go on your second date, the very next morning after your first date. Like I said, relationship."

Shaking my head, I laugh at him and head for the front door. "See you later, fuckface."

"Later, Evie's bitch."

I flip him off before closing the door.

I get in my rental truck, my board and wet suit already in the back, and turn on the engine. Driving the McLaren with a surfboard is about as impractical as it sounds, hence the need for the truck.

As I pull out on the road, the sound of Beyoncé and Jay Z's "Crazy in Love" fills the truck. I turn it up loud, the song igniting the nervous excitement I'm feeling at the thought of seeing Evie again.

She's seriously gotten under my skin.

I've never felt like this about a girl before.

But if it had to happen, making me break my cardinal rule, then I'm happy as hell that it's with Evie.

I pull up to Evie's apartment building to find her already waiting outside.

I wind my window down as she approaches. She's wearing pink flip-flops, jean shorts that are frayed at the bottom, and a pink T-shirt. I can see the bikini string tied around her neck, it's white, and it has my mind wandering to all kinds of hot places. Her hair is down. It's the first time I've seen Evie's hair down. It looks beautiful. And I can't help but imagine how all that long wavy hair would look spread out on my pillow.

"Hey," she says. She has the biggest and most beautiful smile on her face.

*And it's all for me.*

I feel a strange swelling in my chest.

"Hey." I smile back at her. I reach my hand out, curling a lock of her hair behind her ear. I give it a little tug. "First time I've seen your hair down. I like it."

She gives me a shy smile, touching a hand to her hair, as her cheeks turn pink. "Thanks. I haven't seen your hair down either. You always have it tied back."

Grinning, I pull the tie from my hair and shake my hair out. "How does it look?" I give her a cheeky smile.

"Good. Really good."

The way she's looking at me makes my shorts start to feel tight. I shift in my seat to rearrange the big fella.

Refocusing my attention, I say, "You didn't have to wait out here. I would have come up to get you."

"My dad and sister are still sleeping. I didn't want to wake them. Anyway, it's a nice morning to be outside." She reaches up on her tiptoes, leaning against my door, and her fingers curl around the open window. "Good morning, by the way."

"Morning," I whisper. I slide my hand around the back of her head and guide her lips to mine.

She tastes like toothpaste and strawberries.

*Fucking delicious.*

Leaning back, she stares into my eyes. Hers are wide and innocent.

My heart starts to pound, and my cock is definitely paying attention. God, I want her innocence. I want to hide it from the rest of the world and keep it for myself.

I'm pretty sure Evie's a virgin. I got that from the tentative way she kissed me last night. I've kissed a lot of girls, and I'm good at recognizing the inexperienced ones, not that I've ever fucked a virgin. That's something I wouldn't ever do. I don't want the responsibility of being a chick's first time.

But Evie…the thought of being her first…fuck yeah. I want to be her first…and last.

*And listen to me.*

*Only one date, Gunner. You're not even her boyfriend yet.*

*Yet?*

"So, is this another car?" she asks, tapping a hand on the frame.

"It's a rental. The McLaren's not practical for getting my surfboard around, so I rented the truck. I could use Max's truck, but I like to have my own. Hate relying on other people."

"Yeah, I get that. That's why I wish I could drive, so I wouldn't have to catch the bus. I don't mind riding the bus to work, but I hate the waiting around. That's why I come to the beach for that hour—to kill time instead of sitting waiting for it."

"Lucky me that you can't drive."

"Yeah, I guess we wouldn't have met if it wasn't for me catching the bus."

"No, we'd have met. I would have found my way to you somehow."

And I'm turning into a pussy-quoting fool. But honestly, I can't seem to find the will to care about that around her.

As long as I'm making her smile the way she is right now, then I'm happy.

"So, you wanna get in my truck and go catch some waves? Or stay here and make out? Just so you know, I'm happy with either, but my vote does sway heavier with the second option." I give her my best smile, the one that always gets me laid—not that I expect that to happen with Evie anytime soon.

"Surf." She grins at me and then starts to make her way around the truck. "There will be plenty of time for making out later, but the waves won't wait," she adds, climbing into my truck.

She's right even though I would happily ditch surfing to make out with her, which says a lot. I wouldn't normally miss a wave for a girl, not even for a blow job.

"Can we stop by Grady's on the way to the beach?" she asks. "My surfboard's there."

"Sure, but will it be open at this time?"

"No." She starts buckling up. "But Grady's house is behind the Shack, and me and the others who work at the Shack all leave our boards in his garage. Saves taking them home, especially with me riding the bus."

"Will Grady be awake?"

She gives me a crazy look. "He'll already be out surfing. He's usually out there the second the sun starts rising."

Putting the car into drive, I pull out of the apartment parking lot and head back toward the beach.

"So, I'm guessing you're not from Malibu," Evie says as I drive.

"What gave me away?" I smile.

"The fact I've never seen you around before." She smiles back at me. "So, where is home?"

"Beverly Hills." I glance at her.

I see a flicker in her eyes. If anything, it looks like discomfort, not the impressed look girls usually give when I tell them where I'm from.

I don't want Evie to feel intimidated by the money I have—well, that my parents have—so I quickly change the subject. "So, you have a sister?" I ask, well aware that she's never mentioned her mother.

"Yeah, Casey." She smiles big, and I get the impression that Evie adores her sister. "She's seven."

"Big age gap."

"Yeah, my folks struggled to have another baby after me. My mom had a few miscarriages, and then Casey came along. She was our miracle baby." Her happiness fades a little. "She's been sick though, but she's on the mend now," she adds, sounding a little brighter.

"What was wrong with her?" I reach my hand over, taking hold of hers, and I link our fingers together. The feeling is electric. Every time I touch her, the sensation increases. There is nothing like it.

"She had an ependymoma, grade two, brain tumor. The doctors did surgery on it, and she had radiotherapy."

"God, I'm sorry," I say.

"She's doing much better now, but yeah, it was a pretty rough time. We'd lost my mom only a few years before in a car accident."

*Her mother died.*

"Jesus, Evie." I squeeze her hand.

"Oh my God, I'm so sorry. Listen to me talking about my woes, and it's only our second date."

"Don't ever be sorry. I want to hear about it…I want to know *you*," I tell her in all seriousness.

She rests her head against the seat, looking across at me. All I want right now is to hold her in my arms and kiss away every bad thing that has happened to her.

She lets out a breath before speaking. "My mom and dad were in the car on the way back from the mall. They'd been out buying my birthday presents. A truck driver had a heart attack behind the wheel, went through the median, and hit their car."

Her eyes are filled with tears, and my heart contracts in my chest.

"Mom died on impact, which I'm glad for—you know, because she didn't have to suffer any pain." A tear runs from her eye, and she brushes it away. "Dad was in the hospital for a long time. Severe head trauma. He has problems with his short-term memory, and he lost use of his right arm. So, he can't work anymore."

*Jesus.*

Now, I'm seeing the reason she works so many hours at Grady's.

It makes me want to give her every cent I have.

She lets out another breath, swiping her fingers under her eyes. "Look at me, getting teary. I really am sorry."

"Like I said before, don't ever be sorry." I clear my clogged throat. "I think you're amazing and so strong to have gone through all of that and still have the ability to smile that beautiful smile of yours."

I bring her hand to my lips, pressing a kiss to it. I rest our bound hands down on my thigh, and I don't plan on letting go of her for the rest of the drive. Or maybe ever.

"What about your family?" she asks. "Do you have any brothers or sisters?"

"I'm an only child."

*Don't ask about my parents,* I silently wish.

I don't want to tell her who my mother is. People always change toward me the instant they know, and I want to keep things with Evie just the way they are. I want her to stay looking at me the way she is right now, like she sees only me and not my mother.

"What about your folks? What do they do?"

*Fuck.*

*No getting out of it now. I'm not going to lie to her.*

I blow a breath out. "My mother…she's an actress."

"Cool. Stage or TV? Although, I don't get a chance to watch TV, and I don't go to the theater, like ever, so I might not know her. I apologize in advance for my ignorance." She smiles at me, wide, and it's the most beautiful thing.

She is the most beautiful thing I have ever seen.

*Keep looking at me like that, Evie. Please don't ever stop.*

"My mother is Ava Gunner."

I keep my eyes on her for as long as I can. I see the recognition of my mother's name flicker in her eyes.

Then, I wait for it—the change.

But it doesn't come.

"So, does that make you Adam Gunner?"

*Huh?*

"Well, I'm not James Bond." I laugh, a little unsure of what to do in this moment.

"Hey, smart-ass!" She gives me a light jab in the arm. "I meant, I didn't know your surname, and I know actresses can have stage names, so I wondered if that was your surname or if you have a different one. What's wrong—"

It's at this point that I've slammed on the brakes. Luckily, the road is clear of cars behind me.

I lean over and grab her face, and I kiss her, hard.

I kiss her because she doesn't care who my mother is. She cares who I am.

And to me, that is everything.

When I break away, I'm breathing heavily. Evie's breaths are coming out in sharp, short little gasps, and her cheeks are flushed.

"Wow. Okay," she murmurs. "Not that I'm complaining—because…*holy kiss*—but…what was that for?"

I press my forehead to hers and stare deep into her eyes.

"I just told you that my mother was Ava Gunner, and you didn't care."

Her eyes soften on me. "Do people always care?"

I curl my fingers around her ears, taking her hair behind them. "Mmhmm."

"I do know your mom is really famous, but I'm not a big movie person. I don't really get time to watch films, except for Disney movies with Casey. Now, if you'd told me your mom was Stephen King—well, not your mom because that would be weird if your mom was a dude, but you know what I mean. But, yeah, if she'd been him, then it would have been a different story. I would have jumped your bones for sure."

"You'd have jumped my bones?" I raise a brow.

A stain appears on her cheeks. "Well, maybe not jumped your bones, but I'd have definitely been excited."

"Good to know."

She presses her small hands to my face. "Sure, it's cool that your mom is Ava Gunner, and I'm sure she's a really nice person. But, honestly, all I care about is who you are. And from what I know already, I really, really like you."

I brush my thumb over her lips. "I think you're fucking amazing, you know that?"

"I remember you once telling me that, yeah." She bites her lower lip.

"And she's not."

"Who's not, what?" Her eyes are on my mouth.

"My mother. She's not nice."

Her eyes lift to mine. "Oh."

"But that's a story for another day." I give her another gentle kiss before putting the truck back in drive and pull out onto the empty road, feeling a lot lighter than I did a few minutes ago.

We decide to go to Surfrider Beach, which is not far from my house, so I take the car back home where we change into our wet suits. Knowing that Evie is changing in the next room from me, that she is naked in there…it does all kinds of crazy things to me.

Then, we walk down the beach, and Evie tells me all about how Grady taught her how to surf and that he was a pro surfer in his day.

I can't wait to get out on the waves with her and see what she can do.

She's so different compared to the girls back home. I can't imagine one of them getting out on a surfboard. They might break a nail or something.

"Here good for you?" I ask her. Stopping, I assess the waves, which are looking good.

"Yeah." She puts her bag on the sand, standing up her board. "Could you fasten my wet suit up for me?" she asks.

She has the wet suit on fully, but she didn't zip it up all the way. I knew that because, as we were walking here, I couldn't help but notice the bare skin on her back or the small bikini string through the gape.

"Sure."

She turns her back to me. I put my towel and sunscreen next to her bag and then put my board down.

She already tied her hair up back at the house, so I brush her ponytail over her shoulder and see that my hands are shaking.

*What the hell is wrong with me?*

It's not like I've never touched a girl before, and all I'm doing is zipping up her wet suit, for God's sake.

*Get a grip, Gunner.*

Taking ahold of the zipper, I pull it up to the top.

"Thanks," she says when I'm done.

I notice she sounds a little breathless.

"Do mine?" I ask.

"Sure."

She's not even touching my skin, and my cock starts to get hard at the feel of her being so close behind me, her hand pulling up the zipper.

And seriously, a hard-on and a wet suit do not go well together.

I need this boner to disappear.

*Naked old ladies. Hairy, wrinkly naked old ladies.*

*My mother.*

That does it.

"Ready?" I ask.

"I was born ready." She grins, and then she suddenly takes off for the water, her board in hand.

Laughing, I chase after her.

Something in my gut tells me that I'll probably always be chasing after Evie, one way or another.

"You were great out there," I tell her, drying off my hair with my towel.

We've finished surfing and just rinsed off under the outdoor showers, and we are heading back to our stuff on the beach.

I shake my towel out before laying it on the sand, and I peel my wet suit off. I've got my board shorts on underneath. I pull my hair back, tying it up, and then I drop down onto my towel.

Evie has laid her towel out next to mine.

Kneeling on it, she says, "Can you unzip me?"

Sitting up, I take hold of the zipper. I slowly pull it down, the sound loud between us.

Zipping her up before was deliciously tough. Lowering her zipper now…exquisite fucking torture.

The beach is quiet with some people still around, but as far as I'm concerned, there is only her and me.

When the zipper touches its base, I stare at the exposed skin at the bottom of her neck. It looks so soft, so enticing. I want to know how she tastes. And I can't help myself, I press my lips right there.

I feel a shudder run through her body.

"What are you doing?" she asks softly.

"Tasting you," I breathe against her skin. "Is that okay?"

"Yes," she whispers.

Moving closer, she presses into me. My arm slides around her waist as I trail a path of kisses up her neck—until she turns her face to mine. I stare into those whiskey eyes for a long thrilling moment, falling somewhere unknown. Then, I take her mouth with mine. I kiss her gently at first until she's moaning in my mouth and turning in my arms. Her fingers slide behind my neck, linking there, holding me like she never wants to let me go.

And I know for sure that I don't want to let her go.

Then, she breaks the kiss. I see her cheeks are flushed, her lips swollen.

She runs the tips of her fingers across my overgrown stubble. "I can't believe we're making out on the beach."

"Too much too soon?"

She stares into my eyes and shakes her head. "No."

"Good, because I plan on kissing you anytime I get the opportunity."

I want her, so fucking much. And it's not just the kissing even though that rocks. It's more than that. It's her. I want to be around her, to talk to her, to learn everything I can about her.

I have a feeling, when it comes to Evie, nothing will ever be enough. I'll always want more, need more.

"So, what do you want to do for the rest of the day?" I ask, threading my fingers through her hair. "Aside from making out."

That earns me a giggle.

"I don't mind." She lifts her shoulders, looking right at me.

No one has ever looked at me like Evie does. It's like she really sees me. And that makes me feel like a fucking king.

"So long as I'm with you, I'm good," she says.

My heart skips over.

"The feeling is totally fucking mutual, babe."

And it really is.

Two days, and I'm already crazy about her.

She's hit me like a bulldozer. And I don't even care. If anything, I'm happy about it because I have her, and nothing has ever felt better, or more right.

*Evie*
## BEVERLY HILLS · JULY 2015

"Evie."

The sound of Adam's deep voice behind me has the hair on the back of my neck standing on end.

Slowly turning around from the coffee machine I was cleaning, I face him.

He looks just as imposing in here as the last time I saw him, but at least he doesn't look like he's here to yell at me again. Well, that's what I'm hoping.

Honestly, I'm surprised to see him here. I haven't seen him since our talk a week ago. I know he's been avoiding me. I thought I was the last person on earth that he would want to see right now.

But here he is.

Also, I was pretty sure I'd locked the door when I turned the Closed sign. Apparently not.

"We're closed," I say. I don't know why I said that…unless he is actually here for coffee.

"Yeah, I got that from the Closed sign." A small smile touches the corner of his lips.

A warm glow erupts in my chest. *God, I've missed his smile.*

"I'm not here for coffee."

"What are you here for?" I put the cloth in my hand down on the counter.

"We need to talk."

"About?" I'm probably being a little stern. I just don't want a rehash of the other day. I know I deserve it, deserve whatever he has to fire at me, but I've only just recovered from our last encounter.

Well, recovered might be overstating it, but last night was the first night since our talk that I didn't cry myself to sleep. I don't want to start again.

He looks over his shoulder at the door, as though he's expecting someone to come in, and then he looks back to me. "Not here."

I cross my arms over my chest. I don't miss his eyes going to my boobs as they get pushed up. Oddly, it brings me a sense of self-satisfaction. He might hate me, but he still likes my boobs.

*God, get a grip, Evie.*

"Why not? There's only me here, and I don't see a problem with us talking—unless you plan on yelling at me again, because that I could do without."

His eyes flicker to mine. "It's not me yelling that I'm worried about."

"Me?" I let out a laugh. "Why would I yell? I've got nothing to yell about—unless you scratched my car, which I would be kinda pissed about—"

"We're still married."

My brain freezes.

"I'm sorry, what?" I let out an awkward-sounding laugh. "For a second there, I thought you said that we're…still married."

"I did. And we are."

"I-I…what?" All I can do is blankly stare at him. "We're married? I don't understand."

"I never filed the annulment papers that you so kindly left for me. So, yeah, that means we're technically still married. I thought you should know."

It's right then when my head explodes.

"You thought I should know? We-we're married. We've been married for the last ten years. Jesus Christ! I can't…even…" I'm struggling to make sense as well as breathe.

For the last ten years, I've believed my marriage never existed in the eyes of the law even though it meant everything to me. And now, I'm hearing that's not the case at all.

*We're still married.*

My body and brain are jumping between confusion to elation to betrayal, which is funny coming from me because I betrayed him in the worst possible way.

Pinching the bridge of my nose, I take some deep breaths.

After a long moment, I look up at him. "You never filed the annulment papers?"

He slowly shakes his head, eyes fixed on me.

"Why would you not do that?" My words come out on a whisper of hope.

*Hope for what? That he still loves me?*

I almost smack myself in the face for that one.

Adam shrugs.

That sets me off again.

"Jesus, Adam! I'm really confused here! I know I left you, and I did a horrible shitty thing by doing so, but…hell!

I've—we've been married all this time, and I didn't know. There's just something fundamentally wrong with that. What if'—I'm mentally searching around for something to throw at him—"I'd gotten married to someone else?" I have to stop myself from laughing at that one. I've been on exactly one date in the last ten years, so a second marriage wasn't exactly on the cards, but that's beside the point. And for some reason, right now, I want a reason to be mad at him. "You would have made me a freaking bigamist!"

"Look, I'm sorry—"

"You're sorry? Well, that's okay then!" I throw my hands up. "How could you have done this?"

I see fire light behind his eyes.

His palms slam down on the counter, and he leans close to me. "Apparently, as easy as you fucking leaving me without a word."

My eyes widen. "You did this for revenge?" My words come out on a gasp.

I see a muscle pop in his jaw as he works it.

"Nice. Good to know what you think of me, Evie. No, it wasn't for fucking revenge. I was hurt and in denial that you'd left me. I searched everywhere for you, hoping that you'd come back to me. So, filing those papers was the last thing on my mind. By the time I realized what I'd done, the time had lapsed to allow me to file. I had no fucking clue where you were, so it's not like I could call you up and let you know, was it?"

He's got me there. I don't know what to say to that.

I look at the floor, shifting on my feet, feeling instantly shitty again. I wrap my arms around myself. "I guess…that makes sense."

He lets out a humorless laugh. Then, I see his hands lift from the counter. By the time I look up, he's on his way to the door.

"You're leaving?" I hear the panic in my voice. I really hope he didn't.

Stopping, he turns back to me. He looks suddenly weary.

My heart aches for him. Well, everything in me aches for him.

He rubs his forehead with his hand. "I came to tell you about the mistake I'd made. I needed to be honest with you." Those words feel so incredibly pointed, and that's probably because they are. "I've done that. Now, I'm going home."

"You don't think we need to talk about this? Discuss what we're going to do."

"Yeah, we probably do. But not right now. Right now, I just want to have a drink and go to fucking bed." He moves the distance back between us, pulling something from his inside jacket pocket. "My cell and office numbers." He places a business card on the counter and slides it toward me. "Call me tomorrow, and we can talk."

Then, he's gone.

And I'm still married.

Adam and I are still married.

*Holy. Shit.*

I lift the card from the counter, looking down at it.

### ADAM GUNNER

### CEO, GUNNER ENTERTAINMENT

I already knew he worked for the studio.

One time, about five years ago, I looked up his profile on Facebook, using Casey's profile. I couldn't see much as he had it set to private, but I did see his work info, showing that he worked for the studio. I remember how sad I felt at the time. I knew how much he hadn't wanted to be a part of that world. I had been his reason to stay away, and my leaving had sent him straight back.

I had always hoped that he would fight back, stay away. But he didn't.

And I was to blame for that.

The choice I made was to blame for that.

But we weren't supposed to still be married.

Honestly, I don't know how to feel about that.

We're still bound by marriage.

I guess I'm terrified and...thrilled.

I'm still Evie Gunner.

Well, legally anyway. But in my heart, I always have been. It's why I could never move on.

But I know I'm no longer in Adam's heart. He let me go years ago.

I guess it's time for me to let him go now.

*I*'m so done for.

The way I feel about Adam, after knowing him for such a short amount of time, can't be good for me. I mean, it feels good, but it's definitely dangerous.

We've been seeing each other for a few weeks now, and I'm smitten, totally smitten. I'm a smitten kitten. And clearly a massive geek.

We're at the beach. It's early morning, and I have to be at work in a few hours. But we're all here this morning, surfing at the beach just outside Adam's house. Max is out there with Grady, Base, Tad, and Paige. Adam and I quit surfing a while ago. We're sitting up on my rock, and I'm sketching a picture of them all surfing.

Adam is here, with me. He's wrapped around me from behind, his chin resting on my shoulder, while he watches me draw.

His lips skim over my shoulder, and his teeth graze my skin, making me shiver. His fingers trace over the skin on my stomach where they've made their way under the hem of my tank top.

We haven't done anything more than kiss.

He knows I'm a virgin. I told him that on our fourth date. We were making out, and it was getting pretty heavy. I didn't want to lead him on, to think he'd be getting sex, which I wasn't ready to give to him, so I was honest with him. And he was really cool with it. He told me he'd wait for when I was ready. I don't know when that will be, but trust me, if I'm going to lose my virginity to anyone, it will be with Adam.

But my inexperience in that department does worry me a little because I know Adam is very experienced. He hasn't told me that, but I just get the feeling that he has been around the block a few times. I'm not surprised. Looking like Adam does, he could have his pick of girls. So, knowing he's choosing to spend his time with me, sans sex, makes me feel pretty damn special.

And seeing the way Max is with girls also leads me to believe that, prior to me, that was how Adam was spending his time. In the last few weeks, I've seen Max with four different girls, each one exiting his bedroom.

But, man-whore aside, I like Max. He's cool, and even though I've come in and invaded his and Adam's time here together, he has had no issue with it.

I'm not precious when it comes to my virginity. Just right now doesn't feel like the right time. I want to spend more time with Adam, get to know him more, before I go all the way with him. But that doesn't mean I don't want to do other stuff with him. This past week especially, all I've been able to think about is taking things a little, or maybe a lot, further.

And the way he's touching me right now with the heat of his breath on my skin has me tingling in all the right places, making me want his mouth in other places than just my shoulder.

Putting my pencil down on my paper, I lift my hand to his face, scratching my nails over his scruff, until I'm cupping his cheek. I tilt his eyes up to mine.

He smiles at me, and my heart clenches, as do a few other parts of my anatomy.

The way I feel about him…I've never felt anything like it before. In a short space of time, he's become beyond important to me, and I'm struggling to remember my life before him.

But I do remember that it was gray. Now, with him in it, it's filled with color, all varying shades of brightness illuminating my days.

I press my lips to his, giving him a soft kiss.

"So, I've been thinking…"

"About?" he murmurs over my lips, his eyes closed.

"Well…I'm still not ready to have sex, but…I was thinking that maybe…we could do, you know, other stuff."

I feel his body stiffen, and his eyes open to meet mine. "Define *other stuff*."

A blush creeps onto my cheeks. I feel a little embarrassed, talking about this. To be honest, I can't believe I brought it up.

"I don't know…just…all I do know is, when you kiss me…I want more."

"More," he echoes.

"Mmhmm…more." My gaze flickers down.

"When? I mean, there's no rush—"

"We could…now." I bite my lip, suddenly feeling a little more than nervous.

Adam is up on his feet before I even get a chance to blink.

"Um, where are you going?" I stare up at him.

"You said now. And, well, I'm not doing *more* with you now, on this rock, with an audience." He gestures out to the surf. "I thought we could go back to the house. Max will be out here surfing for hours, so we'll have the place to ourselves."

A thrill runs through me. "Okay." I shove my sketchpad and pencil in my bag.

Adam climbs down the rock. I follow, loving the feel of his hands on my waist as he helps me down the last part. His hand grazes my ass.

"Copping a feel?" I smile.

"Totally." He grins at me.

Linking his fingers through mine, he leads me on the short walk to the beach house.

By the time we reach the house, my body is a riot of nerves.

We've just gotten through the door when Adam has me backed up against it, his mouth on mine.

My bag drops to the floor. My hands go to his hair.

God, he smells amazing, like the ocean. I can taste the salt on his lips, and it just fuels me, making me want him even more.

This kiss is so different, compared to our others. There's a need and urgency that hasn't been there before, and I love that he wants me so badly.

His hands find my ass, and he lifts me. I wrap my legs around his waist.

He carries me upstairs to his bedroom.

It's not the first time I've been in here, but somehow, this feels different...because things will be different. We might not be about to have sex, but we're going to reach a whole new level of intimacy.

He lays me down on the bed, coming down with me. Between my legs, his hips press to mine.

*Holy hardness.* I can feel how much he wants me, and from the feel of this thing, it's a *lot*.

He's still kissing me, less ragged but still needy. His fingers find the hem of my top.

"How far do you want to go with this?" he asks, sounding breathless. "What is more? Are we talking second or third base here? I need to know because I don't want to make a mistake with you, and screw this up."

I press my hand to his cheek. "You could never make a mistake. And, honestly…I've never…" I bite my lip, lowering my eyes. I slide my hand from his face. "I've never done anything but kiss before, so I don't know. And I know how lame that makes me sound."

His fingers go under my chin, bringing my gaze back to his. I stare into his eyes, and the look in his is intense.

"It doesn't make you lame, babe. It makes you mine."

He takes my mouth again, kissing me as intensely as the look was in his eyes.

His tongue seeks entrance, so I part my lips. He groans into my mouth, and I feel it low in my belly.

Taking my face in his hands, he starts to press soft kisses over my lips. "Evie…have you ever made yourself come?"

"Oh my God!" I blush. Pushing away, I turn my face from him.

"Hey…don't be embarrassed." His hand forces my face back to his, but I still can't look at him. "It's me, Evie. Just you and me here, and there isn't anything you can't tell me. Okay?"

"Okay," I breathe out, face still flaming. I run my hand through my hair, feeling all kinds of awkward. "And, to answer your question…no, I haven't ever done *that*…to myself."

He's silent for so long that I have to look at him, worried that he's disgusted with me because I'm sure most girls would have done that by now.

But he doesn't look disgusted. He looks...well, he looks like he wants to devour me. I take that to be a good thing.

"You've never come?" he asks, his voice sounding rough.

I shake my head.

He groans. Those intense eyes of his darken further.

He runs his thumb over my lower lip, which I'm apparently biting again, and frees it from my teeth.

"Do you want me to make you come?" His voice is husky, and as sexy as hell.

I squeak, and his lips lift into a heartbreaking smile, leaving me spinning.

My stomach is practically doing backflips.

"I guess...yes. I mean, only if you want to."

He dips his head to mine. "Oh, I want to. I want nothing more."

He brushes his lips over mine, and I feel his fingertips run along the sliver of exposed skin between my top and shorts.

"But you have to tell me to stop if you don't feel comfortable."

"I will," I breathe.

His hand slips under my tank top. Moving up my stomach, he reaches my breast. Then, he's cupping it over my bikini top.

I'm breathless, and I can't imagine that I'll be telling him to stop anytime soon.

His hand feels so very good there. His finger is now tracing a path around my erect nipple through the fabric of my bikini.

His hair caresses my face as he kisses a path down my neck.

I raise my arms, letting him know what I want. He removes my tank top. I hear the soft thud of it hitting the floor.

He kisses down my chest, between my breasts. The whole time, his erection is pressed up against me, and he's moving ever so slightly, creating this amazing friction. I'm starting to feel hot all over, and all I know is that I want more of what he's doing.

I need more.

His tongue traces over the rise of my breast before he presses a kiss there.

Suddenly feeling brave, I reach back and loosen the string tied behind my neck. Then, I untie the string behind my back, letting my bikini fall away.

I watch his face as he takes me in for the first time, his expression almost undoing me.

So many emotions, it's hard to capture one, but all of them are good, and they are making me feel amazing.

"God, you're beautiful, Evie. So very fucking beautiful. And you're all mine." Then, he's kissing me again with the same ferocity as he did downstairs. His tongue is in my mouth, claiming me, just like his words did.

His T-shirt-covered chest is pressed on my bare one, and it kind of feels unfair.

It's not that I haven't seen Adam shirtless before because I have plenty of times at the beach, and seriously, his body is smoking, but I want his shirt off right now more than I want my next breath.

I need to feel his skin against mine.

Grabbing the hem, I drag it up. Adam breaks away from my mouth long enough to let me get it over his head, and then he's back, kissing me.

And we're skin to skin, and I have never felt anything like it in my life.

Then, when his head moves to my chest and he takes my nipple into his mouth, a feeling so intense brings my hips up off the bed and has me squirming. I'm pressing against his erection, needing the friction.

His tongue is swirling around my nipple, and my hands are in his long hair, pulling at it, as it tickles my skin.

"I'm gonna take your shorts off now. Is that okay?"

I love that he's checking with me, but it just serves as a reminder that I don't have many items of clothing left on.

I swallow, feeling a little nervous, and give him a nod.

"Are you sure?" He looks me in the eyes. "You have to be sure about this, babe."

I bolster my confidence. "I'm sure."

His eyes linger on me.

"I promise," I reassure him.

He's seemingly happy with my words as his fingers find the button on my shorts. Without taking his eyes from mine, he undoes them and slides them down my legs.

I'm lying here in only my bikini bottoms and my blush as he stares down at me.

"Beautiful," he murmurs.

And I feel it—not just because of his words, but also because of the way he's looking at me, like I'm the most precious thing in the world to him.

He leans down and begins kissing a path up my stomach, starting at my belly button. When he reaches my mouth, he pauses. "I've never wanted anyone like I want you, Evie. I know we've only known each other for a few weeks, but...I'm crazy about you."

I curl my fingers into the strands of his hair. "I'm crazy about you, too. I wouldn't be doing this if I wasn't."

A growl escapes him. "You have no fucking idea what hearing that does to me...what *you* do to me."

His hand moves down my stomach, his fingers tickling, as he reaches the edge of my bikini bottoms. Then, he slides his hand inside and he's touching me there, and lights explode behind my closed eyes.

"Oh," I moan, pressing my head back into the pillow.

He starts to move his finger over that spot, which feels so very good.

"That's it, babe," he whispers over my lips. "Let me make you feel good."

"Oh God, you are. You really are." My hand grabs hold of his arm.

The sensations he's creating in me with that magic hand of his has me feeling like I need him to stop but also never, ever stop touching me there again. It's so confusing.

I feel like I could climb out of my own skin. I'm restless and needy, searching for something I don't understand.

My other hand curls into the bedding, gripping it like a vise.

My body is tingling, and my sole focus is narrowed down to that one spot between my legs and what his hand is doing there. I feel like I'm climbing toward something unknown—but something really freaking good.

"Evie, I need to taste you."

*What?*

"Your pussy. I want to go down on you," he says the words so easily.

Me? My face feels like it's currently on fire.

"You want to"—I gesture south with my hand, my eyes still closed, unable to look at him—"go…down *there?*"

I hear his deep chuckle.

"Evie, look at me."

I force my eyes open to find him staring back at me.

"Yes, I want to go down on you."

Something dark and hot flashes through his eyes, making me tremble.

"I want to taste you. It's all I can think about." He brings his mouth to mine, his lips brushing softly. "But more than anything, I want the first time you come to be in my mouth. So, what do you say?"

*Holy shit!*

*Really, what am I supposed to say to that?*

I part my lips, and what comes out is, "Ermahgerd."

Adam laughs a sexy-as-hell sound. "Babe, I don't speak anything other than English, so you're gonna have to clarify for me."

I clear my throat, pretty sure my face is the brightest shade of red known to man. "I mean, yes. I would really like…you to do that to me, please."

*Yes, I would really like you to do that to me, please.*

*What the hell is wrong with me?*

I sound like he's just offered to give me a shoulder rub, not put his mouth on my girl parts.

*Jesus, Evie! You could at least try to be sexy. You are in bed with the hottest guy in California. He's offering oral sex of the best kind—or so I've heard—and you're acting like a total doofus.*

Seemingly unaffected by my lack of sexiness, Adam gives me a panty-melting grin and then starts to move down my body, his eyes pinned on mine.

Every part of me tightens.

He hooks his fingers into the band of my bikini bottoms, and I swallow.

Then, very slowly, he pulls them down.

My bikini bottoms now on the floor, Adam settles between my legs.

*Oh God.*

I'm stuck somewhere between total embarrassment and awe right now.

Biting his lip, which is such a sexy look on him, he runs a finger up my center, making me shiver.

"You're soaking wet, Evie. It's really fucking hot."

*Sweet baby Jesus.*

I bite my lip.

Then, he puts his mouth on me.

And reality ceases to exist.

I lose my mind. It goes, *kaboom!*

And for the next minutes, hours, days—I'm not actually sure—I experience the kind of pleasure I didn't even know existed.

His tongue is magical. Out-of-this-world amazing.

I want to marry it.

Then, I feel his finger pressing against my entrance, testing, asking silently for my permission.

"Yes," I moan, pushing against it.

And then his finger is inside me.

*Oh my God!*

His tongue is licking me, his finger moving in and out of me, and I'm gripping his hair, fairly sure I've pulled some of it out. My hips start bucking up off the bed as I scream his name so loud that I'm pretty sure that everyone in the western hemisphere can hear me.

*Oh. My. God.*

I'm panting, and my heart is racing. Every muscle in my body is locked up tight, and I just feel…incredible.

*I just had my first orgasm. And it was the best thing ever!*

I feel Adam press a kiss to my stomach and then one between my breasts.

Then, his lips touch my mouth.

I can taste myself there.

I open my eyes. He's looking down at me with such tenderness that my chest opens up, and my heart exits, going straight into his and taking up residency.

"You're amazing." He brushes my hair back from my face with his hand.

"Um…I think that award goes to you." I give him a goofy smile.

He chuckles as he settles back over me. I feel his very prominent erection pressing against my hip.

And I know now what I want to do, more than anything.

"I want…can I touch you?" I ask him.

Something deep flickers in his eyes.

"You don't have to. That's not why I did this."

"I know." I touch his face with my fingertips, tracing the line of his brow. "But I want to. I want to make you feel good."

"I already do feel good."

"Well, I want to make you feel *gooder.*"

He lets out a laugh. "Is that actually a word?"

"Probably not." I grin. Then, I slide my hand around the back of his neck and bring his mouth to mine. "I want to make you come."

That has an effect on him. The next thing I know, Adam's on his back, and I'm on top of him, my legs on either side of his hips. His hands are in my hair, my lips crashing down to his.

He kisses me deeply. And I kiss him back, needy. My hands pressed against his hard chest, I start to move them lower. I feel the tremble in his body, and it gives me the confidence I need.

When I reach the waistband of his board shorts, I move off him. Fingers hooked, I start to ease them down. He lifts his hips, allowing me purchase.

He's naked beneath his shorts, which, of course, I expected. I just didn't expect him to be…so big.

I haven't ever seen a penis in real life before. I know. I sound like the virgin I am.

There's just something fascinating about it—the size and strength of it, the thick veins running through it, how it looks so very hard yet soft and silky at the same time.

Adam kicks his shorts off the rest of the way, but I barely notice. I can't stop staring.

And he doesn't seem abashed by the fact.

"Can I…touch it?"

"You don't have to ask. I'm all yours, babe. Do whatever you want." He puts his hands behind his head, a confident smile appearing on his face.

Reaching a nervous hand out, I touch him, running a finger up the shaft.

A hiss escapes him.

Looking up, I see his eyes have darkened with lust, and they are fixed on me, that hunger on his face again.

Shifting my position, I kneel between his legs and wrap my hand around him. Then, I do what I think is right. I start to move my hand up and down.

*God, I'm so nervous.*

I look at him to make sure I'm doing this right.

"Just squeeze a little harder," he tells me, his voice rough.

I tighten my grip a little and keep my hand moving.

"Fuck yeah, that's it, Evie. Jesus…" He groans, a flush rising on his cheeks.

I love that I'm doing this to him. It gives me a sense of power.

"I'm not gonna last, babe. It's been…a…long while. Fuck."

His hips jerk up, then, he starts to move himself up and down, pumping his cock faster in my hand, so I quicken my movements to give him what he needs.

I can feel that need between my legs again, and my body starts to tremble.

"Jesus…Evie…fuck, I'm gonna come."

I feel his cock jerk in my hand, and then hot spurts hit my skin as he comes. I keep moving my hand until I'm sure he's done.

I look down at the sticky mess covering my hand and his stomach.

I made him come. My hand made Adam come.

I mentally high-five myself.

I glance up at Adam, and he's staring down at me with awe written all over his face.

I'm feeling pretty awestruck myself.

"Come here," he says.

Letting go of him, I lift my sticky hand up. "Do you have anything I can clean myself with?"

"Oh, sure." He gives a little laugh. Reaching over, he grabs some tissues from the bedside table and hands them to me.

I wipe my hands clean, and then I clean up his stomach. I can feel his eyes on me the whole time.

Adam takes the used tissues from me and deposits them on the bedside table.

Feeling kind of funny, being totally naked, I reach down and get his T-shirt from the floor. It's his favorite shirt, which makes it my favorite. It's a black Rolling Stones T-shirt, the one with the tongue sticking out of a mouth.

I pull it over my head, covering my body. It smells like him, and so do I.

It makes me feel all warm and gooey inside.

"I like my shirt on you," he says, holding his arms out to me.

I crawl into them, loving the feel of his arms wrapping around me.

"But I like you naked an awful lot more."

I grin up at him. "You do realize, you're not getting your shirt back, right?"

He pulls the covers over us and presses a kiss to my forehead. "I have no problem with that, babe, so long as I'm the one who gets to take it off your body."

"Oh, you definitely will be." I press a soft kiss to his mouth, loving as he hums a delicious sound of assent beneath my lips. "And if I haven't told you this already, I like you, Adam Gunner—a whole lot."

His eyes smile into mine, and it's beautiful. He's beautiful.

"And I like you a whole lot, too, Evie Taylor." His lips press to mine again. "I think you're fucking amazing."

Smiling and happy in a way I've never felt before, I tuck my head under Adam's chin, burrowing closer to his body, not ever imagining myself being anywhere else but here with him.

# Adam
## BEVERLY HILLS · JULY 2015

"Adam, your mother's on her way up. Serena did ask her to wait, so she could call up to make sure you weren't busy, but Ava ignored her and bypassed reception. Do you want me to head her off?" the voice of my assistant, Mark, fills my office.

*For fuck's sake.*

I let out a sigh. Then, I press the button on the intercom, answering him, "No, it's fine. Let her in when she arrives."

"Okay, will do. Just to let you know, I'll be away from my desk for a few minutes after that. I need to go see Simon in HR."

"Sure, no probs."

I let out another sigh, a tired one this time, as I lean back in my chair. I haven't been sleeping well all week, and I could really do without a visit from the devil.

I wonder what Ava wants this time. I only see her when she needs something from me.

And my lack of sleep has nothing to do with the fact that I haven't heard from Evie all week. I went to see her on Monday, and it's now Friday. I told her to call me the next day, so we could talk, and she hasn't.

And it's pissing me off.

When leaving the hotel, I've seen her at the coffee shop, but there is no fucking way I'm going back in there to ask why she hasn't called me.

*Maybe she doesn't think us still being married is a big deal. I mean, she didn't care ten years ago, so why would she care now?*

Well, whatever. I did my part. I told her the truth, unlike what she has done with me.

The ball is firmly in her court now.

I hear the familiar click of Ava's high heels on the wood floor outside my office. It makes my skin prickle, and annoyance grows in my chest. Funny how just the sound of Ava walking can piss me off.

I hear her speak—or should I say, I hear her talking down to Mark.

The door opens, and I repress another sigh.

*Here we go.*

"Adam." There isn't any niceness in her tone, not that I'm surprised. She's spoken to me with the same level of intolerance ever since I can remember.

"Ava."

She narrows her eyes at me. She doesn't like it when I call her by her first name. Fuck knows why. It's not like she enjoys or cares to be my mother—well, apart from when I can give her something or do something for her, which is clearly why she's here.

"What do you want this time?"

She frowns at me—well, frowns as best as she can with all the Botox and skin-tightening she's had done over the years.

She takes the seat at the other side of my desk. "Is that any way to greet your mother?"

I tip my head to the side. "Sorry. I'll rephrase. What the fuck do you want this time, Ava?"

Tut-tutting, she shakes her head at me, flicking her hair over her shoulder. "You really are such a disappointment. Other children treat their mothers with respect."

"Other children don't find their mothers having a threesome with their best friend's parents."

I never did tell Max that. I didn't know how to. I mean, it's not something that comes up easily in conversation.

*Oh, by the way, I came home from school the other day, and my mother was fucking your mom and dad.*

Honestly, I was afraid he'd blame me, and I would lose him.

I was thirteen, and Max was all I had in the world.

Sighing, she rolls her eyes. "Ancient history." She flicks a hand at me.

I can't suppress the laugh of disdain that escapes me.

History. Denial. Ignorance.

Ava's best defenses.

I release a sigh. "I'm busy, Ava. What is it you want from me this time?"

Examining her nails, she says, "Well…it's been a while since I worked."

"I thought you were taking a break."

"I was, and now, I want to work."

"Well, I haven't got anything for you. You could always try another studio."

*God, wouldn't that be a fucking dream? Let someone else deal with her.*

Ignoring my suggestion, she says, "I heard that *Avalon* is going ahead."

121

*Avalon* is a script that came to me a few years ago. Originally, I was on the fence about it. It wasn't the right time. But the market has shifted, and I think it's the right time to put it into production. It's a take on the legend of King Arthur, starting with his fight with Mordred at the Battle of Camlann where Arthur was wounded and thought to have died. It progresses to show his recovery at Avalon, revealing that he lived and returned to lead his people against their enemies.

"It is."

"I want the part of Morgan le Fay."

I laugh loudly. Then, I stop laughing, and say in all seriousness, "No."

Her eyes glower at me. "I'm perfect for it, and you know I am."

"You're about thirty years too old for that part."

Anger ignites over her features. "I might be a little older than Morgan would have been, but I don't look my age."

I lean forward, arms on my desk. "The public knows how old you are, no matter how young you might look. You playing Morgan won't work. End of story."

She crosses her arms over her chest. "Your father would have given me the part."

"But Eric's not here, and I am. You forced me to take over this shitty company, so now, you have to put up with how I run it."

"I need to work, Adam," she says this in her nice voice, the one she uses when she's trying to get her own way.

But I'm not playing today.

"Popularity fading, Ava? Have you lost followers on Twitter?"

"You are a spiteful child, Adam. You always have been."

*There's the Ava I know.*

"Yeah, well, I learned it from the best."

Looking down, she takes in several deep breaths before looking back up at me. "Fine. You won't give me the part of Morgan. Give me another part."

"No."

"I'm still a part of this studio!" she yells, her hard plastic face turning bright red.

I sit there, unrattled. "Technically, you're not. You're just the woman who was married to my father and the woman who gave birth to me, and you're here for no other reasons than those. You're lucky I don't call security and have them toss your ass out on the street."

Her mouth twists into a bitter sneer. "You know, when I first got pregnant with you, I wondered if I was making a mistake, being married to your father and having his child. One day, not long after finding out I was pregnant, I found myself outside an abortion clinic." She flexes her hand out in front of her face, examining her nails again. Then, she lowers her hand, and cold eyes meet mine. "I didn't go inside. I really should have."

When I was younger, shit like that hurt me. Now, it just rolls right off me.

It's nothing she hasn't said before to me.

And the truth is, there is no way Ava would have stood within a hundred yards of an abortion clinic. I was her meal ticket. But that's not why she can no longer hurt me.

I stopped feeling when Evie left. Nothing will ever feel worse than that.

And this is how it always goes with Ava. I say no. She dials up the bitch a few notches and says some venomous hurtful shit. We argue, and she leaves. Later, she calls and plays nice, and then I say yes to whatever she wants.

*And, really, what's the fucking point?*

Honestly, I'm just tired. Evie coming back has just knocked the fight out of me.

Right now, I just want peace.

I rest back in my seat. "Yeah, you probably should have aborted me. Saved us both the fucking misery."

Leaning my head to the side, the cool leather of my chair pressing against my cheek, I stare out the window at the Hollywood sign in the distance.

"You can have the part of Viviane, the Lady of the Lake. It's not the lead, but it's prominent. Jason McAllister is in charge of casting. I'll make the call and let him know. Check in with him tomorrow."

There's silence for a moment.

Then, she says, "What's the catch?"

I let out a humorless laugh. "You're welcome." I slide a glance in her direction. "Now, get the fuck out of my office."

She quietly gets up from the chair and heads for the door, which is not like her. Maybe she's finally learned to keep her mouth shut when she's got a good thing.

When she reaches it, I say to her back, "And, Ava, I don't want to see you for a long time. A *really* long time."

Turning, she smiles. It's a twisted kind of smile with just her lips tilting up, no expression on her face at all. "That'll be no problem. Not having to see you has always been the easiest thing for me to do."

She pulls open the door, and my Uncle Richard is standing on the other side of it.

Uncle Richard is my father's younger brother. He's CFO, and he's actually a nice guy. It's so strange that two brothers could be so very different.

"Richard." Her tone screams cool.

It's no secret that they intensely dislike each other.

"Ava. Good to see you leaving, as always."

She sniffs at him like he's dirt on her shoes as she brushes past, heading for the elevator.

I exhale in the knowledge that she's gone.

There have only ever been two women in my life that could fuck with my head.

One is the devil who just left. The other is Evie.

Thank God I don't have to see Evie today. I might end up offing myself if I did.

"Sorry to intrude. Mark wasn't at his desk."

"It's no problem." I gesture for him to sit down.

He takes the seat Ava just vacated.

"So, what did the devil want?" He jerks his head in the direction where Ava just left.

I laugh. It's my first real laugh in a while.

Sometimes, I think Richard should run this company. Well, I think it all the time.

He actually likes this industry and loves this company.

I often have this dream of signing over the company to him, and then I just run away. Far away.

But, I always wake up.

Even though this place makes me miserable ninety percent of the time, if I didn't do this, I don't know what I would do.

I guess I could surf every day and lead a quiet reclusive life, which is sounding quite appealing right now.

"She wanted to play Morgan le Fay."

His eyes widen. "I hope you told her that she's a fair amount of decades too late for that part."

"Yeah, I did."

"Knowing Ava, she didn't take it well?" he checks.

"Nope." I drum my fingers on my desk, my eyes averted. "I've given her the part of Viviane."

"Adam, you could always just tell her no and mean it. You owe her nothing."

"Yeah, I know. But what's the point? I figure it's just easier to give in now than later. Saves me a lot of hassle."

He nods in understanding. "Anyway, I just came up to bring you last year's numbers that you were looking for. They were on my desk after all." He hands the folder containing the papers to me.

"Thanks."

He gets to his feet, about to leave, and then he seems to change his mind. He turns back, his hand holding the back of the chair. "You always were a good kid, Adam. You just got the shit end of the stick when it came to your parents. And I know you probably think you just caved, and Ava won again, but she didn't."

"No?" I give him a disbelieving look.

"Ava wanted to play Morgan. You didn't give her the part. You've never done that before. In the past, you've always caved completely and given her what she wants."

That's not exactly true.

There was one time, a long time ago, when I told Ava no, and I stuck to it. But that was when Evie was still mine, and I had something to fight for.

"Well, there's always time for me to cave." I give a dry laugh.

He stares at me with a serious look on his face. "Even still, I'd call this one a win. I'm proud of you, son."

From out of nowhere, I feel an ache in my chest. It's so severe that I press my hand to it.

Then, my cell starts ringing on my desk. I'm not familiar with the number, but something tells me that it's Evie.

"I have to take this," I tell Richard. "Oh, and thanks," I say when he's reached the door.

I'm not just thanking him for bringing papers.

"No problem." He smiles.

I wait until he's shut the door before I answer, "Adam Gunner."

"Adam...it's Evie."

She didn't have to identify herself. I'd know her voice anywhere. And I hate the way it still affects me, even now.

"Are you still there?" she asks softly.

I realize I haven't said anything in response.

"I'm here."

There's a brief pause on the line. I can hear her gentle breaths.

Then, she says, "I was thinking it's probably time we talk."

I blow out a breath. *My mother and Evie in one day. I guess someone up there really hates me.*

"But we don't have to…if you're busy," she adds quickly.

"No, it's fine. Did you want to do this over the phone or face-to-face?"

"I thought face-to-face, if that's okay with you."

"Fine. When?"

"Are you…busy now?"

I can just envision her as if she were in front of me right now, biting on her lower lip, the way she does when she's nervous.

I look at the paperwork on my desk and the emails filling my screen. "I'm always busy. But I guess now is as good a time as any. Where do you want to meet?"

"Um…I don't know. I didn't get that far. It's taken me a week to find the courage to call you, so…" She trails off.

And that ache is back in my chest again but stronger this time.

I press my fingers against it. "Do you know Rock and Reilly's Irish Pub?"

"The one on Sunset Boulevard?"

"That's the one. I'll meet you there in twenty minutes."

"Okay. See you then."

I hang up, and the first thing I do before putting my cell into my pants pocket is save Evie's number into my Contacts.

Don't judge me. I might need to get in contact with her again.

I mean, we are still married after all.

After grabbing my car keys, I get my jacket and pull it on as I exit my office.

"Mark, I'm heading out," I tell him, passing his desk.

"Will you be coming back, or are you done for the day?"

Stopping at the elevator, I press the button. "Done for the day."

Pulling up outside of Reilly's, I park my car and get out. I lock up and head into the pub. Max and I come here all the time. We've been drinking here since we got our first fake IDs at sixteen.

Back then, I would never have guessed that I'd be coming in here to meet with my wife to discuss the demise of our ten-year marriage that technically only lasted for one week.

I push open the door and step inside the pub. I immediately see Evie, as the place is empty, except for her.

She's sitting in a corner booth by the window, staring into a small glass of wine. She's not in her work uniform. She's wearing a plain T-shirt and jean shorts. I know for a fact that she'll be wearing flip-flops on her feet. It always was Evie's preferred choice of footwear.

Since seeing her again, this is the first time that I've seen her in normal clothes. And once again, I'm thrown back ten years.

She looks beautiful.

And my cock appreciates the fact.

That was always my problem when it came to Evie. I thought with my heart and my cock.

But not anymore. She will always look beautiful to me, but it's irrelevant. She broke my heart, so it no longer works, and I'm shutting my cock down.

I'm thinking solely with my head.

She lifts her eyes from her wine, instantly meeting with mine. She gives me a hesitant small smile.

I ignore the burn in my chest. Keeping my expression blank, I walk over to her.

"I got a drink already. I wasn't sure how long I'd be waiting," she says, like she expected me to keep her waiting or maybe not turn up at all.

Maybe I shouldn't have.

"I would have ordered for you, but I wasn't sure what you'd want…" She trails off.

*Well, you would know, if you'd stuck around all these years.*

I stop myself from saying what I want to say, and instead, I turn to the bartender and say, "Bottle of Bud, please."

I take the seat opposite her. My cell starts to ring in my pocket. I pull it out, and without checking the screen, I silence it before putting it back.

I see her eyes on my phone, and then they lift to mine.

"Thanks for coming," she says softly.

"You don't have to thank me, Evie. We're here because I fucked up, and we have a mess to sort out."

She meets my eyes. "But you wouldn't have fucked up in the first place, if it wasn't for me."

"No argument from me there." *Jesus, Gunner, quit with the bitter.*

I don't miss the flicker of pain that passes over her face.

Maybe that's why I backtrack—not that I owe her anything, but seeing her hurt has always bothered me. "I probably shouldn't have said that. I think we're past the blame game by now."

"Are we really?" She lifts a brow.

She always could see through my bullshit.

I let out a dry laugh. "Probably not, no." Then, I give her a serious look. "But I want to be. I want to put this behind me and move on. It's time."

That's almost the truth. I just keep thinking if I say it enough, it will happen.

And, really, where is there to go from here but forward? To what, I just don't know.

The bartender puts my beer in front of me. When I look back at Evie, her face is turned away from me, staring out the window.

"That's why I called today," she says in that melodic voice of hers. "You're right. It's time to move on." She brings her eyes back to me. "I got in touch with a divorce lawyer and started proceedings."

Have you ever been shot?

No? Me neither. But what I'm feeling right now, I'm guessing, is pretty close to that.

I'm not surprised. It's the logical thing to do. It's not like we can get an annulment now. And we're not together. We haven't been for a decade. It's not a real marriage.

But still, it hurts like a motherfucker.

"Okay," I manage out, trying to keep my composure.

"I just thought I should tell you face-to-face. I wasn't sure if you had started proceedings or not?"

"I hadn't." I blankly stare back at her.

"Oh. Okay. Well, it's good I'm telling you then. I mean, I didn't want you to get any papers from my lawyer without me letting you know first. So, this is a good thing, right? I know you must want to be free of me, so I thought it was the least I could do for you—to start divorce…proceedings." She has her hands on the table, twisting her fingers together. Babbling and finger-twisting was always a tell when Evie was nervous. "And, of course, I've taken full responsibility on the divorce petition. It's termed something like, 'fault-based divorce due to abandonment.' But you'll see that on the papers when my lawyer gets in touch with yours. So, if you'll let me know your lawyer's details, mine can get in touch, and then…I guess they'll deal with it until it's…finalized."

I clear my throat. "I have a lawyer, but he's not a divorce lawyer. I'll find one, and I'll let you know the details."

I feel like I'm on autopilot at the moment.

A fast flowing stream of words is going through my mind, none that I'm saying and none that make sense.

I feel exactly like I did the moment when I realized Evie had left me.

Panic. Fear.

It's like I'm reliving that all over again.

Losing her again.

I'm panicking over losing her when I don't even have her.

*What the fuck is wrong with me?*

"Okay. Well…I guess…I guess there's nothing else to say. So, I won't take up anymore of your time." She's standing up and getting her bag from the seat before hanging it on her shoulder.

All I can do is watch her, the fear of losing her increasing. Closing up on me, like a hand around my throat.

A big part of me, the nineteen-year-old part of me, wants to beg her to stay.

She moves out from behind the table. She stops beside me.

I look up at her.

"I am sorry, Adam," she whispers. "I'm ten years' worth of sorry. I just wish…"

She bites her lip. I see the glisten of tears in her eyes. My heart twists painfully.

"I wish we'd had a chance."

I catch sight of the tears falling down her cheeks before she's gone and out the door.

In my mind, I'm chasing her out of there and demanding to know why she's so upset, wanting to know what she meant by wishing that we'd had a chance. I would force her to tell me why she ended that chance, why she really left, and then I'd beg her to stay.

But in reality, my ass is still planted firmly on the seat, exactly where it should be.

*Why would I beg her to stay when she fucked me over so badly?*

She was the one who abandoned me. She went against our marriage vows.

She's done the right thing by starting divorce proceedings.

My head knows. My head agrees.

I wonder why the fuck I didn't do it myself the moment after I'd told her that we were still married.

My heart—that's why.

He's hanging on to the past.

Seems the little fucker has decided to come back to life after all these years, and he wants to have an opinion.

And my heart...he wants Evie—no matter what, no matter the cost.

My heart has always wanted her.

I just can't let my heart win this time.

I'm thinking with my head all the way.

And my head says, *Divorce.*

# Adam
## MALIBU · OCTOBER 2004

It's Sunday, and Evie's finished work for the day. It's raining out, so we're staying home and watching movies, but none that have been made by my family's studio.

We have popcorn, chips, and soda, and we are halfway through our first film, cuddled up on the sofa. We're watching *American Pie*. Evie's never seen it before.

She snuggles closer, sliding her hand over my stomach. My muscles instantly tense.

She lets out a content sigh. "It's official. I am the comfiest I've ever been. You make for a great pillow. I'm never moving again."

"Works for me." I drop a kiss to the top of her head.

"Jesus, you two are like a Hallmark card, and I don't mean that in a complimentary way," Max grumbles.

I turn my head to see him walking in from the kitchen, a can of soda in his hand.

Evie lifts her head from my chest and looks at him. "Aw, Max, just think, this could be you one day, in a Hallmark card all of your own," Evie teases.

"Fuck no!" He frowns at her. "No fucking way is that shit happening to me."

Evie starts to laugh.

She and Max get along great, and that makes me happy. Well, she makes me happy all the time.

And she's making me happy right now while she's laughing. I can feel the vibration of her laughter through her hips, which are pressed up nicely against my cock. Of course, my cock responds in the way he always does around Evie.

He gets hard.

I know the second she feels my erection. Her body stiffens, and she slowly moves her eyes to mine.

We silently stare at each other, the air thickening all around us.

A flush rises in her cheeks, lust filling her eyes as they flicker down to my lips.

"So…I'm feeling kind of tired," Evie says, giving a fake yawn. "Wanna go take a nap?"

I know the last thing she wants to do is nap. She wants to fool around. And I am totally on board with that.

"I could take a nap," I say casually, aware that Max is still here.

Evie and I haven't had sex yet, but we've done everything else. Honestly, I don't care that I'm not having sex. I'm getting plenty of blow jobs, and that's not something to scoff at. Blow jobs from Evie are nothing short of amazing.

Everything she does is amazing.

I'm crazy about her.

*Do I love her? Without a doubt.*

I just haven't quite told her yet. I haven't found the right time.

"Seriously?" Max laughs. "That was weak, guys. A nap? Why not just be honest and say that you're going upstairs to have sex—or at the very least, oral?"

Max knows Evie and I haven't had actual sex. He's saying this to wind her up.

I don't discuss our sex life with him, but he's also my best friend. When Evie and I first got together, he pushed to know if we'd done it, so I told him that Evie was a virgin, and we were taking it slow.

At that point, I think he realized how serious I was about her.

Evie's face goes bright red, and she drops her head to my chest, letting out a mortified-sounding laugh.

I lift a hand, giving Max the middle finger. "Fuck you very much, dickwad."

"Love you, too, man." He blows me a kiss. "Have fun, kids, and play safe. I'll be in the game room if you need me."

"Not likely," I mutter.

He laughs again before disappearing through the door.

"Is he gone?" Evie mumbles into my shirt.

"Yep."

She lifts her face, a blush still staining her cheeks.

I run my finger over the soft skin there. "You still wanna go fool around?"

"I want to, I just…feel kind of weird, knowing that Max knows what we're doing."

"Just ignore him. But we don't have to if you don't feel comfortable."

She reaches up and presses a kiss to my lips. "You're perfect, you know that?"

"It's been said before." I grin.

She playfully slaps my chest. I catch her hand, and bringing it to my lips, I kiss the tips of her fingers. Then, I catch the top of one with my teeth.

She shivers, and her eyes darken. "You know, I'm not feeling so embarrassed anymore."

"No?" I suck the tip of her finger into my mouth, nibbling on it.

"No," she says on a breath. "Let's go upstairs."

Evie limbers off me, getting to her feet. I stand, and then I take her face in my hands. I kiss her long and deep. Then, I grab her hand and lead her in the direction of the stairs, listening to the sound of her sexy giggle.

I've just gotten up the first step when there's a knock at the front door.

"Who could that be?" Evie asks.

I shrug. "Max probably ordered takeout. I'll get rid of whoever it is."

I give her a quick kiss and then head for the front door.

I pull it open, and my heart sinks.

*Fuck.*

Ava is standing there. Over her shoulder, I see her limo parked on my driveway, her bodyguard standing beside it.

"Ava," I say her name like a bad taste is in my mouth. "What are you doing here?"

I haven't seen her since I left Beverly Hills back in July, and even those few months haven't been long enough.

"It's nice to see you, too, and call me mother. You know how much I hate it when you call me Ava." She sweeps past me, walking into the house.

I release a sigh and close the door. My eyes immediately seek out Evie, who's still standing at the bottom of the stairs.

My mother's eyes are on her like a lion stalking a gazelle. I feel a nasty twist in my gut.

"And who have we got here?" Ava asks me without taking her eyes off Evie.

"Nobody. She's just a friend."

Evie's eyes immediately flick to mine, and I see the hurt flash through them.

Her pain strikes me like a blow to the stomach.

I didn't mean that. I just don't want Ava to know that Evie is my girlfriend. Ava knows I don't do girlfriends, and if she knows Evie's my girlfriend, then she'll know that Evie means something to me. And the minute Ava knows that, she'll have more power over me. She'll wield Evie like a weapon against me.

I can't let that happen, so I need her to think that Evie is just another girl.

Evie knows my mother is a bitch and that we're not close, but she doesn't know the extent of what a fucking devil she is.

I want to protect Evie from her, but protecting her will become a hell of a lot harder if Ava knows I care for her.

"A friend," my mother echoes. "And does your friend have a name?"

Evie seems to come to life, the hurt quickly masked in her eyes. "I'm Evie Taylor." She steps forward, holding her hand out to Ava. "It's really nice to meet you, Mrs. Gunner."

My mother looks down at her hand. Then, ignoring Evie, she sweeps past her and into the living room.

Evie's face drops. And it's another blow to my gut.

I really fucking hate my mother.

"So, this is what my money's paying for," Ava says, looking around the beach house.

Ignoring her, I say in a quiet voice to Evie, "I'm really sorry. I had no idea she was coming."

"Why do you need to be sorry about your mother turning up at your house?"

I run a hand through my hair. I should have told her before what Ava was like. I just never wanted her to know the kind of fucked up my family is.

137

"Because she's not a good person, Evie."

Evie only knows good people. She doesn't know the kind of evil my mother is or what I grew up around.

"I can't explain now, but I will later, I promise."

I just need to get Evie out of here—now. She can't drive, so I'll have to take her home and then come back and deal with whatever Ava wants from me. Because, without a doubt, she wants something.

"Ava, I'm just going to take Evie home, and then I'll be back."

"No need for her to rush off. Stay, and visit with me a while." Ava sits down on the sofa. A false smile is plastered on her face as she pats the space on the sofa beside her.

Evie glances at me in question and then tentatively walks into the living room before taking the space beside Ava.

I sit on the arm of the chair, facing them.

"Oh, happy birthday, by the way," Ava says to me.

"My birthday was three weeks ago," I respond blankly. "You know, September thirtieth."

My fingers go to the pendant around my neck that Evie got me.

It says, *Surf. Sleep. Repeat.*

It's the best gift I've ever received.

"Of course I know when your birthday is." Ava fakes a laugh. "I was there. Most horrendous day of my life. I'm not forgetting that in a hurry."

Evie's horrified gaze lands on my mother.

I just let out a sigh.

"So, what brings you to Malibu, Ava?" I say in a bored tone.

"We'll get to that soon." She flicks a hand at me. "First, I want to hear all about this one here." She turns her body toward Evie, who still has a look of absolute horror on her face.

Evie clears her expression and offers my mother a smile.

"So, how long have you and my son been seeing each other?"

"Not long," I answer. "And we're not really seeing each other. Are we done here?" I stand up.

Ava ignores me, and I try to ignore the look of devastation in Evie's eyes, the devastation that's crushing my insides.

"Hush, Adam." Ava gives me a look before turning back to Evie. "He's always kidding around like this. Don't take him seriously. You must be important to him. I know my son, and I've never seen a girl with him at four in the afternoon. He usually brings them home late at night, and then they're gone before breakfast."

I didn't know Ava paid enough attention to me to know my routine with girls. Then again, she never lets anything slip by that might be useful to her.

"So, how long have you two been seeing each other?" She reaches over and squeezes Evie's hands, which are clutched firmly in her lap.

Evie looks like she doesn't know how to answer the question. Maybe she doesn't. I am treating her like shit, and she's probably unsure of what to say.

"Since July," she edges the words out slowly.

"Since July? Wow…" Ava's eyes meet with mine, and I see it written there.

She knows I care for Evie, and she's going to use that against me in one way or another.

"Well, I think I should probably get going." Evie gets to her feet, pulling her hands from my mother's. She gets her bag from the side of the sofa and hooks it on her shoulder.

"I'll give you a ride home." I can tell her everything then—how sorry I am, why I've treated her this way in front of my mother. And I can tell her that I love her.

I need to tell her.

"No. It's fine. I'll get the bus." She won't meet my eyes.

*Fuck.*

The word is echoed in my ears in the sound of Max's voice.

I turn to see him standing in the doorway, his eyes on Ava.

"Max," Ava greets him.

"Mrs. Gunner. What brings you to Malibu? Was hell too warm, so you thought you'd come cool down here with the natives?"

And this is why I love Max. He just says whatever he wants to her, which isn't usually anything nice.

The smile is tight on my mother's lips. "You are funny, Max. You really should consider a career in comedy." She turns her eyes to me before looking back at him. "So, how are your parents doing nowadays?"

I freeze. She's taunting me, not Max.

She can't punish him for what he just said, so she's taking it out on me.

She knows I never told Max what happened, what I saw that day when I came home from school early.

She knows how important Max is to me, and she knows I'm afraid to lose him.

"Wouldn't know. I haven't spoken to them in a while." Max shrugs, moving farther into the living room. He eyes the situation—Evie on her feet, ready to run, while I'm tense, looking like I'm about to explode any second. "Everything okay?" he asks me.

"Fine," Ava says brightly. "Just meeting Adam's new girlfriend."

Max's eyes widen on me. He knows I don't want Ava to know that Evie's my girlfriend or be anywhere near her.

"I was just heading home," Evie says in a quiet voice to Max.

"I'll take you," I tell to her.

Evie finally looks at me, and the look is hard. It cuts me to the quick, but it is nothing less than I deserve right now.

"No. I'll take the bus." Her chin defiantly juts out.

"I'll give you a ride," Max says to her.

She glances over at Max, and I see her relax a little.

"That'd be great. Thank you."

*Well, fuck me.*

I try not to take that personally, but I do. It actually makes me want to punch a hole in the wall.

But I want Evie away from Ava more than I want to throw a temper tantrum right now.

Max grabs his keys from the coffee table.

I follow them to the front door.

Hooking my fingers into Evie's shirt, I pull her back to me. "I'm so sorry," I whisper in her ear, sliding my hands over her waist. "I'll come over later and explain everything."

She doesn't say anything. She just pulls away and walks out the front door without looking back.

"You okay?" Max asks me.

"I said some stuff. Didn't want Ava to know that Evie's important to me. Evie doesn't understand why. I've never told her what Ava's like," I say in a quiet voice.

"I'll try to do damage control on the drive home. Just get rid of the devil as soon as you can, and then get your ass over to Evie's. You want me to come back after I've dropped Evie off? We can tag-team Ava."

He's being a good friend, but I know the last place he wants to be is here. Can't blame him for that. Ava is like poison.

"Nah, it's cool, but thanks, man. I'll let you know when the coast is clear."

He pats me on the shoulder. "Whatever Ava wants, Adam, tell her no." He fixes me with a stare.

He knows what Ava's like. And he knows what I'm like. I always cave to what she wants simply because it makes my life easier.

141

I stand at the door, watching as Max pulls his truck out of the driveway.

I will Evie to look at me, but she doesn't.

It hurts, and right now, I'm blaming Ava for that.

When Max's truck is out of sight, I slam the front door shut.

I take a deep breath, preparing myself to deal with Ava. Then, I walk back into the living room.

I find her perched on the arm of the chair, sitting like she's about to take a scene.

That's Ava. Everything's a movie to her. Life is fucking a movie.

"There's no alcohol here," she complains. "I want a martini."

"Sorry to disappoint, but I'm not old enough to buy alcohol. I'm only nineteen, remember?" I dig at her forgetting my birthday.

She lets out a sarcastic laugh. "Don't give me that shit, Adam. You've been buying liquor since you were sixteen."

I fold my arms over my chest. "Okay, let's cut the bullshit. What are you doing here?"

"Visiting my son." She folds her arms, mirroring me. "Your little girlfriend seems...nice." She screws her face up on the word *nice*.

"She's not my girlfriend. I'm just fucking her."

"Well, I think it's sweet that you've found yourself a little piece of trailer trash to play with while you're here."

"Don't talk about her like that," I snap on reflex.

Ava smiles a winning smile, and I know I've screwed up.

"Awfully touchy about some girl you're just fucking."

"I'm not doing this with you. Just tell me what you want, and then you can get the fuck out."

"Honestly, the way you talk to me." She laughs easily, shaking her head, like I've just told some joke. Then, she unfolds her arms and places her hands flat on her thighs. "So, I need a teeny, tiny favor."

I snort.

The last teeny, tiny favor I did for her involved me flying to Vegas to get Eric. My father had spent the weekend with some male hooker in the apartment he owned there, fucking him and getting high on coke. Then, the hooker waited until Eric had passed out from the drugs before handcuffing him to the bed and robbing him of everything he had. The hooker did leave the phone on the bed so that Eric could call for help and the keys to the handcuffs on the bedside table so that I could unlock him.

How kind of him.

Ava wanted to keep the incident out of the press, so I was sent to go help him.

Walking in and seeing my father handcuffed to the bed, butt naked, with used needles on the bedside table and a dirty condom still on his cock was not a scene any kid should have to deal with or see. And it's one I've sadly never quite been able to scrub from my mind.

"Is Eric in trouble again?"

"Not exactly. I mean, he's always in trouble. But this isn't trouble as much as this is business. A favor will help him and ultimately you, as the studio will be yours one day. It's a mutually beneficial kind of favor."

I fold my arms and lean back against the wall, readying myself for the bullshit.

"Do you remember Mandi Becker?"

I cringe when I hear the name. Mandi was a few years younger than me. Total psycho. She had this massive crush on me. Used to follow me around like an annoying puppy dog. Tried to get it on with me a few times, but of course, I always blew her off.

One time, a few years ago, I'd passed out at a party, and I woke to find her straddling me, undoing my jeans, attempting to get my cock out. I went absolutely mental on her. I was sixteen. She was thirteen at the time. Why the hell she was at the party in the first place, I'll never know.

The girl is a nutjob—a nutjob who is now famous. She won a talent show on TV and became this big star.

"I remember. She's a singer now, right? Won that show."

"That's her. Well, your father is doing a film about a poor girl, trailer-trash sort, who wins a talent contest and becomes a singing sensation overnight—worldwide fame, that kind of thing. Sort of like what happened with Mandi."

"Except Mandi was hardly trailer trash. She grew up in Beverly Hills."

"Semantics. And you know how people love a good rags-to-riches story. Anyway, it's not a biographical film. But Mandi would be perfect for the part with her being a talent-show winner. She has a huge following here and internationally. She can actually sing, so we wouldn't need a voice-over. She'll be perfect for the part."

"And what does this have to do with me?"

"Well, the studio's been struggling these last few years. We haven't had a box office hit in a long time. A lot have been straight-to-DVD movies. You would know all of this if you paid attention to the business that will one day be yours instead of wasting your time out here, on the beach, playing with your little surfboard."

"Were you in any of the films?" I ask her.

"A few. Why?"

"That's why they flopped. You're getting old, Ava. People don't want to see you on-screen anymore."

Her lips press together. So, tightly I'm surprised they haven't turned blue.

*Wow.* What she needs from me, she must really need because she didn't bite.

"The studio needs a big hit, and this film will be it. Your father had a meeting with Mandi and her people the other day, and she's close to signing on for the film. But she has a condition…"

"Which is?"

"You."

"Me?" I laugh. "What does she want me for?"

"Well, you know how she's always had a thing for you…" She lifts a brow.

"You can't be serious." I push off the wall. "She wants me? For what?"

"To date, I'm guessing."

"Why? I'm sure she's not struggling for dates nowadays."

Ava shrugs. "I have no clue. But she is fixated on having you. You always have been a beautiful boy, Adam. Maybe it's that. But whatever it is, this girl wants you."

"Oh my God." I drag my hands over her face. "You seriously want to pimp me out to this nutjob singer, so she'll do a movie for Eric."

"I wouldn't call it pimping out."

"No?" I throw her a look. "What would you call it?"

"Oh, stop whining, Adam. Do you know how many boys your age would kill to be in your position? All I'm asking you to do is fuck a hot famous singer and keep her happy so that she'll make the movie. Then, once she's contractually bound to the movie, you can dump her ass and come back here to your little trailer-trash girlfriend. I don't see the problem in that."

"The fact that you don't see a problem is the problem in itself. You do know that Mandi is sixteen, right? You're basically asking me to fuck a minor—you know, commit a felony, statutory rape." I give a humorless laugh. I should be surprised, but I'm not.

"So, don't fuck her. Just keep her happy until she signs the contract."

I stare at her for a long moment, wondering how this woman is actually my mother, how I grew inside her for nine months, and how I somehow managed to come out normal—well, as normal as I can be after growing up with this fucking monster.

"Are you seriously asking me to do this?"

She gives me a look, telling me that she is.

"You're insane. I'm not doing it, Ava. No fucking way." I turn from her, walking toward the kitchen.

I need a drink. And there is alcohol here. I lied before. She just looked in the wrong place.

"I think you're forgetting your place in this family," she snaps, cold and low.

I whirl on her. "I think you've forgotten yours!" The words burst from me.

Her eyes go wide.

I never yell at Ava like this, and I never tell her no. I just do what she asks to make my life easier.

But enough is fucking enough.

She's screwing with my relationship with Evie asking me to do this, and I won't let Ava destroy what I have with her. I'm not losing Evie because of her.

"You forget that I'm the next in line for this shitty fucking studio that you and Eric love so much! The day Eric dies, that studio is mine. Your career is mine. You'd do well to remember *that*, Ava." My heart is pumping hard. My body shaking with rage.

She folds her arms, her eyes like lasers on me. "You will do this, Adam. Or there will be no studio left to inherit. Your father has made some bad business decisions over the years, and the studio is failing."

I let out a dry laugh. "Like I give a fuck. Let it go to shit, for all I care."

I turn back away and get one step farther from her when she says, "If you don't do this for me, then I will cut you off, dry. You'll have nothing. No money. *Nothing.*"

Ah, the age-old threat, the one that I'm wise to now. And tonight, I actually have the balls to say it, the thought of Evie giving me the courage.

Slowly, I turn back to Ava and shake my head. "You won't cut me off. And do you know why?" I take a step toward her. "Because you need me. You cut me off, and when Eric eventually dies—which won't be long if he keeps up using drugs the way he is—with no son to inherit the studio, the studio goes straight to Uncle Richard. And you know how much he hates you. With Richard in control, your career will end as quickly as it began because Richard will put your ass out on the street. Then, all you'll be is just another washed-up has-been who was once famous." My chest is heaving. I'm so fucking angry.

She stares at me for a long moment. If she looks could kill, I'd be stone-cold dead.

Then, she picks up her purse and stands. "Don't ever threaten me again, Adam. It would be a mistake to do so."

She turns and walks out of my house.

I don't breathe until I hear the front door slam shut, knowing that she's gone.

I'm shaking. I clench my fists in and out, trying to calm myself. My only thought now is being with Evie.

I wait another minute, making sure Ava is gone, before grabbing my car keys.

I climb into the McLaren and turn the engine on. "Hotel California" by The Eagles is playing on the radio, and I can't help but laugh at the irony.

That's me. I can check out anytime I want, but I can never leave.

I can come to Malibu and hide here for a year, but ultimately, I'll go back because I have to. It's my predetermined fate.

I can never get away from the fact that I'm a Gunner.

147

Hands gripping the steering wheel, I lean my head forward against them and close my eyes. I take deep breaths in and out through my nose.

*Evie.*

She's my way out. She's so strong, so full of life. She's my light at the end of this dark fucking tunnel called my life. I can get out with her by my side.

I lift my head, feeling a sense of purpose I've never felt before, and then I'm out of there and heading straight to her place.

I've never driven so fast before in my life. I'm surprised I don't get pulled over.

I pull up with a screech of tires outside her building. I run inside, taking the stairs two at a time. I bang on her front door, trying to catch my breath.

Her dad opens the door.

"Mr. Taylor," I say, out of breath. "Is Evie here?"

"Adam, for the hundredth time, call me Mick." He chuckles. Then, his expression turns a little more serious. "Is everything okay? Because Evie came home in a less than happy mood earlier."

"Yeah, everything's fine." *Aside from my devil bitch of a mother turning up, and in my attempt to protect Evie from her, I ended up hurting her feelings.*

I hold his steely gaze, my own giving nothing away.

He gives me a dubious look and then pushes the door open wider, standing aside, letting me in. "Evie's in her room. And you know the rules. Door stays open."

"Yes, sir, Mr. Taylor—I mean, Mick. Hey, Case." I wave to her as I cut through the living room, heading for Evie's room.

"Hey, Adam." She lifts her head from her book, giving me a wave and a smile.

I walk down the short hall toward Evie's bedroom. Stopping outside her door, I hear the angry sounds of

Christina Aguilera's "Fighter" coming from inside her room.

Definitely not a good sign.

Taking a deep breath, I knock on her door.

"I'm sleeping, Dad!" she yells. But her voice sounds off.

I open the door, letting myself in. She's turned away from me, facing the wall her bed is set against.

"Hey, babe," I say softly.

Her body stiffens at the sound of my voice. Her response to me makes me feel ill.

"Can I come in?"

"What are you asking me for? You're already in my room without my permission." She sits up and turns the music off. Then, she presses her back to the headboard, her knees bent, arms around them.

I examine her face. Her eyes are red. She's been crying.

My heart twists painfully in my chest.

I move across the room, sitting beside her. "Evie."

I reach for her, but she wards me off with her hands.

The rejection stings like a bitch.

"I don't know what just happened back there, at your house, but I didn't like it. Max told me a little, that your mom is a bitch—his words, not mine—"

"She is a bitch."

"I know you've told me before that she's not a good person. But you never talk about your family. All I know is that your mom is Ava Gunner, the movie actress, and your dad owns a movie studio that will be yours one day, but you don't actually want it. And that's all I know.

"Then, your mother turns up today, and I have never been more uncomfortable in my whole life. The way she talked to me—and worse, the things she said to you—it was awful, Adam. But what was worse was the way you treated me. You said that"—her eyes fill with tears again, her lip trembling—"I was *nothing*. A friend. Your friend, for God's

149

sake. Is what we've been doing what friends do? You told her that we're not really seeing each other.

"So, what was that, Adam? Your way of blowing me off? Or...or are you...are you just ashamed of me because I don't come from money, like your family?"

Tears openly run down her cheeks, and my chest feels like it's cracking wide open.

"Fuck no. Jesus, Evie." I take her face in my hands, not letting her push me away this time, forcing her eyes to meet mine. "I could never be ashamed of you. I love you."

Her eyes go wide, blinking at me. "You...love me?"

I take a deep breath. "Yeah, I do. Not exactly the way I envisaged telling you, but it's the truth. I love you. I'm in love with you. And the only people I'm ashamed of are me and my mother. I'm sorry I said those things, but you don't understand. Ava wrecks everything she touches. She's poison. And I don't want you anywhere near her. I don't want to lose you. I can't lose you, Evie. You're everything to me."

I press my forehead to hers, my eyes closed, and I just breathe her in.

"You won't lose me," she says softly, her hands resting against my arms. "I'm in love with you, too, Adam. And I'm not going anywhere."

Then, she kisses me.

And nothing has ever felt so good in my whole life as hearing Evie tell me that she loves me.

In this moment, I know that I'll never recover from her, and I don't ever want to.

This is it for me. She is it.

*Evie*
# BEVERLY HILLS · AUGUST 2015

"*Y*ou don't have class today?" I ask Casey, not taking my eyes off the TV screen where Aria and Ezra are totally heating it up.

It's my day off, and I'm spending it watching *Pretty Little Liars*.

I know my life is lame. People usually spend their days off with their friends or boyfriend, not in front of the TV with no other plans than that.

But I don't have any friends here, except for Angie. And she's not a close friend, just a work friend. As for a boyfriend—ha!

I'm currently in the middle of getting a divorce from the only man I ever loved…still love. But let's not get into that right now.

Back to Ezra…

"Yeah, I'm heading out in a few." Casey sits on the edge of the sofa, totally blocking my view of the TV.

Sighing, I look around her. Holding up the remote, I pause it.

"Where's Dad?" she asks me.

"The library."

"Again? Good to know he's getting use out of the Kindle we got him for his birthday."

"Ah, cut him some slack. It's good for him to get out and about. Anyway, I think he has the hots for the librarian."

"Really?" She lifts an eyebrow.

"Yep. She's pretty, too. I saw her when I went with him the other day."

Dad hasn't shown interest in anyone since Mom died. It's nice to see him recognizing that the opposite sex does exist again. Maybe I should take a page out of his book.

I reach down and grab my water. After taking a drink, I put it back down.

As I shift back to my spot, I see Casey staring at me. "What?" I say.

"Are you...okay? You just haven't seemed like yourself lately."

"I'm fine."

"It's only ten a.m., and you've already polished off a tub of Chunky Monkey." She taps the empty carton with her foot.

"I was hungry."

"And the Cheetos?" She indicates the super-size bag on the coffee table, sitting there waiting for me.

"Brunch." I grin at her.

"So, you don't plan on moving at all today?"

"Nope. Now, if you don't mind"—I nudge her with my leg—"I have some TV to watch, and you have class to get to."

152

She doesn't budge. She's still staring at me. I know my sister. I know she's considering saying something to me.

"Come on, Case, just spit it out. If you want to say something to me, let's get it over with, so I can get back to watching my show."

She tilts her head to the side, her blonde bangs spilling into her gray eyes. She has Mom's eyes. Sometimes, she reminds me of Mom so much that it hurts.

But it would hurt an awful lot more not to have Casey here.

If only I could have Mom here, too.

And Adam.

Then, life would be totally perfect.

But perfect and me don't go together.

"I heard you telling Dad that not long after we moved here, you saw Adam."

Every muscle in my body tenses.

Casey knows Adam and I were married, and then we weren't. And that's all she knows, all she needs to know.

"And?" I can't help the frown that pulls on my face.

"Well, I'd say that's a pretty big deal, seeing the man you loved, the guy you married and then left a week later, after all this time. It had to have been at least a little weird."

"Not really."

"No? It would have been for me."

"It's not a big deal because it's ancient history." *It's such a big deal that I could cry right now from just talking about it.*

"History can be painful to relive. I know something went down with him, and you've never really gotten over it—even though you'd never tell me," she says pointedly.

"There's nothing to tell. We were married, and then we weren't. And I got over it." I sigh, looking at the wall.

Lying to Casey sucks. I've always hated doing it.

But sometimes, you have to protect people from the truth they don't need to know.

My life is one big, fat lie.

Since the moment I told that first lie ten years ago, I've done nothing but lie since. It gets pretty tiring sometimes.

"Sure you got over it," she scoffs, folding her arms. "So, when was the last time you had a boyfriend again, Evie?"

"Um…"

"Exactly." She laughs. "Last time you went on a date?"

"Jesus, I don't know!" I throw my hands up.

"It was five years ago, and it's the only date I can remember you going on. You only went because it was a double date with Terri, that girl you worked with at the coffee house, and she'd set you up without you knowing. The last boyfriend you had was your husband."

"He's not my husband." *Okay, that's not exactly true.* But I'm not telling her that.

Dad knows, but Casey doesn't need to. I told him after Adam came to see me. I needed someone to talk to. And Dad knows all the sordid history. I know I can trust him, and I can tell him anything without any judgment.

But if I tell Casey, then I'll have to explain a whole lot of other things that I can't explain, things she doesn't need to know.

"Ex-husband. Whatever. But it must have been hard to see him. I might have been young and still sick at the time, but I remember, Evie. I remember how bad it was for you after we left Malibu and moved to San Fran. You were like a ghost for that first year."

*I really don't want to talk about this.*

"Seeing him wasn't hard, Case. A little weird, yes. Hard, no." *The only thing harder was leaving him in the first place.* "Can we stop talking about this now?" I can feel myself starting to crack.

"Why? Because he was the love of your life?"

"No, because I want to watch my show. And he was not the love of my life, FYI." *God, I sound like a teenager.*

"Sure. So, you just married some guy you kind of liked when you were eighteen years old?"

"Puppy love. You've heard of that. Marrying Adam was a mistake, and I got over it."

"You're such a bullshitter. You never got over him."

"Oh my God!" I blow up. "Yes, I did!"

Sometimes, I feel like I've been more of a mother to Casey over the years than a sister. But it's at times like this when I'm reminded that I'm definitely her sister.

"You keep telling yourself that. But you've been acting weird since you saw him, and now, you're spending your days off on the sofa with Chunky Monkey for company, which is on your face, by the way."

I touch a hand to my face, and yep, there it is. Ice cream smeared on my cheek. *Classy.* Lifting my T-shirt—which is actually Adam's old Rolling Stones T-shirt that I had claimed as mine when we first started dating—I wipe the ice cream from my face.

"Look, what is your problem here, Case? Why the big interrogation about Adam?"

Her face drops, and I instantly feel like shit.

"I'm just worried about you, that's all," she says quietly, sounding wounded, making me feel even shitter.

"Case, I'm okay," I tell her softly, placing my hand on her arm.

I know why she worries. Since Mom died and since her illness, she has this innate fear of losing Dad or me. It can make her thoughts irrational at times, especially when she gets something in her head. She probably thinks that Adam being back in my life is hurting me. And she will have, unintentionally distorted it her head, to it being a way that she could lose me.

"There is nothing to worry about, honey. Adam has nothing to do with anything." *Except that he has something to do with everything.* "He's just someone I used to know."

I have to stop myself from breaking out in song.

"Just promise me, you'll talk to me if you need to?"

I brush her hair back off her face. "I promise."

She stares at me for a long moment.

Then, she picks up her bag and stands. "Okay, well, I'll see you later." She bends down and kisses my cheek. "Try not to eat yourself into a coma, okay?"

"Okay." I press Play on the remote as I hear the front door close.

Wouldn't you believe it? My cell starts ringing—well, vibrating against my butt.

*Mothereffer!*

Lifting up, I retrieve my cell. I check the screen. It's Stan, my divorce lawyer.

I connect the call and put the phone to my ear. "Hey, Stan. Everything okay?"

"Hi. Well, I guess it depends on how you define *okay*."

"Usually, right along with something awesome."

"Well then, I have something awesome for you—or should I say, I have awesome news."

My bat signal turns on. "What's the awesome news?"

"I just heard from Adam's lawyer. He's agreed to the divorce, which means it'll go through nice and quickly."

"Okay." Even though I knew Adam would agree, I still feel a sinking loss in my stomach.

"But that's not the awesome. The awesome is that he's agreed to the divorce on his terms, and they are in your favor."

"My favor?"

"Yes. Massively in your favor. He is giving you *a lot* of money, Evie."

"I'm sorry. What?"

"Money. He's giving you a large amount of money as part of the divorce settlement."

"But I don't want a settlement. I never asked for that. Why would he do that?"

"I don't know, and I wouldn't questions it. Adam is offering to give you pretty much his net worth. He's keeping Gunner Entertainment and his house, and that's all he wants. The rest is yours."

"His net worth? I'm sorry. I don't understand." My tongue feels like rubber in my mouth.

"His net worth is his total assets, minus outside liabilities, negating the studio. And as he personally owns only one house, Adam's asset is cash and lots of it."

"I know what net worth is. I just…" I can't get my brain and mouth into the same gear.

It doesn't matter though because Stan is on a roll. "We're talking millions here, Evie. Nine figures. This divorce is about to make you a very rich woman."

*Millions? Nine figures?*

I sit up so quickly that the remote goes flying off my lap and into the coffee table with a loud thud.

"He's giving me all his money?" I gasp. "But why? It doesn't make sense."

"Sense or not, it's about to be yours."

"But I don't want his money!"

"Well, whether or not you want it, he's determined to give it to you."

I press my shaking hand to my muddled head. "Can I contest his terms?"

Stan coughs out a laugh. "You can, but I can't see why you would." He sounds confused. He's not the only one.

And he probably thinks I'm mental, but I don't care. The only mental one here is Adam. He's clearly lost his freaking mind.

I don't want his money. I never did.

I have no clue as to why he's doing this.

"I want to contest. You send those papers back and tell him no way am I divorcing him on those terms."

There's silence, and then Stan roars out a laugh. "I have to say, this is the strangest divorce case I've ever dealt with.

157

Normally, the husband is holding back on funds, and the wife is fighting for them. Never have I had a husband offering everything and the wife wanting nothing."

"Yeah, well, nothing about my and Adam's marriage was ever conventional." I sigh, dragging my hand down my face. "I just don't understand why he's doing this. Is he being forced to?"

"Forced? By whom?"

"I don't know. The law? I mean, in Cali, is there a law that says he has to give me money?"

"Technically, the law states, if there's no prenuptial agreement, then assets will be split fifty-fifty. But because of your unique circumstances—the fact that you filed on abandonment, putting yourself at fault, along with the length of time you've been separated, and you leaving him ten years ago—then no. There isn't a judge that would award in your favor."

"And his lawyer would have told him all this?"

"I would imagine so."

"I just…" I rub at my head. "None of this makes sense."

"Don't make sense of it. Just be happy, and start thinking about how you're going to spend your money. Look, I have to go. I have to be in court in fifteen minutes. We'll talk soon."

Then, he hangs up before I get a chance to reiterate that I want him to tell Adam no freaking way to his terms.

I'm staring down at the cell in my hand like it's an alien.

*What the hell is Adam doing? Why would he try to give me all of his money? It makes no sense.*

Well, if my lawyer won't tell him no, then I will.

Getting up, cell still in hand, I head for the front door. I shove my feet in my flip-flops and grab my car keys off the key hook, and then I'm out the door.

As I make my way down the stairs, I Google the address for Gunner Entertainment on my phone.

Wilshire Boulevard. It shouldn't take me too long to get there.

I push out the door of my building and quickly cross the lot to my car. I get in and take off.

As I drive, I just get more confused, and then, quiet frankly, I get pissed off.

*I mean, what the hell does he think he's doing? He knows I couldn't give a shit about his money. Is he doing this on purpose to mess with me? If he is, then it's working.*

Traffic's pretty clear, so I'm there in no time.

I pull up outside the building. I'm out of my car and heading for the entrance.

I practically blow up into his building. I'm so angry that I feel like I could punch someone—preferably him.

I march over to the reception desk.

The, of course, gorgeous, mega thin blonde-haired receptionist lifts a finger, halting me, as she says into the mouthpiece, "Connecting you now."

Then, she presses a button on the phone and flicks stony eyes to me.

I watch as she looks me up and down, a sneer appearing on her perfectly made-up face.

It's then I remember that I'm still wearing Adam's old Rolling Stones T-shirt and my ratty old jean shorts that I might have had since I was seventeen. I haven't shaved my legs today, and my three-day dirty hair is in a messy knot on top of my head. I quite possibly still have ice cream on my face as I didn't look in a mirror after cleaning it off.

*Oh God.*

I've just marched into Adam's building, looking like a homeless person. *Great. Just effing great.*

"Can I…help you?" she says with as much distaste as is shown in her expression.

Maybe I should just back up and leave the building. I still have time.

No, I'm here now, and I need to know what the hell he's playing at.

Anger wins out over vanity this time.

*Just pretend you belong here and don't currently look like a hobo.*

"I'm here to see Adam," I say with as much confidence as I can.

"Adam?" She frowns.

"Yes. Adam Gunner, the guy whose name is on that sign hanging above your head." I point my finger in the direction of the sign.

"I'm well aware of who Mr. Gunner is and what his first name is," she says icily. "Now, what I want to know from you is, do you have an appointment?"

"No, I don't have an appointment—"

"Then, you can't see him," she says smugly, cutting me off. "No one sees Mr. Gunner without an appointment."

She pulls her headset off, swings her chair around, and gets up, walking over to the desk behind her.

*Okay, now, she has seriously pissed me off. She's like a fucking guard dog that I can't get past.*

"Hey, Pit Bull Barbie." I slam my hands down on my hips.

She turns slowly to face me. The look on her face is pretty pissed off.

Like I care right now.

"Are you talking to me?" Her eyes narrow, her lips twisting.

"Apparently so." My hands leave my hips to bang down on the fancy glass top, praying to God I don't crack it. I lean forward. "Now, be a good little receptionist and call upstairs to tell Mr. Gunner that his *wife* is here, and she wants to see him *now*."

Pit Bull Barbie's eyes widen at the term *wife*. She actually stumbles back a little, grabbing hold of the desk behind her. "W-wife?" she stutters.

She seems pretty affected by this news.

A stabbing thought suddenly enters my head.

Maybe she knows Adam like I know Adam. Maybe she's his girlfriend—or at the very least fucking him.

*Oh God.*

I know nothing of Adam's life now. He could have a girlfriend, and she could be it.

And that stabbing sensation enters my chest and centers on my heart, piercing straight through and slashing from side to side.

I have to curl my hands around the edge of the desk to stop from falling over.

"Yes. His wife." I hear the tremor in my voice.

*Come on, Evie. This shouldn't matter to you.*

But it does. It really fucking does.

She lets out a sarcastic laugh. "Yeah, and I'm the next Queen of England. Mr. Gunner is not married. I would know if he were."

*Yep, they're fucking. And I think I'm going to hurl.*

*Jesus, this hurts like a motherfucker.*

I let my pain morph into anger. The images of her and Adam *together* are aiding that.

"Well, you might want to check your facts because I am, without a doubt, his wife. Now, do your job, and call upstairs. Tell my husband that I'm here to see him, and be quick about it." I flick my fingers at her in a derogatory manner as I take a step back.

Okay, maybe that was overkill with the my-husband bit. And I honestly don't ever treat people like I've just treated Pit Bull Barbie here. Being in the service industry, I'm treated like this regularly, so I always make sure to be respectful to people. But she's really pissing me off, and if she and Adam are—well, whatever. I just don't like her.

She strides back to the desk in front of me, sits her ass in the chair, and picks up her earpiece before putting it in. Then, she presses a button on her phone. "Mark, I have a woman here claiming to be…well, she says she's Mr.

161

Gunner's...*wife*." She flicks a look at me. "To be honest, she..." She spins her chair away from me, like she thinks doing that will mean I can't hear her. "Well, she looks like a homeless person. Maybe she's a mental patient who's escaped from a facility. Should I call security?"

There's a long silence while I stare at the back of Pit Bull Barbie's head.

"Well, yes, she is small, I suppose. And she does have blonde hair, but it's kind of disgusting—fine, okay." She shoots me a glance over her shoulder. "What's your name?"

I fold my arms over my chest, letting out a sigh. "Evie."

She relays my name down the phone, and we go back to silence again.

Maybe I should just get my cell out and call Adam myself. Now that I think of it, I probably should have done that in the beginning.

"Are you sure?" she says. "Because—I'm sorry, what?" she gasps, her back going rigid. Then, more silence. "Fine," she snaps. "Tell Mr. Gunner I hear his message loud and clear."

She spins her chair back to me. Looking like she's just been slapped on the face, her cheeks bright red, she bites out the words to me, "Take the elevator to the eighth floor. Mark Evans, Mr. Gunner's assistant, will meet you there."

"Thank you," I say primly, giving her a smug look even though I really want to give her the middle finger.

I swivel on my heel and march over to the elevator. I press the call button. The doors immediately open. I step inside and press the button for the eighth floor, which also happens to be the top floor.

The door closes, and I crumble against the elevator wall.

*Holy shit!*

I can't believe I just did that.

I just announced to Adam's receptionist—and quite possibly a woman he's fucking—that I'm married to him.

Me and my big mouth.

I really shouldn't have done that. I can't imagine that she's going to keep that piece of news to herself.

And Adam, though not celebrity famous, is a notable person. He's the head of Gunner Entertainment, for God's sake. It's newsworthy.

If this gets out…I'm screwed.

And as the elevator ascends, taking me closer to Adam, my stomach drops right back down to the ground.

*I*t's Christmas—well, almost. It's Christmas Eve. Adam and I are at the supermarket, shopping for a turkey and all the trimmings.

We've left our food shopping pretty late, but between school and working every available shift I can at Grady's in the run up to Christmas, I haven't had a chance to get to the store. And Dad hasn't had time to get out as Casey's been sick with a touch of the flu, but she's on the mend now.

Max has gone home for the holidays. I got the impression that he didn't want to, but he had no choice.

Adam isn't going home, so he is spending Christmas with us. As far as I know, he hasn't spoken to his mother since she came in October. Adam hasn't told me what went down with his mother after I had left, but I get the feeling

SAMANTHA TOWLE

that it wasn't good. If he wants to talk about it, then I'll listen, but I'm not going to push him.

He hasn't mentioned his dad, but I know they're not close. Adam's dad is not the kind of father who calls up for no other reason than to have a chat with his son.

I'm just happy that he's spending the holidays with me.

Dad is even letting him spend the night at our apartment tonight, so we can all wake up together tomorrow morning to open presents.

Adam will be sleeping on the couch.

We still haven't gotten to the actually-having-sex stage in our relationship, not that Dad would let Adam sleep with me if we had gotten there. Not a chance in hell.

And I want Adam. I really do. I'm crazy about him. I love him. But I'm just not there with the sex thing yet. The thought kind of terrifies me. I've seen the size of his cock, and I honestly can't wrap my head around how the hell it's supposed to fit inside me, not that I've said that to Adam.

He's just so patient with me. It's amazing. He's amazing.

"I've never done this before," Adam says, pushing the cart alongside me.

I continue to deposit food into it from off the shelves. "Done what?"

"Shop for Christmas food."

"No?" I give him a surprised look.

"Nope. The house staff always got the food and prepared it. Believe it or not, I didn't actually have to shop for food until I moved here with Max."

"That's tragic." I laugh.

"Yeah," he agrees, laughing.

"So, what did you do for Christmas?" I imagine, with the money his family has, they probably spent it in Aspen or somewhere equally as nice.

His eyes lower. "Christmases were usually pretty shitty in the Gunner household. If Ava and Eric weren't fighting

166

over one thing or another, then Eric was getting drunk and waiting for the moment he could leave. We weren't really the open-the-presents-around-the-tree kind of family. I usually spent most of each Christmas up in my room.

"When I was around thirteen, I started spending Christmas alone. Ava and Eric decided I was old enough to fend for myself, so they would go off—separately—to do whatever with whomever, so I would be home alone. There was the staff, but I would let them go home, so they could spend the day with their families. And I would just eat whatever our housekeeper, Millie, had made for me before she left, which was always something nice."

"Your parents left you alone on Christmas?" I gasp, my heart hurting for him.

He shrugs like it doesn't matter. Averting his eyes, he picks up a pack of cookies and starts examining them.

But I know it bothers him, and it makes me ache for him.

"I mean, I only spent two Christmases alone before Max found out, and he never let me spend another Christmas alone again, so it wasn't all bad. Christmases got better after that. Max would take me to his house. Even though his parents are as close to fucked up as mine, they're always home for Christmas. And it didn't matter 'cause I was with Max, and we always had a laugh."

I hate his parents. I've never even met his dad, and I hate him already.

No, I don't hate them. I loathe them.

I mean, what kind of people leave their kid alone at Christmas?

The fucking evil kind—that's who.

Stopping in the middle of the aisle, I walk over to where he is and wrap my arms around him from behind, hugging him tight. "Thank God for Max. I'm going to let him know how much I appreciate him when he gets back after the break," I say into his shirt.

167

Adam turns in my arms and looks down at me. "I hope you're not going to show your appreciation in the same way you show me that you appreciate me."

I laugh, slapping his shoulder. "No, dork. I'm just going to thank him."

"You don't need to."

"I know. I just…" I reach up on my toes and press my hands to his cheeks, his scruff tickling my palms. "I hate that you didn't have the kind of Christmas you deserve. So, I'm going to make sure this year is your best Christmas yet, and then every year after this one, I'm going to make sure we top the year before. I mean, we're going to spend every Christmas together from now on, right?" I don't want to sound presumptuous.

I know he's as serious about me as I am about him. But I also know he'll be leaving for school in the fall next year, which means he'll be moving to the other side of the country, and we haven't talked about what that will mean for us.

He leans down and brushes his nose against mine. "You can bet your hot ass that we'll be spending every Christmas together. I don't want to be anywhere but with you, babe."

He gives my behind a squeeze, and I giggle. My fingers work their way into his long hair as he brushes his lips over mine, kissing me.

"So, that's what you would have done this year, if you hadn't met me? You'd be at Max's?"

"Yeah."

"You don't think he minds you spending the holiday with me?"

"Nah, Max is cool."

He kisses me one more time before releasing me. I get back to filling the cart.

Christmas is the one time of year I don't have to scrimp on the food I buy because, as a Christmas bonus, Grady gives us supermarket vouchers.

*God bless Grady.*

My cell starts to ring in my pocket. I pull it out and see it's Dad.

"Hey, we shouldn't be much longer—" That's when I hear the siren in the background. My heart stops. "Dad?"

"Evie, we're in an ambulance. Casey—she-she was fine, talking to me about what kinds of mashed potatoes she was gonna have you make for dinner tomorrow. Then, all of a sudden, her speech went all slurred, and-and then she collapsed and started convulsing. She was having a fit, Evie." His voice breaks, and tears fill my eyes. "The paramedics stabilized her, and now, we're heading to the hospital."

"Wh-which hospital are you going to?"

"West Hills."

"I'll be there as soon as I can. I-I…love you, Daddy."

He shudders out a breath. "Love you, too, baby."

I hang my phone up.

"Evie?"

I turn to Adam, and my lips tremble. "Casey…she-she collapsed." My voice is wobbling all over the place. "She had a fit. Da-dad called from an ambulance. Th-they're on their way to the hospital."

There's no hesitation in him. "Let's go."

He grabs my hand, taking charge, and we abandon the shopping cart before heading for the parking lot.

"Which hospital?" Adam asks as we're climbing into his truck.

"West Hills. Her neurologist is at the UCLA Medical Center, but maybe they're taking her to West Hills because it's closer. I don't know."

"Don't worry. We'll get to her soon, and then we can find out what's happening," he reassures me.

Adam pulls out of the lot, speeding as he does. I should tell him to slow down a little, but I don't because I want to get to Casey as soon as possible.

I press my head back into the headrest, shutting my eyes, as I suck in a breath.

I know what this means. The tumor is back.

I feel Adam's hand curl around mine. I open my eyes and turn my head to look at him.

"She's gonna be fine, babe." He looks at me with love in his eyes.

I numbly nod my head, squeezing his hand in return, but I don't feel his words.

I've been here before, and she got better the last time. But now, she's sick again, and I have a terrible feeling deep inside that things could be worse this time.

Dad is pacing the waiting room in the ER when we arrive.

"Hey." I hug him. "How is she doing?"

"She's having a scan done at the moment," he tells me, releasing me. "She was conscious and talking when they took her through. I'm just waiting for the doctor to come and tell me what's happening." Dad turns to Adam, acknowledging him, "Adam."

"Sir, I'm really sorry to hear about Casey."

"Call me Mick, please." My dad gives him a weak smile. "And thank you. And thanks for getting Evie here so quickly."

"No problem."

"Dad…" I catch his attention. "Is it…back?"

He knows what I'm asking. His eyes lower. "I don't know, honey." He shakes his head. "I don't know."

Adam reaches over and squeezes my hand. I step back into him, really needing the safety and warmth that only he can give me. He puts his arms around my stomach, and presses his lips to my hair.

"Do either of you want anything?" Adam asks.

Both Dad and I say, "No."

Then, we fall into this quiet silence. We're all just standing there, lost in our thoughts, waiting for news on Casey, while we're surrounded by other people waiting on news of their loved ones, too.

Fortunately, we don't have to wait too long.

"Casey Taylor's family?"

We all turn at the same time. The doctor looks to be fortyish and is on the wrong side of hair loss but is faithfully clinging to what he has left.

"I'm Dr. Prestwich," he says, addressing us as a group. "I'm the doctor who has been treating Casey since she arrived here."

"I'm Casey's dad, Mick." My dad reaches over and shakes his hand. "And this is my eldest daughter, Evie, and her boyfriend, Adam."

The doctor nods at us as a greeting.

"Right. Well, as I said, I've been treating Casey. She was taken down for a scan not too long ago, and while she was there, I familiarized myself with her history." He looks down at the folder he had tucked under his arm. "Now, Casey was diagnosed with an ependymoma, grade two, brain tumor a year and a half ago. She received surgery and radiation therapy, which she finished just under a year ago, and the treatment was successful."

"That's correct," my dad says.

"She's been fine since? No signs of any recurring symptoms—headaches, tiredness, slurred speech, random bouts of vomiting?"

"No. She's been fine, like she used to be before the tumor. I mean, she's had a touch of the flu recently, but that's it. Today, she was complaining of feeling a bit tired, but I put it down to all the Christmas excitement. She was talking to me while I was wrapping Evie's present. Then, just out of nowhere, she just fell to the floor and started…started having a fit."

Dad's eyes glaze with tears. Hearing his words and seeing the tears in his eyes bring tears back to my own. I have to look away and bite my lip to stop from crying.

Adam's arm comes around my shoulder, pulling me into his side. He presses his lips to my temple.

"Okay. So, the scan results came back, and I've looked at them. I'm not a neurologist specialist, but…there is definitely something showing on Casey's brain—a shadow. I have spoken with Casey's neurologist…Dr.…." He starts scanning his paperwork.

"Hemmings," Dad finishes for him.

"Hemmings, yes. Thank you. So, yes, I spoke to Dr. Hemmings over at the UCLA Medical Center. I have had the scan sent over to him. He wants to have Casey transferred to UCLA first thing in the morning, so they can do more tests. So, she will stay here for the night."

"So, the tumor is back?" I manage to get out.

The doctor looks at me. "I can't say for sure exactly what is wrong with Casey without having further tests done. But given her history of a prior cancerous tumor to the brain…yes, it is possible that is the case. But I will emphasize not to panic because, even if the tumor has returned, it does not mean it's cancerous this time."

All I can hear is, *The tumor has returned.*

*It's happening again.*

"When can we see her?" I ask, desperate to see my sister.

"Casey will be transferred to the children's ward shortly. I'll arrange for you to see her before she goes up. You can stay the night with her, if you wish, Mr. Taylor?"

"Yes, I'd like that. Thank you."

"Right. Well, a nurse will be through soon to take you to see Casey."

"Thank you, Doctor," Dad says.

The doctor disappears back through the door he came in through.

Dad turns to me.

I can see it, the fear, in his eyes.

My heart starts to break. I force myself to keep strong for Dad's sake. He needs me now more than ever.

"Mr. Taylor?" I turn to see a dark-haired lady walking toward us. "Sorry to bother you right now, but we need you to fill out some paperwork for us."

Dad lets out a tired-sounding breath, running his hand through his hair.

"Is it anything I can do?" I volunteer.

"No, it's fine, Evie," Dad says. "I can do it. Why don't you and Adam grab us some drinks to have while we wait to see Casey?"

"Okay," I say. "Coffee?"

"Perfect. You need some money?"

"No, I got this." I pat my purse.

Adam and I walk down the hall to where we saw the coffee machine.

"I'm so sorry, babe," Adam says as we walk. He catches my hand, holding it.

"Yeah, me, too. It's not going to be much of a Christmas for you, I'm afraid. We'll be spending it in the hospital with Casey. Maybe you should go see Max—"

He stops me in the middle of the empty hall and turns me to him. "No way am I leaving you. I can't believe you'd suggest it."

"I just want you to have a nice Christmas," I say, thinking back to what he told me in the supermarket.

"I will have a nice Christmas because I'll be with you. I don't care where I am, Evie, so long as I'm with you."

Tears prick my eyes again. I'm so lucky to love him and have him love me back.

173

I slide my arms around his back, hugging him, and I press my cheek to his chest. His strong arms come around me. I can hear his heart beating strong and solid through his shirt.

"I love you," I murmur.

"I love you, too." His fingers brush through my hair.

We stand there for a moment, just holding each other, until I reluctantly let go, and we start walking to the coffee machine again.

I reach for my purse, but Adam stops me. "I'll get these. What do you want?"

"Coffee, please."

Adam gets three coffees, and I carry mine and Dad's while Adam carries his own as we head back to the waiting room. We're just passing by a room when I hear my dad's voice inside, bringing me to a stop.

"I really am sorry that I don't have my credit card with me. It's in my wallet at home, and I left in a rush with Casey."

"Like I told you before, Mr. Taylor, it's not a problem." It sounds like the lady from before. "Just make the payment whenever you can. You can come in and make it, or just call, and we can do it over the phone. And here's the leaflet that I was telling you about. It describes the available payment plans. It might be worth looking into them with the level of care that Casey might need."

"Thank you." My dad's voice comes closer toward us, so I duck behind a partition wall with Adam following me.

*Payment plan.* I didn't even think about the cost for Casey's treatment.

We're barely managing to get by as it is. This is going to break us.

I close my eyes, releasing a sigh.

"Your dad doesn't have insurance, does he?"

I shake my head. Then, I open my eyes. "No. He had it when he was working, but after that, he didn't get any.

Casey's first round of treatments wiped us out, and we couldn't afford to get insurance after that, as the premium was higher because she was already diagnosed with the illness. I don't know how we're going to manage the payments for her treatment now."

"Let me help."

My eyes flash to his. "No."

He puts his coffee down on the floor. Then, he takes both the cups from me, putting them next to his.

He takes my face in his hands. One hand is warmer than the other from the coffee he was holding.

"You don't need to struggle or worry about this. I have the money to pay for whatever treatment Casey needs. Then, you can just focus on being there for her."

"It's not your money. It's your parents' money." That came out sounding way harsher than I'd intended.

He drops his hands from my face and takes a step back.

"I'm sorry." I blow out a breath. "I didn't mean that the way it sounded."

"You're right. It is their money. And they do nothing good with it. I never have. Let me do something good. Let me help Casey and you and your dad."

"We're not a charity case, Adam."

"I didn't mean it that way, and you know it."

"I know. God, I'm sorry." I press a hand to my head. Everything I'm saying to him right now keeps coming out wrong and bitchy.

I reach for his hand, and he lets me take it.

"I appreciate your offer to help. I love you for it, but I can't accept it—not just me, but my dad, too," I say quickly when he parts his lips to speak. "He's a proud man. It's hard enough for him that I work to help us make ends meet."

"Accepting help isn't a weakness, Evie."

"I know, but…just let me handle this."

175

Letting go of my hand, he stares down at the floor, his fingers pinching the bridge of his nose. Then, he looks back up, a determination on his face, and steps into my space, pressing his body to mine, holding my face with his hands. My hands go to his waist.

"Okay, Evie. We'll do this your way…for now. But if things get too hard, then I'm helping, no matter what you or your dad say, you hear me?"

I curl my fingers into his shirt. "Okay," I say.

But as his lips touch softly to mine, I know I just lied to him for the first time because there is no way I'll take his money.

This is my family, and it's my problem to solve.

## Adam
## BEVERLY HILLS · AUGUST 2015

"Adam?" Mark's voice comes through on the intercom. "A woman in reception is claiming to be…well, she says she's your wife, and she's demanding to see you. As far as I know, you aren't married, but I wanted to call you first before I have security escort her from the building."

"Is she blonde, tiny, and goes by the name Evie?"

"One minute. I'll check with Serena."

He's back a few seconds later. "Yes to all three."

I can't help the smile that crawls onto my lips. Evie telling people that she's my wife, demanding to see me, can only mean one thing. She's pissed. She always was feisty when she got going. Guess that hasn't changed.

"Let her up. And, Mark, I don't want this being public knowledge. Tell Serena that if I hear one word about this from anyone else or see anything in the press, she's fired, without references, and I will personally make sure she never works in this town again."

"I'll relay the message."

I release the button on the intercom and lean back in my chair.

I'm not ashamed that Evie is my wife. God, the day we got married, I wanted to shout it from the rooftop.

But Serena is a fucking gossip. She could rival Perez Hilton. And she's made it more than clear that she wants me to fuck her. I never have for two reasons. One, she's blonde. And two, I don't fuck my staff. Too messy.

The reason I want it kept quiet is because I don't want Ava finding out. Not for me though. I couldn't give a shit. I'm protecting Evie. If Ava finds out that Evie and I are still married and on our way to divorcing, she'll go after Evie.

On principle, Ava won't like that I'm giving Evie my money, but she'll let that go. What she won't let go of is the studio. And I know the way her mind works. She'll see Evie as a threat to that. According to the State of California, Evie is legally entitled to fifty percent of my assets because we got married without a prenup, which would put the studio in some jeopardy if Evie decided to go after half of everything I owned.

But she never would. I know that. However, Ava judges everyone by her own standards, which are pretty low. So, she would hurt Evie in any way she could to keep the studio.

So, I want Ava to stay blissfully ignorant until the divorce is finalized, and then I can have the pleasure of telling her about giving Evie the money as a side bonus to telling her that I've signed the studio over to Richard.

The fact that Evie's here and pissed means she's found out about the terms of the divorce settlement.

I confirmed the details with my lawyer yesterday, much to his grievance—he nearly fainted when I told him of my plans—so I knew Evie would be hearing about it soon enough.

And I knew if she was the same Evie I knew all those years ago, then she'd be pissed that I was giving her all my money. I guess I was right on that count.

*Why am I giving it to her?*

Well, partly, if she is the same person I knew, then at least I'll get to piss her off, in the biggest way possible, one last time.

The main reason though began, as I sat in the office with my lawyer, talking over the divorce settlement and my finances, with my life laid out on paper in front of me. It was then I realized that was all I was—money.

I have nothing to show for my life in twenty-nine years, except for a handful of hit movies under my belt and my parents' money.

They're still controlling me even now.

I haven't done any of the things I wanted to do.

I'm running a business I don't give a shit about. I've been living day to day, one fuck to the next fuck, and I'm just tired.

The last time I was happy, truly happy, was with Evie, and for that, I owe her.

But it's more than that.

In those days, Evie gave me freedom. When I married her, turning my back on it all—well, trying to—I gave up the money and went against my parents.

But I went crawling back after she'd left. I went back to what I knew.

It was that or face the world alone, and I didn't know how to do it.

*Better the devil you know, right?*

And coming back to this life…well, I blamed Evie for that, but it was my own weakness. I could have stayed away and built a life for myself, even without Evie there.

But I was a coward, and I went back to what was easier.

It was my fault.

But no more. I want out.

And I'm doing that by getting rid of the money I received from my trust fund and the money I've earned over the years from selling my soul to the devil.

Giving it to Evie might seem like a strange thing to do because I know she's never cared about money, but she's struggled financially her whole life.

I'm guessing things haven't gotten any easier for her, considering she's driving a twenty-year-old Pontiac Grand and is working as a waitress in a coffee shop. Also, Casey is starting at UCLA, and I know that won't be cheap. I know Evie will be paying for it. It's not that her dad and sister are freeloaders, but it's just the way she is. She takes care of them.

She took care of me for a time, too.

Now, I can finally take care of her. I can make her life a lot easier.

As for the business, I'm signing that over to Richard. As soon as the divorce is finalized, I'm giving it to him.

And then I'm going to…well, I don't know what's at the end of that sentence, but I do know that it's time to let go of the past, to let go of Evie, and move on.

And I guess that starts right now.

Getting up from behind my desk, I walk to the front of it and lean against it, crossing my legs and curling my hands around the edge, as I await Evie's arrival.

I can't deny that I'm nervous. My heart is pounding.

No one can get to me like she does. No one ever could.

I hear Mark's voice outside my door, and then it opens with Evie walking in.

She looks like she just got out of bed. And she looks fucking beautiful.

Her hair is tied into a messy bun on the top of her head, and her face is free of makeup, not that she ever really wore much. Her eyes are full of ire, and they're blazing. Everything in me pays attention, especially my cock.

Angry Evie is hot Evie. Well, any version of her is hot. But I always did get off on it when she was all fired up.

"Mark, hold all my calls, and cancel my eleven o'clock," I tell him without looking away from her.

"Sure thing," he says. Then, he closes the door behind him, leaving Evie and me alone.

There's a brief moment of silence. The emotions are so thick in the air around us that you could reach out and grab them.

That was the thing with Evie and me. We always did feel too much around each other.

"So," I say, lifting my brow, breaking the silence, "you're my wife, huh?"

Her cheeks stain pink, like they do when she's embarrassed. "Mmhmm…yeah, sorry about that." She twists her hands in front of her.

"Don't be."

"I just needed to get up here, so I could talk to you," she explains, gesturing with her hands. "And your Pit Bull Barbie receptionist wouldn't let me through."

"Pit Bull Barbie?" I laugh. "Guess that is a pretty accurate description of Serena. But you could have called if you wanted to talk. It would have saved you the trouble of coming here." I don't mean that. Her coming here, even if because she's angry with me, means something. I just don't know what that something is.

"I wanted to talk face-to-face about this."

"And what is *this*?" I uncross my legs and stretch them out in front of me.

A frown appears on her face. "The divorce settlement, Adam. Have you lost your damn mind?"

"Quite possibly."

She folds her arms, which pushes her tits up, and of course, my eyes go straight to them.

181

That's when I see what she's actually wearing. I registered that she had on a T-shirt, but I didn't focus on the T-shirt itself.

It's mine—or it was mine. She claimed it in the early days of our relationship. I loved seeing her in that shirt. I always felt like it somehow branded her with me, so no other man could ever touch her.

Seeing her wearing my old T-shirt causes something primitive to tear open inside of me, and all I can think about is ripping that shirt off her body and fucking her senseless.

"Nice T-shirt," I say, lifting my eyes back to her face.

She glances down at the T-shirt. Her fingers curling around the hem. "I always liked wearing it," she says softly.

Hearing her say that elicits a thousand memories. I feel the pleasure and pain of each one in every part of my body.

"I remember." My voice is rough. *I remember how many times I pulled it off your body right before I made love to you.* "I also remember it was mine."

Her eyes meet mine. "It was."

"And so were you."

Some unnamed emotion flickers through her eyes. She turns her face away. When she looks back at me, her eyes are devoid of emotion. "We need to talk about the settlement. I don't want the money, *Adam.*"

The way she said my name was like a punishment, so I return the reprimand.

"Those are the terms, *Evie.*" I fold my arms over my chest. "You take the money, or I won't sign the divorce papers."

Frustration and anger gather up on her face. Being the sick bastard that I am, I get even more turned on by it.

"Why are you doing this?" She lays her palms out, almost like she's pleading with me.

"Because I can."

"Is this—is this some weird sort of test, or is it your way of punishing me because I left you?"

I let out a dry laugh.

She's right though. Part of me is doing it to punish her. She knows me too well.

Unfurling my arms, I stand up straight. "Only you would think five hundred million is a punishment."

"Because I don't care about your money! I never did. It was never what I wanted from you."

That blows a fuse in my brain. "Then, what the fuck did you want from me? If it wasn't the money, what the hell was it?" I yell.

"You!" she shouts back. "All I ever wanted was you!"

"Then, why the fuck did you leave me?"

We're standing here, yelling at each other, and I know Mark can hear us, but I don't care.

I care about what she's about to say next.

A flash of something I can't discern passes over her face.

Then, her anger is gone as quickly as it came, and she's retreating, backing up. "I can't…this wasn't a good idea. I shouldn't have come."

She turns to leave and I let out a harsh laugh.

"Running for the door again, Evie? What a fucking surprise. It's become your specialty, babe. Tell me, does it get easier each time you leave, or was it already easy in the first place?"

Then, she does something that surprises me.

She stops. Her hand on the handle, she presses her forehead to the door.

For a second, I'm not sure what's happening.

Then, I see her body tremble, and I hear a sniffle.

She's crying.

*Fuck.*

I'm moving toward her without a thought. Stopping, I'm only inches from her.

Seeing her like this, crying…it's like a vise is around my chest, squeezing.

I want to touch her so badly. But I don't.

Instead, I ball my hands into fists at my sides. "Evie?"

"It was never easy." Her voice is a whisper.

My heart stills. "What wasn't?"

She exhales a sad-sounding breath. "Leaving you. No part of that was ever easy."

"Then…why?"

She shakes her head from side to side, her forehead still resting against the door.

"Talk to me," I urge gently.

"I can't."

Frustration slams into me, but I somehow manage to control it. "Okay, so don't talk to me about that. At least tell me why you're crying."

I hear her take another breath, and then she turns to face me.

The sight of the tears staining her cheeks wrecks me. I never could bear to see Evie cry.

Unable not to, I reach over and brush my fingers over her cheek, collecting her tears.

The feel of her skin is electric against mine. And I don't miss her sharp intake of breath.

Her eyes lower, like it's too hard to look at me. "I'm crying because I'm sad. And I'm sad because all we do when we see each other is fight and hurt one another. Mostly, I'm sad because I miss you. I've missed you for ten years, and I'm tired of missing you, tired of this hollow space in my chest where you used to be."

When she lifts those whiskey eyes to mine, I see all the raw pain in them, and I know she's telling me the truth about that.

Something changes in this moment, and things that seemed important to me before don't seem so vital anymore.

But what is important are those words she just spoke.

I've waited ten years to hear her say those words, to say that she's missed me.

Now, she has.

Maybe it's because she said she missed me or because she's wearing my shirt or because I've finally lost my damn fucking mind, or maybe it's all those things combined, but I can't stop myself.

I kiss her.

I kiss her fiercely. I kiss her with ten years of pent-up anger and need and longing and desperation.

And I know, in that second when my lips touch hers, that I won't regret one moment of what's about to happen. Even when it hurts so badly that I think I'll regret it, wish it had never happened, I won't.

There's no hesitation as Evie kisses me back. It's like she needs this as much as I do.

Her lips part on a moan, the sound vibrating all the way down to my cock, and all hell breaks loose.

Pure primal need to reclaim what is mine slams into me, and I'm helpless against it, helpless against her.

Lifting her, I slam her back against the wall. Her legs come up and wrap around my waist.

And it's like no time has passed at all. Everything about her is the same—her taste, her scent, how she feels under my hands.

I want more. I want all of her, more than I should allow myself to have. But I have always been a sucker for the kind of pain that Evie provides.

And if I'm not inside her soon, I will actually fucking die.

The feel of her lips moving against mine, her tongue in my mouth…nothing has ever felt so good, so cathartic. It's like coming home, like waking up from the worst kind of nightmare.

I know this is just a Band-Aid over the bullet hole she put in my chest, but I need it.

I need her.

I couldn't stop now even if I tried. And I don't want to. I really don't.

Evie always has been my drug of choice.

History is pulling me right back in with its steely claws, and I'm more than happy to let it. I'm shackling myself to that motherfucker and letting it lead me straight into hell.

Our mouths are going at it. Lips, teeth, and tongues, the urgency and desperation of it all remind me of the inexperienced teenagers we used to be.

The memory of how amazing it felt to be inside her makes my cock even harder, and I was already as hard as stone.

Reaching over, I turn the lock on the door. Then, I grab the hem of her T-shirt, lifting it. She raises her arms, so I can get it over her head.

She's wearing a pink lacy bra underneath.

I let out a groan at the sight. Pulling a strap down her shoulder, freeing her tit, I cup it with my hand, and I start kissing her again.

My tongue is deep in her mouth, licking. My hand is squeezing her tit, fingers pinching her nipple.

The moans escaping her, entering my mouth, are making me painfully harder.

I haven't been this hard since I was last with her.

She's pressing her hips against mine, trying to find the pressure she needs.

"Adam…I need…"

She doesn't have to say it. I know exactly what she needs.

I know Evie's body better than I know my own.

Putting her to her feet, I undo her shorts. She kicks off her flip-flops. I pull her shorts down her legs, taking her panties with them. Then, I drop to my knees before her.

"Adam…"

I glance up at her.

She looks needy and vulnerable. It turns me on like nothing before.

I slide my hand under her thigh, lifting it, and I hook it on my shoulder. Then, I put my mouth on her pussy.

She cries out my name, her hands gripping my hair. The sound drives me crazy. It drives me on.

She tastes exactly the same, feels exactly the same.

Fully aware of how she likes to be touched, I run my tongue up her center and then suck her clit into my mouth as I slip a finger inside her.

Mouth still on her, I look up at her. She's staring down at me. Her eyes are glazed and filled with wonderment and lust.

Knowing I'm doing this to her, making her feel this way, has me feeling like a king.

She always could lift me up.

I know it's only a temporary, fleeting feeling, and when it's over, I'll come crashing back down, but I'll take what I can right now. I need this. I need her, more than I realized or wanted to admit to myself.

Closing my eyes, I get back to it, giving her what she needs and taking what I want in return.

I lick and suck her with my mouth and fuck her with my finger.

Moments later, she's blowing apart against my mouth.

Pulling my finger from her, I run my tongue around her, licking her clean. Then, I suck my finger into my mouth, too.

Her eyes are staring down, watching my every movement.

She looks so fucking perfect. Her body is trembling with aftershocks of her orgasm, the orgasm I gave to her. Half of her bra is hanging down, exposing her perfect tit. Her pussy is glistening and throbbing because of me.

I have a flashback to the first time I made love to her.

She was perfect then.

She's perfect now.

Evie will always be perfect.

But I know, underneath all that perfection, is a heart of ice.

Tears and words aside, Evie walked out on me without looking back once. And someone with a heart couldn't do that.

It makes me want to break her. Fuck into her every ounce of pain that she made me feel, the pain I've carried with me every single day since she's been gone, until she feels my pain like it's her own.

Pushing up, I get to my feet. I need inside her now. And I don't intend on taking her gently.

I'm going to fuck her hard. I'm going to punish her for leaving me. I want to make it so that all she remembers, all she knows, after I've finished with her is me and how good my cock felt inside her.

Loosening my tie with purpose, I remove it, tossing it to the floor. I open the top few buttons on my shirt, then, I reach behind, grab hold of my shirt, and tug it over my head. I let it join my tie on the floor.

I see Evie's body still, and when I look at her, her eyes are wide and staring straight at my chest.

And I know I'm fucked.

*My tattoo.* I didn't even think about it.

"You-you…had a tattoo done?" Her voice shakes.

I never had any tattoos when we were together. But I know that's not what's caught her attention or making her voice tremble. It's what the tattoo says, what it represents.

In scripture, across the center of my chest, right over my heart, are the words,

AND FOR THAT WONDROUS BRIEF MOMENT IN TIME,
SHE WAS MINE, AND I WAS HERS.

Directly beneath are the letters *E* and *A*, our initials, entwined.

It's a play on the words we both had inscribed on our wedding rings.

The tattoo wasn't done out of bitterness. It was done because of loss and pain. I was hurting. I needed something to remind me of her, of us, aside from the physical reminders I have at the beach house. I wanted something of Evie with me all of the time.

I never regretted having it done, not once.

Not until this moment.

Evie seeing it causes all kinds of wounds to open up inside of me.

I feel exposed, vulnerable, like my heart is lying there, bleeding, at her feet.

I steel myself against the agony.

But then she touches me, and I have to fight to stop myself from falling apart.

Her fingertips trace over my ink, over the words that scream my feelings for her.

My heart is racing. Her touch burns. I close my eyes against the pain.

"Adam?"

I open my eyes. Hers are filled with emotion and need.

And my desire for her blows up like a grenade hitting pavement.

I kiss her hard without restraint or reserve.

*I need to be inside her.*

I rip open my pants and shove them and my boxers down over my hips.

"Are you on birth control?" I ask roughly.

"Yes."

"I'm clean," I tell her. "I get regular checks."

I see a flash of something in her eyes, but it's gone before I can figure out what it is.

"I'm…clean, too," she says on a whisper.

I lock eyes with her. I'm fighting against the thought of any other man touching her, fucking her.

I grit my teeth.

I need to mark her as mine again.

My hands go under her thighs. I lift her, her back sliding up the wall, and I slam straight inside her.

She cries out.

"Fuck," I hiss, pressing my forehead to hers.

She's so tight. It's like fucking her for the first time again.

"Jesus. You're really tight, Evie."

Her body tenses around me, and she closes her eyes. "Just fuck me, Adam, please."

That, I can do.

Taking her mouth again, I claim her with my tongue and my cock.

I fuck her madly and desperately, driving her against the wall with each hard thrust I give.

The feel of her tight wet warmth surrounding me, her scent, her soft skin, just *her*…it's too much, sending me to the brink of madness.

I can't see straight. All I can see is Evie.

All I need is her.

I have her. I'm buried deep inside her, and even this doesn't feel like enough.

She sinks her nails into my back, scratching across my skin, moaning my name into my mouth, and I nearly explode. I know I'm not going to last much longer. I'm surprised I've managed this long.

"Evie…" I huff against her lips. "Tell me you're close. I can't hold off much longer, and I need you to come with me."

It was always that way with her. I always needed her orgasm with mine. Her pussy squeezing my dick, making me come so fucking hard—there was nothing like it.

"I'm close," she pants. "Just keep…doing…that—ah, fuck, Adam. That's it…I'm coming!"

She buries her scream in my shoulder by sinking her teeth into my skin, and I blow apart, coming harder than I can ever remember coming, even with her.

I'm literally seeing stars. My head is spinning. My legs feel like jelly.

I press my head against the wall, breathing hard.

Evie's panting against me, trying to catch her breath.

As our breathing slows, the sexual fog lifts, and reality seeps back in.

I just had sex with Evie.

A multitude of thoughts scream at me. Emotions burn in my chest.

I was expecting regret to come first, but surprisingly, it hasn't made an appearance yet.

I guess having her here in my arms after all these years, is what's keeping the regret at bay.

And the feel of my cock still inside her makes me want to fuck her again.

*I can't fuck her again.*

Forcing my head up, I look at her face.

Her eyes look moist, her expression pained, and my first thought is that I hurt her. I was pretty rough.

"Did I hurt you?"

"No." She moves her eyes to mine.

We're staring at one another, and I have no clue what to say or do, what my next move should be.

I know what I want to do, I want to take her mouth again and kiss her until I can't breathe.

*Again, not a good idea, Gunner.*

This is the first time I'm stuck on what to do or say when I've just screwed a woman. Usually, I'm pulling out and looking for my exit by now.

Only, she's not *just* a woman.

She's Evie.

The only woman I've ever loved.

The woman I married.

The woman who broke my heart.

That thought sobers me. I pull out of her, lowering her to her feet, and I see her wince.

"Are you sure I didn't hurt you?"

"No, I'm fine," she says, not meeting my eyes.

Moving away from her, putting some distance between us, I pull up my boxers and pants, fastening them.

By the time I've turned back to her, Evie's already got her T-shirt on and is pulling on her panties.

The air is tense and uncomfortable. That's probably my fault.

I've distanced myself from her, physically and emotionally. I feel so confused right now. I don't know what to do or say.

Evie pulls on her shorts, and she's dressed.

I've never seen her dress that quickly before. It actually pisses me off. It's like she can't wait to get her clothes on and get away from me.

I have to grit my teeth to stop from saying something. *Really, what would be the point?* And it's not like I'm exactly helping the situation, standing here like a fucking mute.

"So…that happened." She's struggling to look at me, her hands twisting in front of her.

Her teeth bite her lower lip so hard that I'm surprised it isn't bleeding.

"It did." My voice is cold. I know it is because that's the intention.

I'm angry with her. I'm angry with myself.

"I'm guessing…we probably shouldn't have done that," she edges the words out softly.

"No, we shouldn't have. Then again, we shouldn't have gotten married, and we did. We're not exactly known for our good decisions, Evie."

Pain lances across her face, her eyes instantly filling with tears.

And I feel like shit.

I shouldn't have said that. I didn't mean it. I let my anger get the better of me.

Her throat works on a swallow. She blinks, and a tear runs down her cheek.

*Fuck.*

*But didn't I want to hurt her? Hasn't some part of me wanted to hurt her the way she hurt me from the moment I saw her standing there in the coffee shop?*

But seeing her like this, crying, in pain…it doesn't make me feel good. It didn't before I fucked her, and it sure as shit doesn't now. If anything, I just feel worse.

"Evie—" I start.

But she cuts me off, "It's fine." She forces a bright smile. Drying her face with her hands, she pushes her feet into her flip-flops. "You're right. We're not known for our good decisions, especially when it comes to us."

She reaches for the lock on the door, clicking it open.

"Evie…wait." I take a step toward her. She turns back to me, and something that looks a lot like hope lights her eyes.

*What am I going to do? Say?*

*Ask her to stay? For what reason, other than another fuck?*

*Or do I ask her where it all went wrong for us?*

*What would be the point? I already know the answer.*

It went wrong for us the day she decided to disappear and pretend like we never happened.

So, what do I say?

The only thing I can.

"I'm sorry."

The light in her eyes dims, and she releases a sorrowful breath. "Yeah, I'm sorry, too." Then, she opens the door, and she's gone.

Again.

# Adam
## MALIBU · MARCH 2005

*I*'m nervous. And I'm not nervous often. But right now, I am seriously fucking nervous.

It's Evie's birthday. She's turning eighteen today. And what that means for us is sex.

Evie told me a few weeks ago that she was finally ready, that she wanted to have sex.

Gotta say, I nearly came on the spot when the words left her mouth.

But then I thought about it. I knew her birthday was coming up soon, and I wanted this to be special for her. So, after talking it through, we both agreed for it to happen on her birthday.

She's in the bathroom, changing right now—or I'm guessing preparing for it, as women do. I don't know why.

She was perfect as she was, but she insisted on getting changed, said she had a surprise for me.

I should be jumping for joy right now. I mean, my hot girlfriend, whom I'm crazy in love with, is in the bathroom, getting ready to have sex with me.

And I'm a nineteen-year-old guy who's been sexually active since he was fourteen, having sex on a regular basis for all those years, and I haven't had sex since I met Evie eight months ago.

I waited for her because she's all I want.

But now, it's finally going to happen, and I'm scared shitless that I'm going to somehow fuck it up for her.

Taking a girl's virginity is a big thing. Taking Evie's virginity, because of how much I love her, makes that big thing huge.

And the thought of hurting her…

*Jesus, I don't know if I can do this.*

It's going to hurt her. I know that. I just wish there were some way I could stop that from happening.

I get up from the bed where I'm sitting and put a CD on. Semisonic's "Secret Smile" starts to play softly out of the speakers.

I turn to the window, looking out at the darkness.

I took Evie out for dinner earlier to celebrate her birthday. She insisted we come straight back here afterward. She didn't want to wait any longer.

Seriously, if Evie had her way, we'd have skipped dinner altogether and spent the night in here.

But I wanted to do this right. I want this to be perfect for her and for me.

She deserves everything, especially considering how hard things are for her and with Casey being sick.

Once Casey was transferred to UCLA Medical Center, they did more tests on her, and Evie's worst fear was realized. The tumor was cancerous, and it was more aggressive.

Casey had surgery right after Christmas to remove the tumor.

The morning Casey went in for surgery was a hard day for both Evie and Mick.

I know they've been through it once before, but I think this time was even harder. Evie put on a brave face, but I could tell she was so afraid. I know her inside out. And I wanted to help her, make her feel better, but all I could do was be there for her, so I that was what I did. I stayed there with them until Casey came out of surgery.

Once Evie knew Casey had come out of surgery okay and that they'd managed to remove a large part of the tumor, she allowed herself to shed a few tears.

But we still have a long road ahead with Casey undergoing chemotherapy at the moment.

I know the hospital bills are racking up, and Evie is working as many hours as she can while still going to school.

I just wish she would let me help her financially.

I considered just going to Mick and offering him the money, but when I said that to Max, he said it wouldn't be a good idea. Evie might feel like I had gone behind her back.

So, I didn't do it.

All I can do for her is try to make her happy, and I want to give her the best birthday I can.

I glance over at the easel and pencil set I bought her for her birthday. I set it up in the corner over by the other window, so she can come up here and sketch whenever she wants.

I can't wait to sit and watch her sketch on it. Seriously, there is nothing hotter than watching Evie draw.

"I love this song."

I turn at the sound of Evie's voice.

*Holy fuck.*

Actually, I take that back. There is nothing hotter than the way Evie looks right now.

She's wearing a pale pink nightgown that stops just a few inches down her thighs. A silky-looking bow that I can't wait to untie sits below her tits. And the material covering those beauties is lace. I can see her nipples poking through.

She is the hottest thing I have ever seen.

I've seen Evie in a bikini before. I've seen her naked when we fool around, which is often. But this, her, now—*holy fucking shit.*

She looks stunning.

I clear my throat. "I know. That's why I put it on. I really like your nightgown by the way."

"It's a baby-doll nightie," she corrects me with a smile.

"Well, I really fucking like your baby-doll nightie." I grin as I start to walk toward her, a prowl in my step, even though my insides are trembling like mad.

Evie looks so much more confident than I feel.

You'd think I was the virgin out of the two of us with the way I'm behaving.

Reaching her, I link my fingers with hers, and that's when I feel the tremble in her hand.

"Babe, we don't have to do this tonight." I tuck her hair behind her ear with my free hand.

"No, I don't want to wait anymore. I want this with you—tonight." Her voice sounds so sure, but I can feel the nerves in her body.

"I want this, too," I tell her. I dip my head and softly kiss her just once.

I lead her by the hand over to my bed, stopping when we're beside it.

"You have a lot of clothes on," she says, fingers tugging on my shirt button.

"I didn't know you'd be wearing so little," I tease, grinning.

"Do you like it? I bought it especially for tonight...for you."

Staring into her eyes, I say, "I like it a lot."

She smiles at me, and it punches me straight in the chest, like all of her smiles do.

She reaches up on her tiptoes and kisses me. Her fingers thread into my hair as I take over the kiss, tilting her head back with my hands, I part her lips with mine. I slip my tongue into her mouth, and she moans softly.

The sound travels straight to my cock.

Her hands move from my hair to my shirt, and she starts unbuttoning it. My hands slip under her nightie to her ass, and I find it bare.

I break from the kiss. I lift the material, peeking over her shoulder and down at her ass.

"No panties?" I grin, looking back to her face.

Her cheeks redden a little. Then, she shrugs and says, "I didn't see the point."

*That's my girl.*

"God, I fucking love you." I grab a handful of her hair and take her mouth again.

She undoes the last of the buttons on my shirt and pushes it off my shoulders.

I have to let her go for a second to get it off, and the fucking cuffs get stuck on my wrists. I toss it to the floor, and my hands are straight back on her, touching her soft skin.

I start to kiss her neck. It's Evie's sensitive place. All I have to do is run my tongue over the skin just beneath her ear, and she's crying out, hips pressing into mine.

I lick my way up her neck, to the sensitive spot, and she turns to putty in my hands.

"I want you now," she moans, her hands going for my pants.

I stop her because I don't want to rush this.

It's her first time. I want it to be one she'll always remember.

"Not yet." I kiss her mouth again.

Then, I lift her and lay her down on my bed. I climb up between her legs before lying on her. I support my weight on my elbows, so I don't crush her. Then, I take her sweet mouth in a kiss again.

Her legs come up, wrapping around me, pressing her sweet pussy against my bare stomach. She's hot to the touch and so fucking wet.

I slide my hand along her thigh. Gripping her hip, I kiss down her neck, loving the way she squirms against me, and I pull down one strap, revealing her breast to me.

I take her already hard nipple into my mouth, laving it with my tongue. My hand leaves her thigh, pulling the final strap down, exposing her other breast to me, and I pay that one the same attention.

"Adam, God, that feels so good," she moans.

Lifting up, I stare down at her.

She looks so beautiful, and she's all mine.

"Even though I like this nightie, babe, I like you naked a hell of a lot more." I start to pull it down her body.

She loosens her legs from around me and lifts her hips, allowing me to remove the nightie.

Once it's gone, I lie back between her legs, and I start kissing her again.

"So, how are we going to do this?" she asks me between kisses.

I know she's nervous. Hell, I am.

"Really well, I hope." I chuckle.

She playfully swats my back.

"I mean, what do we do? Do we just get right to it, or…I don't know."

I run my thumb over her lower lip as I talk to her, "I'm going to make you come first, help loosen you up. You're going to be tight, babe, and I want to make this as painless as possible."

"It's going to hurt, Adam. There's nothing you can do about that." She cups my cheek with her hand.

"I know. But if I can help make it hurt a little less than I will. So, I'm gonna make you come with my mouth." I press a kiss to her lips. "And then I might make you come again."

"Twice?" she says, her pupils dilating.

"Yeah, twice. The more orgasms, the better. You probably won't come the first time we actually have sex."

"Wow, you're really not selling this sex stuff to me," she teases. "Also, you seem pretty knowledgeable about taking a girl's virginity. Just how many virginities have you taken?" She's smiling, but I can hear the hint of worry in her voice.

"None. You're my first—in so many more ways than just this." I give her another soft kiss. "I love you, Evie."

Her fingers curl around the back of my neck. "I love you, too." She brings my mouth back to hers, kissing me.

The kiss quickly turns into more.

Then, I'm moving down her body, taking her pussy with my mouth, licking her and fucking her with my finger, just like I know she loves.

When she blows apart, I climb up her body, lying beside her. Keeping my finger inside her, I kiss her mouth. She returns the kiss hungrily. I push another finger inside her and start moving them in and out again. My thumb moves up to her clit.

She grabs my arm, her thighs pressing together. "I don't think I can come again so soon."

"You can." I slide my leg between hers, pushing them apart. "Let me make you come again." I run my tongue over her lips.

I know I have her when she relaxes, and her legs drop open.

I start massaging her clit again while moving my fingers in and out.

She moans, her fingernails scratching down my arm.

My cock is solid. I could pound nails he's that hard. Trying to get some relief, I press my dick against her hip.

Her hand finds me. She opens the button on my jeans and slips her hand inside my boxers. Her hand curls around my cock, and I groan with the relief of her touch.

I keep working her with my fingers while she works me with hers.

"Jesus, Adam, I'm…I'm gonna come again."

I pump my fingers faster, rubbing her clit harder.

Then, she's tensing and crying out my name in release.

Nothing sounds better than hearing Evie say my name when she comes.

I kiss her lips, her cheeks, her eyelids while she comes down.

Her hand is still around my cock but unmoving.

She blinks open her eyes at me. "Wow," she says.

"Yeah. And it's only going to get better." I give her a wink.

That earns me a smile.

Every single time Evie smiles at me, I feel like I've won something incredibly precious.

Lying on my back, I lift my ass up and push my jeans down, taking my boxers off at the same time.

Then, I turn back to her. She runs her fingernails down my chest, and it makes me shiver.

I reach over to my nightstand and grab the new pack of condoms I bought. I rip it open and get one out, keeping it in my hand.

Then, I come back to Evie, who's staring at me. I can see the nervousness in her eyes.

"Are you really sure you want to do this?" I check.

She lifts a hand to my face, and runs her fingers over my scruff. "I'm sure. I want this with you. I want to feel you inside me."

That's my undoing.

I think I've shown pretty amazing restraint up until this point, but there's only so much a man can take.

Sitting back on my knees, I tear the condom open with my teeth and roll it on.

Evie watches me the whole time, her eyes unreadable.

Then, I move back between her legs.

I frame her face with my hands. "I love you," I tell her.

"I know. I love you, too." She brushes her lips over mine. "Now, stop delaying, and fuck me already."

A laugh escapes me. "God, you're such a romantic, babe. What ever happened to making love?"

"Making love, fucking—whatever you want to call it, I just want it to happen. I don't want to wait any longer." Her hands grip my ass, nails digging in, as she lifts her mouth back to mine. "Make love to me, Adam."

I close my eyes on a groan. I kiss her deeply.

Lifting up on one arm, I take my cock in my other hand and run it up and down her pussy. Then, finally, I center my cock on her entrance.

"Ready?"

"I'm ready," she breathes. Her hands slide up my back, holding on.

She squeezes her eyes shut.

"Eyes open, Evie. I want you with me the whole time."

She opens her eyes, gritting her jaw.

I slowly press my hips forward, my eyes locked on hers.

I watch as they widen while the tip of me slips in.

"Okay?" I check, panting. I'm breathing heavy. This self-control is a motherfucker, and it's really taking it out of me.

"Mmhmm." Her lips are pressed tightly together.

"Try to relax, babe." I can feel her muscles locked up around the head of my cock.

I kiss her again. Hand cupping her breast, I stroke my thumb over her nipple. "You gotta relax and open up, so I can get in."

I feel her start to relax beneath me, so I push in a little more, getting halfway, and then I pull back out to the tip.

"You didn't go all the way in," she says.

"I'm trying to take it easy. I push all the way in, and it's gonna hurt you."

"It's going to hurt either way. Just do it quick, like ripping off a Band-Aid."

"I don't know…"

"Please, Adam. I just want this part to be over with, so we can get to the part where it feels good."

I don't know if that part will come for her this time, but I'll do my best to make it feel as good as I can for her.

"Okay."

I never can say no to what she asks of me.

I ease in a little, going halfway again, and then I pull back out and slam home.

"Ah!" she cries out, her head pressing back into the pillow, her back arching.

"Evie? Fuck, are you okay?"

I cradle her face, seeing tears in the corners of her eyes. "Jesus, I knew I shouldn't have done that."

"No, I'm fine," she pants. "It just hurt a little, but it's gone now. Don't stop. Please don't stop."

I should, but after hearing her begging me to continue, my own need takes over. I start moving, going as slow as I can.

It's hard to keep a slow place because, fuck, she feels so good, so fucking incredibly tight. I've never felt anything like it.

But it's not just that. It's her. What's uniquely her is making me feel so good.

As I move, she starts to relax. Her legs come up around my back. Her hands sliding up into my hair, she lifts her head to mine, kissing me.

With the feel of her tongue in my mouth, her legs wrapped around me, I can't hold back any longer. I start moving faster, pumping my cock in and out of her.

She moans into my mouth, and the sound undoes me.

"Fuck, Jesus, Evie, I'm gonna…come."

My vision blurs as the first hot spurt of my come shoots out of my cock. Then, I'm coming fast and hard inside her body for the first time. And nothing has ever felt better.

My head falls onto her shoulder. Her arms wrap around my neck.

I press a kiss to her soft skin as she starts to thread her fingers through my hair.

Lifting my head, I look at her. Fuck, she looks beautiful. Her face is all flushed, her lips are swollen from my kisses, and her hair is all mussed up.

She's perfect. And she's mine.

"You didn't come," I say.

I knew she probably wouldn't, but that doesn't mean I didn't want her to.

"I know, but we knew it was likely that I wouldn't. But you came. Inside of me." She has a big smile on her face.

"You look pretty happy about that fact."

"I am. No more virgin Evie, which means we can have sex whenever we want now."

I let out a low chuckle. "Sounds fucking awesome to me. Let me just clean up." I give her a quick kiss and then carefully pull out of her.

She winces.

"You okay?"

"Just a little sore. Is that blood?" Her wide eyes are staring at my condom-covered cock, which has little speckles of blood mixed in with her juices.

"Yeah, it's yours from…you know." I gesture to her pussy.

She lets out a groan, covering her face with her hands. "Oh God, that's so embarrassing."

"Nothing to be embarrassed about, babe. It's natural and kinda hot."

She slides her hands from her face, and I give her a wink before going into the bathroom.

I dispose of the condom and clean up. Then, I get a washcloth and rinse it up with warm water. I take it back out to Evie. I sit on the bed beside her and press the cloth between her legs.

"What are you doing?" she asks.

"Cleaning up my girl." I kiss the tip of her nose.

When I'm done, I take the washcloth back to the bathroom and then head straight back to Evie.

Grabbing the blanket from the bottom of the bed, I climb up next to her, cover us both with the blanket, and wrap her up in my arms.

"That was all kinds of amazing," she says, looking up at me.

I shimmy down, so we're face-to-face. "Yeah, it was. Really amazing."

She starts running her fingers through the scruff on my chin. I love it when she does that.

"So, can we do it again?"

A laugh escapes me. "When? Now?" I say at her expression.

She gives me a smile that says yes.

"But aren't you sore?"

"A little, but it's not bad." She runs the tip of her finger over my lips, tickling me.

Capturing her finger, I run my teeth over my lips, alleviating the itch. Then, I graze my teeth over the pad of her finger, and she shivers.

"Well, if you're really sure you want to, then give me ten minutes, and I should be good to go again."

She slides a hand between us and wraps it around my cock.

He pays attention immediately, and she raises a brow at his sudden growth.

*My girl is awesome. Am I the luckiest bastard in the world, or what?*

"Okay, maybe not ten minutes. More like two." I grin.

She laughs as I roll her onto her back, taking the sound in my mouth as I kiss her, and I slip my hand between her legs, getting her ready for round two.

Since that day in Adam's office, the one where I went to yell at him about the divorce settlement and ended up having sex with him before he was harsh and cold toward me—not that I didn't deserve it, but just maybe not at that moment—yeah, that day...well, we've been going at it regularly since then.

Meaning, we've been having sex at any given opportunity. It's been happening for nearly two weeks now.

Don't ask me what it means or what's going on because I have no clue. We don't talk. We just fuck.

And I'm afraid to ask him in case I don't get the answer I want.

When I left his office, I was hurting from his words, but I couldn't think of anything else but him. I couldn't get his smell or taste off me, and I didn't want to.

I'd missed him for ten long years, and I wasn't ready to let go. And as it turned out, he felt the same—well, that, or he just really likes fucking me.

Probably the latter.

The next night, he turned up at the café, right at the end of my shift. It was almost like he knew what time I would be finishing.

He stood there in the doorway. He didn't have to say anything. I was pretty sure I knew why he was there.

But he said, "That he wanted to *talk*."

I said, "Okay."

I locked up the coffee shop and followed him back to his bungalow in silence the whole way. My stomach was churning with nervous excitement, my heart racing.

He opened the door, letting me inside his place.

The moment it shut, I was pushed back up against it, and his mouth was on mine.

Our clothes were gone soon after. I was on his bed with his head between my legs, and I was crying out his name. Then, he was inside me, screwing me like it had been too long since the last time.

When it was over, we both lay there, on separate sides of the bed, staring at the ceiling.

Then, Adam got up and went into the bathroom. When I heard the shower go on, I took that as my cue to leave.

So, I dressed quickly and left.

And we've been doing the same thing every night since. Adam turns up at the end of my shift, and then I follow him back to his bungalow where we go at it for a few hours. Then, he gets up and showers, and I leave.

There was one night when he didn't turn up. My stomach churned, and I felt sick. I felt like I'd lost him all over again even though, in truth, I hadn't really gotten him back.

So, I went to his bungalow and knocked on his door.

He didn't answer, so I left.

And like the idiot I am, I cried myself to sleep that night, thinking about where he was and what he was doing—or *whom* he was doing.

I didn't see Adam for two nights. It was a long weekend.

Then, on Sunday morning, I remembered him telling me that he only stayed at the hotel during the week.

I felt marginally better.

All day on Monday, I waited, feeling like I was holding my breath, and I didn't exhale until I saw him standing there in the doorway, looking like the most beautiful thing I'd ever seen.

Now, it's been three more days of the same. I'm currently lying in his bed, staring at him, and he's looking right back at me.

I haven't left yet.

But I know I'll have to go soon. I always go right after he gets up.

"Come to Malibu with me this weekend."

I freeze. *Is he…is he asking me to spend the weekend with him? In Malibu…where we met. Does this mean—*

"Grady's been asking to see you."

*Oh.*

"Grady? You still talk to him?"

"Yeah. I surf with him every weekend. Max usually comes, too. Grady and I got close after "—he looks away—"you left."

A pain pierces my chest. I feel like I'm bleeding out.

"So, you're asking me to come to Malibu with you because Grady wants to see me?"

His eyes come back to mine. "What other reason would I ask for?"

*None, clearly.* "Will Max be coming?"

It's not that I don't like Max because I do. I think he's great. But I'm guessing he doesn't like me so much anymore after I broke his best friend's heart.

"No. He's got other plans this weekend."

"Oh, okay." I sit up, resting against the headboard. "So, will I need a hotel room?"

I don't want to be presumptuous and think we'll be staying anywhere together.

"No, I have a place. You can stay in the spare room."

*Okay.*

"Great. Thank you. It'll be good to see Grady again."

*Come on, Evie. Sure you want to see Grady, but really, this is about you doing anything you can to spend time with Adam, outside of the bedroom.*

Not that he said we'd be spending time together. He might just leave me to spend time alone with Grady and let me sleep in his spare room because he's a good guy.

Adam gets up from the bed, heading toward the bathroom, like usual.

I slip my legs over the side of the bed, covering myself with the sheet, preparing to go.

"And, Evie"—he stops in the bathroom doorway, turning back to me, his hand resting on the frame—"me asking you to go to Malibu doesn't have anything to do with you and me—not that there is a you and me. Going to Malibu is not some romantic getaway where we get to relive our past and pretend things are okay. Because they're not okay. I've only asked you because Grady's been bugging my ass about seeing you since he found out you were back. Is that clear?"

*Crystal.*

His words are like a knife in the chest. This isn't something I didn't already think. But I had hoped…I don't know what I hoped. He doesn't feel what he used to for me that is obvious enough. I killed those feelings years ago. I know he's just fucking me. But still…it hurts like a bitch. I have to fight the tears from entering my eyes.

"It's clear. But I didn't think there was anything more to it than going to see Grady."

"Oh. Well, good then." He turns abruptly and disappears into the bathroom without another word.

And that's me dismissed.

Taking a deep breath, I pick up my discarded clothes from the floor just as I hear the shower turn on.

As stupid as it sounds, I hate that he showers immediately after having sex with me. It's like he can't wait to get the smell of me off of him.

When we were younger, Adam always said he liked the smell of me after sex. He liked it even more when I smelled like him.

And when he did shower after sex, it was always with me, and he'd end up dirtying us both back up again once we were in there.

But we're not kids anymore.

We're not the same people we were back then. Everything is different, and that's because of me.

And after Adam's little speech, I know for definite that the only thing he wants from me is sex.

I was just fooling myself, thinking maybe he could at some point want more. *But why would he?* I hurt him in the worst possible way.

I dress quickly, so I won't be here when he gets out of the shower. I have a feeling he wouldn't like it very much if I were still here.

I slip my feet into my shoes and grab my bag. Then, I let myself out of his bungalow.

I walk the short distance to my car, which is in the staff parking lot.

When I reach it, I get in my car and turn the engine on.

"Here With Me" by The Killers is playing on the radio with Brandon Flowers lamenting about a lost love that he wants back.

I feel a pinch in my chest and then a sting of tears in my eyes so fierce that I can't fight them.

Grasping ahold of the steering wheel, I drop my head against it, and I cry.

I cry for the choice I had to make all those years ago. I cry for not really having a choice.

Back then, I thought giving up Adam would be the hardest thing I would ever have to do in my life.

Now, I'm not sure.

Because this here right now, having him but not really having him, is far more painful than anything I've ever felt. And I've felt a lot of pain.

Back then, at least I could cling on to the hope that some part of him still loved me, that I wasn't alone in my feelings.

But whatever Adam did feel for me died a long time ago, and I am more alone now than I was in those ten years without him.

There is nothing worse than loving someone when they don't love you back, especially when you have only yourself to blame for it.

The song ends.

I dry my face with a tissue, take a deep breath, and turn the radio off. I put my car in drive, and I stay the whole journey home in complete silence.

## Evie

# MALIBU · JULY 2005

"I can't believe it's been a year." I tilt my head back from its place on Adam's lap, so I can look up at him.

We're on the beach by my rock—well, our rock now. We're celebrating our one-year anniversary with a picnic— well, pizza and sparkling water, like we had on our first date, so it's a less fancy type of picnic. But it's perfect for me, just like he is.

It's a year to the day when we first talked on the beach. I did wonder if our anniversary should have been tomorrow, the day we had our first date, but Adam said it was today. He said the day we first talked was the start of us.

He can say the sweetest things at times.

"I hope you're not saying that like it's a bad thing." He grins down at me.

"Of course not, silly." I tap his chest with the back of my hand. "It's a good thing, a really good thing. Just…time sure does go by quickly."

"Especially when you're having fun." He winks.

He's totally referring to sex, the huge amount of sex we have.

Since we slept together for that first time, not a day has passed when we haven't had sex.

I've had a lot of fun with Adam teaching me all kinds of new things and positions. And I know for sure he's had a lot of fun, too, because he tells me so often.

I stare back out over the water, thinking about time. We don't have much of it left.

Time is creeping up on us. Adam will have to leave for Harvard in just a little over a month.

I'm not ready to let him go. I don't feel like we've had enough time together.

And I worry that he's going to go to Boston, and make a whole new life for himself that doesn't include me, and I'll lose him.

I let out a small sigh.

"What's up?" He taps my forehead with his fingertip.

"Nothing." I look up at him. "Just thinking about when you have to leave for Boston. Stupid really. I shouldn't be thinking of it on our special day."

"Come on. Let's go for a walk."

This is what he always does whenever I bring up Boston—changes the subject or distracts me with something else.

I don't know why he won't talk to me about it. Maybe it's because he feels as sad as I do about him leaving.

But he can't ignore it forever.

Lifting off him, I get to my feet and brush sand off my butt, which somehow managed to sneak onto our blanket.

"What about our stuff? Should we take it back to the house first?" I ask him.

"Nah. Leave it. It'll be fine."

He wraps his arm around my shoulder, so I put my arm around his waist and snuggle into his side.

We walk along the shore for a while in blissful silence. The beach is clear of people, except for a few random joggers.

The only sound is the splash of water washing over our feet as we walk.

"Oh, I can't believe I'm only just asking, but how did Casey do at her scan?" Adam asks.

Earlier today, Casey went to the hospital to have a brain scan done. I couldn't go as I was working, but Dad went with her.

She's nearing the end of chemotherapy, and she had to have the scan done, so they can determine how effective the treatment has been.

Can't say I'm not nervous about it, but I'm trying to remain positive.

"Dad said it went fine, but we won't find out anything until she has her appointment with her doctor, which is next week."

"Sucks you have to wait a week for the results. Can't they see her sooner?"

I shake my head. "It was the only appointment he had. He has other patients, too, I guess." Not that I care about those other patients. I care about only Casey.

Some voices off in the distance catch my attention. At the sound of cheers, I lift my eyes in the direction of them and see there's a wedding happening out on the terrace of one of the hotels along the beach.

"Aw, look at that." I pat my hand on Adam's hard stomach, getting his attention. "A couple is getting married on our one-year anniversary."

I stare at the couple. They look so happy.

I have a thought in my mind, a picture, that the couple could be Adam and me one day.

It makes my insides feel all warm and gooey.

I smile up at Adam, only to see his eyes fixed on the soon-to-be newlyweds.

He's not smiling. He just has this really serious look in his eyes.

Then, he stops walking.

"Hey, you okay?" I ask him.

He turns to face me. "Marry me."

"What?" I stare back at him, unblinking.

I couldn't have heard that correctly. I mean, I know I was just having a mini daydream about future Adam and Evie becoming Mr. and Mrs. Adam Gunner, but he couldn't have said that for real.

He moves closer, taking my face in his hands. "I love you, Evie. I look into the future, and the only thing I see clearly is you. Marry me."

Yep, he definitely did say that.

*Holy. Shit.*

I part my suddenly dry lips, but nothing comes out of my mouth but air.

*What am I supposed to say to that?*

I mean, I know it's either usually a yes or no answer, but—

*Holy crap!*

We're so young…but he's…he's Adam. And I love him so much. I don't see myself ever being with anyone but him.

But we're so young.

"You think we're too young." It isn't a question, and apparently, he can also read minds as well as throw out-of-the-blue marriage proposals out there.

"Aren't we?" I manage to say.

"I don't think we are. I love you, Evie, and that's not changing…well, ever. I want to spend the rest of my life with you. Everything else is just semantics."

"I just…I don't know. I guess I'm just feeling a little blindsided by this. I definitely did not see that one coming. You sure know how to surprise a girl."

"So, is that a yes?" He gives me a smile, but I can see that it's laced with worry.

He's worried that I'll say no.

*Do I want to say no?*

I close my eyes and try to think about this good and hard—well, as hard as I can in the short time frame I have.

I love Adam more than anything. And I do see myself with him, building a life with him, forever. He's all I see.

But he's leaving to go to Harvard.

I open my eyes. "Harvard," I say. "If we did this, I couldn't go with you. I can't leave Casey and Dad, especially not while Casey's still so sick."

He grasps my face again. "I'm not going to Harvard. I'm staying here with you."

"Adam, you can't. It's a great opportunity—"

"That I don't want. I never wanted to go to Harvard. Ava and Eric told me I had to go. Then, I'll have to go work for Eric. I don't want that. You know I don't. All this time, I thought that I was trapped, that I had to do what they said, join the family business, but I don't. I don't have to do anything I don't want to. So, I'm not going to. I'm finally doing what I want, and what I want is to marry you."

He looks so alive in this moment, more alive than I have ever seen him.

And I love it. I love him.

"Can we really do this? Get married?"

"We can do anything we want, babe. You've made me realize that. Being with you has made me realize a lot of things…that *I* can do anything I want. I don't know exactly what I want to do yet"—he chuckles—"but what I am certain of is that whatever I do, I want you by my side."

"Where would we live?" I'm trying to look at this from all angles before I give him an answer. I'm being practical, one of us has to be.

"The beach house. It's paid up until the end of August. We can stay there until we find another place."

"My dad and Casey need me with them though."

"Then, we'll all live together. We don't have to plan everything. We can work the rest out later. All I need right now from you is a yes."

For a long moment, I stare up into his eyes, those turquoise eyes that I adore so much. From the instant I saw those eyes, I knew that I could spend a lifetime staring into them.

"This is crazy. You know that, right?"

"Maybe it is. But I don't fucking care. Just…just say yes, Evie."

My heart is thudding against my ribcage. My thoughts are running a mile a minute. But each time, they circle back to one word.

"Yes."

The look on his face…I'll remember it forever.

"Yes?"

"Yes"—I smile so big that it feels like my face might split in two—"I will marry you, Adam Gunner."

He lets out a sound of total happiness, and then he swoops me up into his arms, his lips crashing to mine. He kisses me so fiercely that I can practically feel his love for me pouring in through his kiss.

My palms are pressed up against this chest, and I can feel his heart racing beneath them.

He lowers me to my feet, but his lips seem reluctant to leave mine as he continues sweeping soft kisses over my mouth.

"I love you so much," he murmurs, his fingers threading into my hair.

"I love you, too." I run my fingers over his cheek. "So, we're really doing this, huh?"

He presses his forehead to mine, our noses touching. "Yeah, we're really doing this."

"And how will we do this? I mean, how and when will we get married?"

A grin appears on those lips of his that I love so much. "How does tomorrow sound?"

"Tomorrow?" I gasp. "So soon?"

"What's the point of waiting? I want to make you mine as soon as possible."

"I'm already yours."

"But I want to make you mine officially, so no one can ever take you away from me."

"No one's taking me away, Adam. The only way I'll leave is if I want to. And there's no way I'll ever want to leave you." I push his hair back from his face. "You really want to do this tomorrow?"

"Yeah, I do. I want you to be my wife sooner rather than later."

*His wife.*

His words touch deep inside of me. "Well then, tomorrow it is." I swallow. "But where in the hell can we get married on such short notice?"

A grin spreads across his face. "Vegas, babe."

"Vegas?" A strangled laugh escapes me.

"Yeah. Have you ever been before?"

"No. I've never had a reason to go."

"Well, now, you do."

"But…Casey's appointment is next week…"

"We'll be back before that with time to spare. I only need a few days of your time, and with you being off work for the next three days, it's perfect. Meant to be. So, what do you say?"

I let my emotions take me over, allowing myself to feel the happiness he's offering me. I wrap my arms around his neck, levering up onto my tiptoes so that we're almost face-to-face. "I say, take me to Vegas, Adam Gunner, and make me your wife!"

He laughs deeply, his smile so big that it almost breaks my heart.

His hands find my ass, and he lifts me off the ground. I wrap my legs around his waist.

"You're my family now, Evie. This is it—you and me forever."

I rest my nose against his, staring into his ocean eyes. "Forever," I echo.

# Adam
## MALIBU · AUGUST 2015

The intro starts to play, and I see Evie freeze in the passenger seat beside me.

It's like the radio is playing a sick joke on me. I *never* listen to this song. Ever. I have successfully avoided hearing it in nearly ten years, and now that Evie's sitting here beside me as we drive to the place where we met and fell in love, our wedding song starts to play on the fucking radio.

Well, fuck Bon Jovi and their fucking "Livin' on a Prayer."

I reach over and change the music station just as Jon Bon Jovi launches into a full warble. And what do I get? Bruno Mars wailing "When I Was Your Man."

*For fuck's sake.*

This is not good, but it's definitely better than listening to the song we got married to. And it's definitely better than sitting in complete silence for the rest of the journey.

We've hardly said a word to each other since I picked Evie up from outside her apartment building in Culver City forty-five minutes ago. She told me she'd wait outside for me. I guess she didn't want her dad or Casey to know she was going away with me.

And yeah, I know how long we've been in the car. I've been watching the clock. There's not much else to do when sitting in the car with your soon-to-be ex-wife, whom you're still fucking, than look at the road ahead, listen to the radio, and continuously check the time.

I'm just thanking God that we're only a few more minutes away from the beach house. Otherwise, I might have to shoot myself.

I guess I didn't think how it would be, actually spending time with Evie since we started sleeping together. Not that we actually sleep. We just fuck. Then, after we're done, I go and hide in the shower until she leaves because I don't know how to deal. Afterward, I spend the rest of the night and the next day telling myself that it won't happen again, that I'm done. Finito, she is out of my system.

Until I find myself standing outside the coffee shop, waiting for her to finish working. Yes, I know her work schedule.

I'm so screwed.

I'm addicted to her again. My obsession is in full flow. I can't believe how stupid I'm being. But I can't seem to stop. I don't know how to stop.

I'm eighteen years old again and at her mercy.

I know it has to stop because I can't keep doing this to myself.

I can feel myself softening toward her, getting close again, and I can't let that happen. I can't risk letting her shred me to pieces again.

I barely survived the last time.

So, after this weekend, I am definitely done. I'm going to tell her that it has to stop. No more.

After this weekend, no more sex with Evie.

*Yeah, sure you are, Gunner. You keep telling yourself that. You're in so deep again that you can't even see a way out.*

I swing my car into my driveway and turn off the engine.

"You still have the beach house?" Evie asks in surprised voice, staring at it through the windshield.

My scalp starts to prickle. "I bought it when I got back from Harvard."

I watch her processing this information, and then she turns her face to me. "It always was a beautiful house."

*You're beautiful.*

I suddenly feel like I can't breathe.

*Fuck.*

I open my door and get out of the car.

*You need to sort your shit out, Gunner, ASAP.*

I get Evie's overnight bag from the trunk and head to the house, with her behind me. I unlock the front door, letting her in first.

I watch her step inside the hall. Her movements are timid, like she's afraid.

Maybe she is.

I am. I'm fucking terrified.

I hadn't considered before now, how difficult it would be to have her in the beach house again.

It's hard. Really hard.

There's an ache in my chest that won't seem to go away, and I have a feeling it's going to be here all weekend.

"You're in the spare room," I say as I walk past her, heading for the stairs.

She follows behind me.

When I reach the landing, I pass by what used to be Max's old room, and it is now mine. "This is me," I tell her, jerking my thumb at the door. "And this is you." I open the door to what she will remember as the spare room.

It's now the guest room where Max usually stays when he's here. With the worst view in the whole house, it overlooks the side entrance to the house, so basically, you're looking at a fence.

When I moved back here, I took Max's old room and made it my bedroom.

I couldn't bring myself to sleep in my old bedroom. Too many memories in there.

But I didn't want anyone else sleeping in there either, so I turned the spare room into the guest room.

"Sorry about the view." I jerk my head in the direction of the window as I put her bag down on the bed.

"No, it's fine. Perfect. Thank you for letting me stay here." She smiles as she sits down on the edge of the bed.

*Evie. Bed. Beach house.*

I have the sudden urge to make love to her, which is definitely not a good idea, considering I'm suddenly calling it *making love* and not *fucking*.

I'm so screwed.

"It's no problem." *It's such a big problem that I can't even begin to explain it to you.* "I told Grady that we'd go see him as soon as we got here. Do you need to freshen up before we go?" I'm backing up toward the door.

"I could do with a quick freshen-up." She smiles at me again, this one a little weaker.

"Towels are in the bathroom. So, I'll see you downstairs when you're ready."

"Okay. Thank you," she says.

Closing the door behind me, I rest my head against it and let out a breath.

*I can do this. Evie being here isn't a big deal.*

Taking a step away from her door, I make my way back downstairs and head out onto the deck to wait for her.

I'm just working through some emails on my phone when she appears. She's wearing different clothes—a strappy white summer dress that has little pink and purple flowers on it that stops just shy of her knees. Her hair is down. Her face is still clean of makeup, except for a little gloss on her lips.

She looks beautiful.

And she sees me staring because she starts nervously running her hands up and down her dress.

Then, she says, "I thought I'd make a bit of an effort. I wasn't sure if we'd be having lunch with Grady or not. Is it too much? I can go change—"

"No, it's fine." I clear my throat. "We'll be having lunch. Not sure where though. It's Grady's pick." I check my watch. "We should go." I pick up my house keys off the table and put them along with my cell into my jeans pocket. "I thought we could walk along the beach to Grady's?"

"Sounds great."

I lock up the back door and follow her down the steps to the beach.

I watch her gaze catch and linger on the rock she used to sit on to sketch. It was the first place I saw her, the first place we talked, the place where I fell in love with her.

I'm moving closer to her without even realizing I'm doing it.

Her hair blows in the breeze, brushing against my chest. I breathe in her scent. She smells of everything that once represented happiness to me.

Standing here with her reminds me of the times we would just stand out on the beach together with my arms wrapped around her from behind, her scent in my nose, our toes buried in the sand. We'd watch the sunset and listen to the waves crashing in against the sand.

"It still looks the same," she says softly. "Like no time has passed at all, you know?"

"Yeah, I know," I say, my eyes fixed on her.

Being here with her, it could almost be like nothing has changed. It's ten years ago, and we're still in love. No anger, no pain, no hate. Just her and me.

She turns to face me, and the past is written all over her face.

And it hurts so very badly. Because I know what the reality is, and it isn't happy. That's for sure.

"Let's go." I turn away and start walking down the beach toward Grady's.

It doesn't take us long to reach the Shack. The walk was a little tense but not as tense as the car journey here. Maybe the sea air is loosening us up a bit. That, and the fact that I know Grady will be with us soon, and he will monopolize all of her attention makes me feel a little better.

When we arrive, I open the door, letting Evie in first, and see that the shop is busy.

Grady is behind the counter. The second he sees her, his face lights up. He's around that counter and sweeping her up into his arms in seconds.

"Look at you!" he says to her. "You look exactly the same. Still as beautiful as ever. God, I have missed you, Evie Girl."

"Missed you, too," she says in an almost whisper, as he lowers her to her feet.

I can see tears glistening her eyes. I didn't think about how hard coming back here might be for her.

I was only thinking about how hard it would be for me.

Base comes out of the stock room, and he immediately spots her. "Holy fuck! Evie Taylor!" He charges at her like a bull and sweeps her up off her feet.

My body stiffens, and I have the sudden urge to take his head off his shoulders. I don't care how big he is.

"Grady said you were back, and you'd be coming in today. But I wasn't believing that shit until I saw you, and here you are," Base says to her.

His face is right in hers, his hands still on her. I can feel my muscles bunching up.

"Yep. Here I am." She gives him a weak smile.

"You here to stay?"

She shakes her head. "Just the weekend. But I only live fifty minutes away, up in Culver City, so I can visit anytime."

*Visit him without me. Over my dead body.*

I don't mind Base. He's a cool guy, but I won't hesitate in busting up his face if he doesn't stop touching what's mine.

*Mine?*

But that's just it. Evie isn't mine, and she hasn't been for a long time.

"Fucking A!" Base yells, hugging her again.

*I swear to God, mine or not, if he doesn't get his fucking hands off her, I'm going to—*

"How are you doing over here?" Grady steps up beside me.

"I'm good," I answer through gritted teeth.

"So, you're sleeping with Evie again," he says in a lowered voice.

*What the hell?*

My eyes flick to his. I hold his stare for a long moment, mine challenging him, but he doesn't back down.

I look away and let out a sigh. "Yeah, I am."

"Are you sure that's a good idea?"

"No, not really."

"Look, I don't want to interfere because that's not my bag, but you've become like a son to me over the years, and I love Evie a whole lot. I don't want either of you getting hurt. I know how bad things were for you after she left. I

229

don't want you going back there. And things like this usually end up going only one way—south."

My chest is tight again. It happens every time Grady calls me son. It's the same when Richard calls me it, too.

I've either got serious daddy issues, or I'm heading for a heart attack. And the way I've been feeling around Evie lately, I'm thinking it might be the latter.

"Neither do I." I meet his eyes. Then, I look back at Evie. "So, how did you know that I was sleeping with her, old man?" Subtly has never been my specialty, but I didn't think I was doing anything outwardly obvious.

He lets out a laugh. "I might be old, but I'm not fucking blind. You haven't taken your eyes off her since you walked through the door, and right now, you look like you're about to rip Base's head off at any second."

"Yeah, well, he's being a handsy motherfucker, and he needs to be taught some manners." I scowl over at Base.

He's finally taken his hands off Evie, but he's got her attention, talking to her about something that requires him to move his hands a lot, and she's laughing at whatever it is he's saying.

*She's laughing.*

My chest starts to ache again.

I haven't heard her laugh once since she came back. Now that I think about it, I definitely haven't seen a real smile from her. I've seen plenty of forced smiles, fake smiles…and sad smiles but not the real thing.

And right now, she's smiling and laughing with him, and I'm jealous.

Yeah, I'm *that* guy.

Because I want to be the one to make her laugh and smile.

But then I'd actually have to be a human being to her to get her to even smile at me, and being human around Evie feels like a huge task that I don't know I can manage.

I know if I want that from her, then something has to change. And I have to be the one to make that change.

I just don't know if I can—or if it's even a good idea.

"Take it easy, son. He hasn't seen her in a long time, and he's just happy to see her. That's all. And I can't have you fighting in my store. My insurance won't cover it."

"I have my checkbook with me." I give him a slow grin.

"Funny. Now, come on, let's pry your girl away from Base, so I can take you both to lunch."

We take our seats at Plate—me next to Evie, Grady sitting across from her. I was surprised when Grady said we were eating here. He's more of a pizza-and-beer kind of guy than healthy organic food.

"So, you going healthy on me, old man?" I say, grinning over my menu at him.

"No, you're paying, and this place is pretty pricey. I always wanted to try it." He smirks at me. "And the doc did tell me to cut back on the fatty foods, so I figured that spending your money and eating healthy is a win-win for me."

"Doctor?" My alert goes up a notch. "Are you okay?"

"I'm fine, kid. Just a checkup. The doc has been telling me to lay off the fatty food and beer for years. I haven't, and I'm still good, still out surfing every day."

I stare at him for a long moment. Nerves twisting in my gut.

"So, what can I get everyone to drink?" the waitress asks, appearing out of nowhere.

"Beer for me," Grady says.

I raise a brow at him.

"I said, cutting back, not giving up."

"Sparkling water for me," Evie says.

"Same for me," I say.

"So, Evie Girl"—Grady leans over the table toward Evie and takes her hand as he looks her in the eyes—"I want to hear all about what you've been doing since I last saw you. How are your dad and young Casey?"

"She's not young Casey anymore. She's eighteen now and about to start UCLA. She wants to be a nurse."

I watch the pride in her eyes as she talks about Casey, and it pulls in my gut.

And that's how lunch goes. I sit there, mostly listening to them catch up on the last ten years. I don't miss how she's cagey about certain things, but Grady's careful and only asks the right kind of questions.

I learn more about what Evie's been doing all this time than I have in the last few weeks since she's been back.

And that gaping hole in my chest widens, making me feel lost.

Then, lunch is over, and we're dropping Grady off back at the Shack.

I watch as he and Evie say their good-byes, and she promises to come back and see him soon.

He comes around to my side of the car. "I'm guessing you won't be out surfing in the morning. So, I'll see you next weekend." He pats my arm, which is resting on the door. "See you soon, Evie Girl, and not in another ten years, okay?"

"Okay." She smiles at him.

I watch him go into the Shack, and then I pull away from the curb. "So, what do you want to do now?" I ask her.

I didn't really think this through, that I would be left with all this time with her after Grady had to get back to work. He couldn't leave the store all day.

She turns her head, resting it against the headrest, and looks at me. "I was thinking…well, I brought a sketchpad with me. I was thinking I might go to the beach and try to draw, see if anything comes to me. I did most of my best pictures on that beach."

"Yeah, you did."

I decide to go surfing even though the tide is low while Evie sketches. It's either that or sit and watch her drawing up on her old rock.

That's a sight I can go without seeing at the moment.

It's hard enough to see when I come out with my board, and she is already up there, sketchpad in hand with her face tilted up to the sky, her hair blowing in the breeze.

It's another flashback to my youth, reminding me of the way I loved her back then, how much I loved her, probably from the moment I had seen her sitting up there.

After I've finished surfing, she's still up there, sketching. I know she said she didn't draw anymore, but she seems to have her mojo back—or whatever it is that artists have—and I don't want to interrupt, so I leave her out there and go inside to take a shower.

When I'm showered and dressed, I head out of my room to see if she's ready for dinner. I was thinking we could order something in.

I walk out of my bedroom, and something makes me look to the left. That's when I see my old bedroom door ajar.

I always have that door locked. I don't want to risk anyone going in there and realizing what a fucking freak I am.

I was in there last weekend, just looking at stuff. I must have forgotten to lock it.

*Fuck!*

My feet are moving toward the door, my heart pumping in my chest. I have to know if she's in there or if it just opened somehow. It definitely wasn't open earlier. I would have seen it.

But if she's in there, then…she'll have seen it. And she'll know that I'm not over her, that I never got over her.

With a shaking hand, I grab the handle and push the door the rest of the way open.

She's here, standing in the middle of the room, with her wedding dress in her hands, her eyes on it.

She looks up at me, startled.

There are tears in her eyes along with a look of confusion mixed with shock.

I feel like I've just caught her reading my diary.

Anger bubbles in my veins. My heart burns. My stomach roils. My hands shake. My head starts to pound. Embarrassment and humiliation stain my skin.

I literally don't know what to do.

So, I do the only thing I can.

I turn and walk out of the room, slamming the door behind me.

## Adam
## LAS VEGAS · JULY 2005

*W*e drove to Vegas in my rental truck, leaving at six this morning, and we arrived at lunchtime. We checked in at our hotel and then went in search of a chapel. We found one close by the hotel, so we booked with them.

We're getting married at six p.m.

Then, we went shopping.

We bought wedding rings. I wanted to buy Evie an engagement ring, but she wouldn't let me. She said we weren't technically engaged since we'd just decided to get married only yesterday, and now, we were here today to do just that. She said she wanted a wedding ring. I knew it was more about not spending my money.

It bothers her, especially since it's technically my parents' money. It bothers me to a certain degree, but it's the least my so-called parents can do, seeing as they pretty much made my childhood miserable, have given me nothing but grief all my life, and will no doubt cut me off after I tell them that Evie and I are married and that I'm not going to Harvard or going to work for Eric at the studio. So, I can justify their money paying for my wedding.

So, there was no engagement ring, but she couldn't argue with a wedding ring. We picked matching platinum bands. Evie's has diamonds set in it. I pushed for that. She would have gone with the plainest and cheapest one, if I had let her.

The jeweler said we could add an inscription on them, if we wanted, as part of the purchase price. That was something we both agreed on.

I asked Evie what we should have, and she came up with the perfect inscription.

HE IS MINE, AND I AM HIS.

So, I had the same to match. Of course, it's worded a little differently.

SHE IS MINE, AND I AM HERS.

And the rings are now in their box, tucked safely in the inside pocket of my tuxedo, while I impatiently wait for Evie to finish getting ready in the bathroom.

I forced her to buy a wedding dress, which I haven't seen yet.

She'd suggested getting married in a white dress that she already had. I wouldn't have that, so I pushed her into a bridal store, after giving her one of my credit cards, while I went into the suit store across the street to buy my tux.

*I'm getting married.*

It might sound crazy to some, considering I'm only nineteen and Evie's eighteen, but I don't care. I've never been this happy in my whole life. From the first moment I met Evie, I knew that she was the one.

Max doesn't know where I am. Well, I didn't sneak off or anything. I just told him that Evie and I were going camping for a few days. It's not a total lie, not if you think that staying in a Vegas hotel is similar to camping.

I don't like lying to Max, but if I'd told him we were coming to Vegas, he'd have guessed. He's not stupid. What other reason would we come here for? It's not like either of us is old enough to gamble or drink. I know Max would have tried to talk me out of it, and I didn't want anyone talking me out of this.

I want this with Evie, badly, like I've never wanted anything before.

I know Evie's mine, and I know that she loves me, but I just want to make her mine in name. I want the world to know she's mine, that she belongs with me, that she'll never leave me.

Evie told her dad the same as I'd told Max, that we were going camping. When we get back, I know we'll have to tell everyone the truth, that we got married. Mick has only just come around to letting Evie spend the night with me at the beach house, so I'm trying not to think about how he will react when he hears the news. I'm just hoping he doesn't own a shotgun.

I hear the lock turn on the bathroom door, instantly pulling my attention to it. I get to my feet.

The door opens, and then Evie's here, standing in the doorway, and I can't fucking breathe.

She looks sensational, beautiful, breathtaking.

There really aren't enough adjectives to describe just how incredible she looks.

Evie's beauty has always been unparalleled. And right now, that has never been truer.

Her gown is simple but stunning—strapless with a tulle skirt that stops at her feet. A pale pink sash is tied around her waist with a bow on her back. With a simple flower wreath on her head, her hair is down, flowing in its natural wave.

"Hey, handsome." She puts the clutch in her hand on the desk as she gives me a smile that stops my heart.

"You're beautiful," I tell her.

"Yeah?" She touches a hand to her hair.

"Yeah." I walk toward her, my heart in my throat. "You're perfect, Evie. You're just…" I'm struggling with my words. I don't know what's wrong with me. "Everything."

A light shines in her eyes. She reaches out and places her hand against my chest, covering my heart. "You're everything, too, Adam, more than I think you realize." She reaches up on her toes and kisses me.

The gloss on her lips tastes like strawberries. But she smells like Evie, like the beach on a hot summer day.

I wrap my arms around her and take the kiss deeper.

She breaks away too soon for my liking. "I'm gonna have to do my lips again," she says breathlessly, a smile on her face.

"You're fine," I tell her.

"You're not." She giggles, touching a finger to my now tacky lips. "I'll grab you a tissue."

She goes to the bathroom before returning a second later with a tissue in hand.

"Here." She reaches up, wiping the gloss from my lips.

My gaze naturally falls down to her tits. They look amazing in this dress. Well, they always look amazing, but all trussed up in her wedding dress, they somehow look even better.

And my body very much appreciates the view, and of course, my cock wakes up and wants to come out to play.

I slide my hands to her hips, gripping with my fingers. "So…we have a little time before we have to be at the chapel. I was thinking that maybe we could use that time efficiently."

She stops wiping my lips and lifts a brow. "And which efficient way were you thinking?"

"A bend-you-over-that-desk-hike-up-your-dress-and-fuck-you efficient way." I waggle my brows as I press my erection against her.

She lets out a soft laugh, shaking her head at me. Then, she screws the tissue up in her hand and tosses it in the direction of the bin, hitting it.

*Score.* My girl has got skills.

"Uh-uh. Not happening. I look damn good, and you're not messing me up."

"I'm hard because you look so good. I won't mess you up, babe. I promise. I'll be in and out. Real quick. No mess."

"Wow." She laughs. "You're really selling this to me. But it's still a no. We're not having sex until you've made an honest woman of me." She slips out of my arms and gets her clutch from the desk.

I follow behind and press my chest to her back, slipping my arms around her waist. I drag my lips over the skin on her neck, and she shivers.

"I'll take you to that chapel and make an honest woman of you, all right," I whisper in her ear. "Then, we're coming straight back here, and I'm going to spend the rest of the night making a dirty woman of you. I'm fucking you until neither of us can walk."

She glances back at me. I can see the desire igniting her eyes. "I'm holding you to that."

"Do. Because it's a promise, as serious as the one I'm about to make to you in that chapel." I give a hard kiss to her lips and then slip my hand into hers. I grab our room key and my wallet from the desk and pocket them.

"You got everything you need?" I ask her.

She stares up at me for a long moment. The look in her eyes makes my chest tighten and my heart race.

"Yeah"—she smiles—"I got everything I need."

Pure happiness, only the kind she can provide, spreads its warmth through me. "Me, too, babe." I squeeze her hand. "Me, too."

I push the door to the chapel open and stand aside, letting Evie through first.

Hand in hand, we walk up to the unattended reception desk. I press the bell on the desk, and "White Wedding" by Billy Idol starts to play loudly.

*That's…different.*

I glance to Evie and then roll my eyes to the ceiling. She giggles softly.

Out of all the wedding songs there is, Idol's seems to be a weird song choice to play at a chapel, considering Billy Idol's talking about his little sister's shotgun wedding— unless they fully promote shotgun weddings here.

I glance around, taking the place in a little more. When we came here earlier, I was still high on the excitement that Evie had agreed to marry me. It was the first chapel we'd seen, and we booked with them.

I didn't really bother to take a good look around. Maybe I should have.

This place is…well, it looks like an actual rock band resides here. There are guitars hanging on the walls. Some appear to be signed. And there are pictures of famous rock bands.

Don't get me wrong. There are wedding-themed things here, lots of it in fact, but it all looks…kind of heavy-metal themed.

*Okay.*

I probably should have paid more attention earlier or maybe even properly registered the name of the chapel— The Love Rocks Hard Wedding Chapel.

*Massive clue there, Gunner.*

But I just thought it meant, you know, love rocks hard because it does. Well, with Evie, it does anyway.

"So, this place is a little…different," I whisper to Evie.

She looks up at me, unfazed. "Hmm…you didn't get that when we came here earlier?"

I shake my head. "I wasn't really paying attention."

"You're silly." She giggles, her eyes bright. Then, her expression drops. "Do you…not want to get married here? Because—"

"No. I do," I quickly say. "I will marry you anywhere, Evie Taylor Soon-to-Be Gunner, literally anywhere."

Her expression softens on me. "Good, Adam Gunner, soon-to-be my husband. But we can go somewhere else if you really want. I just thought you were okay with this place, so I was."

"Do you want to go somewhere else?"

"No. I just want to marry you as soon as possible. And I can do that here, so I'm golden." She gives me a smile filled with love.

And I get that tight warm feeling in my chest that I always get when she looks at me this way.

"Sorry to have kept you waiting." A high-pitched voice comes into my ears.

I turn from Evie to see a middle-aged woman with a Suzi Quatro hairstyle dressed in…well, a leather dress. She bustles through the door behind the reception desk. "There was an incident with leather pants and baby powder, but you don't need to hear about that." She laughs loudly, beaming a big smile at us. "You're Adam and Evie, right? Our six o'clock?"

"Yes, ma'am," Evie says.

"Oh, honey, don't call me ma'am. I'm Trixie. And it's lovely to meet you both. Now, if you'll follow me to our pre-wedding rock room, we'll quickly go over the details and then move on to getting you two married."

*Pre-wedding rock room? Seriously? What the hell have I brought my girl into?*

We follow Trixie into a medium-size room that's decorated exactly the same as the reception area with a small table in the middle and fours chairs around it. "November Rain" by Guns N' Roses is playing quietly in the background.

*For fuck's sake.*

I have to stop myself from rolling my eyes. I have nothing against rock music. I actually like some old rock songs. I just didn't envision marrying Evie to the sounds of a Slash guitar solo.

I sit down beside Evie, and Trixie takes a seat opposite us.

"So, I just need a few things from you." Trixie opens a folder up. "You've gone for the basic package, correct?"

"That's right," Evie answers.

I wanted the most expensive package, only the best for my girl—well, under the circumstances. But Evie said we didn't need the singing-and-dancing package, which literally did include singing and dancing, courtesy of an impersonator of our choice—well, a choice from the small list of impersonators they had.

I wish we had gone for that package now. It might have given me an idea as to the style of this place.

Trixie is flicking through the papers. "And Porsha had you sign all the necessary forms. You've already paid for your marriage license."

I'm guessing Porsha was the woman who took our booking this morning.

"And your bouquet has pink and white flowers, correct?" Trixie checks with Evie.

"Yes," Evie answers with a smile.

She looks at me with that smile still on her face, and my chest grows warm. Her smile gets me every single time.

She curls her hand around my arm, and I rest my hand over hers.

"My husband, Ike"—*God, I hope she doesn't mean Turner*—"will perform your ceremony. He's a minister," she says proudly.

I'm going to reserve the right to pass judgment on Ike—possibly Turner—until I've met the guy.

"Now, you kids are going to need a song to walk down the aisle to. Do you have a song already in mind? Bear in mind, we don't have all that hip-hop or R and B rap music you kids are all listening to at the moment. Then again, I guess you figured that out when you booked the place."

*I wish I had, Trixie. I really wish I had.*

This will teach me to pay attention next time, not that I plan on getting married again. Evie is the only one for me.

"But if you kids do have a special song, I can see what I can do."

"Oh my God. We don't have a song," Evie blurts out, suddenly sounding panicked.

I look at her, and her eyes are already on me, filled with worry.

"Hey…it's fine." I rub her hand, not really seeing the reason to stress. "It's okay. We'll just pick one."

"But don't you think that it might be a bad omen that we don't have a song? I mean, all couples have songs." Evie's voice is getting higher and higher.

I'm seeing the reason for her worry now.

"Evie, it's fine. Not all couples have a song." I squeeze her hand. "And, no, I don't think it's a bad omen."

"He's right. Lots of couples who come in here to get married don't have a song. That's why we have a book of songs, so couples can pick one out together," Trixie says, pulling Evie's attention to her. "I'll just grab the song list for you."

"That'll be great. Thanks." I smile gratefully at Trixie as she gets up and retrieves a small binder from the shelf on the wall.

I can tell the no-song thing is really bothering Evie. So, I take hold of her chin, bringing her eyes to mine. "Evie, you don't need to worry about this song thing. I'm not. We'll pick a song together, and whatever song we choose, that will be ours. It will be the one we get married to, and nothing is more important than that, right?"

"Right." She smiles.

Her expression relaxes just as Trixie puts the folder on the table in front of us.

"Okay." I open it up and start looking down the list of songs.

*Hmm, not much going on here. Mostly heavy-metal bands.*

I flick to the next page.

*Soft-metal bands.*

*Okay...*

"You see any you like?" I ask Evie.

Biting her lips, she shakes her head. I can see the worry creeping back into her eyes again.

I don't want her to worry. I want her to be happy. So, we need to find a song really soon.

"How about we leave it to chance?"

She lifts a brow at me. "Chance?"

"We can pick one at random." I scoot my chair closer to hers and take hold of her right hand with mine. I curl my fingers over hers, leaving only our index fingers pointing out.

"Close your eyes," I say.

She hesitates for a moment and then does as I asked.

"Okay." I press our fingers to the top of the list of the soft-rock page. I figure that's better than heavy metal. Then, I shut my eyes. "You ready?" I ask her.

"Ready for what?"

"We're gonna move our fingers down this list. You're going to say stop when you're ready. And whichever song we land on, we're getting married to it, and that will be our song."

"Okay." She blows out a breath.

"On the count of three, we start moving. Okay?"

"Okay."

"One. Two. Three." I start moving our joined fingers down the list, waiting for Evie to say stop.

It feels like we've been going forever, and I'm starting to worry that we're going to run off the page when Evie says, "Stop."

I stop our fingers and open my eyes. Evie's are already open, and she's giggling.

I glance down at the song to see what we've picked.

*You've got to be kidding me.*

"'Livin' on a Prayer?' You have 'Livin' on a Prayer' as a wedding song?" I flick a look of disbelief to Trixie.

She gives me a confused one back. "Of course. 'Livin' on a Prayer' rocks. It's one of the best love songs Bon Jovi ever wrote."

*Love song?* I wouldn't exactly call two people struggling to make ends meet a love song, but whatever.

I turn to Evie. "We can pick again."

She brings her eyes to mine. There's mirth and happiness in them. "No way." She laughs. "That defeats the purpose of leaving it to chance. We picked it. So, 'Livin' on a Prayer' is the song we're getting married to."

I stare at her face, trying to determine if she's actually being serious.

Yep, she looks pretty damn sure about it.

"'Livin' on a Prayer,' it is," I sigh.

"Excellent choice." Trixie gleefully claps her hands together.

"I kind of like it," Evie says to me. "It's a cool song, and it's different for a wedding song."

245

"It's definitely different." I give her a look.

She shakes her head at me, her lips twitching. "I bet there aren't many people who can say they got married to 'Livin' on a Prayer.'"

"There's a reason for that, babe."

She laughs again, louder this time, the sound filling the room. "Yeah, you're probably right. But I don't care. It's ours, and we finally have our song."

She looks so happy in this moment, and that makes me happy.

"Gosh, you kids are so cute together," Trixie says, beaming at us. "Okay," she says, looking back down at her papers. "The last thing we need to sort out before you two can get married is the matter of witnesses. I'm taking it you don't have any with you?"

"No," I answer.

"Well, you need two. I can be one for you and our impersonator, Nigel, can be the other. He's actually a Jon Bon Jovi impersonator. He also does Axl Rose, Bret Michaels, and Billy Idol, too. But as you've picked a Bon Jovi song to get married to, it'd be awfully nice to have him dressed as Jon Bon Jovi for the ceremony."

"Um, yeah. Awfully nice," I deadpan.

Evie digs her fingers in my am. I flash her an innocent smile.

"And we won't charge you extra for him to dress up as Jon Bon Jovi, as he's already in costume from the wedding we just did, and you two are just the sweetest. You look so much in love. Reminds me of my Ike and me."

"That's really kind of you," Evie says to her.

"I guess it was fate—you choosing a Bon Jovi song and him still being in costume and all." Trixie smiles wide.

"Yep, total fate," I say.

That earns me a pinch, a really hard pinch, on my arm from Evie. I flash her a look this time 'cause that fucker hurt.

"Well, I'll just go tell Nigel that he's needed, and I'll make sure that Ike is all set up and ready for you." Trixie gets up from her seat. "Be back in a few ticks."

"You're being a butthead," Evie whispers as soon as the door is shut.

"Did you just seriously call me a butthead?" I laugh. "And I'm not being a butthead, babe."

"You are. You're being sarcastic and, quite frankly, snobby. I know this place is a little different, but we chose it. And Trixie is being really kind to us. So, stop being an ass, and just be nice."

"You're right. I'm sorry." I give her puppy-dog eyes. "I'm being an ass and a butthead and a snob. And I really fucking hate snobs. Forgive me, babe." I brush my fingers over her cheek.

She lets out a soft sigh. "There's nothing to forgive." She leans close and gently kisses me.

"Right, kids, we're ready for you!" The sound of Trixie's clapping hands startles us both.

I glance from Trixie and back to Evie, my lips lifting into a smile. "You ready to get married?"

Her eyes shine with happiness, and it makes my heart feel like it's going to explode.

"More than ready."

I take her hand in mine, helping her to her feet, and then we follow Trixie to the chapel.

I thought I'd be nervous, walking to the chapel to get married, but I don't feel nervous at all.

I just feel ready and happy, the happiest I've ever felt.

"Okay, so, Adam, you come up to the altar with me." Trixie comes to a stop by a set of red double doors. "Evie, you wait here. When the music starts playing, you come through the door and make your way up the aisle as fast or as slow as you like. Okay?"

"Okay," we both answer at the same time.

Trixie hands Evie her bouquet.

"See you at the altar, babe." I wink at Evie.

I follow Trixie up the aisle to where our minister, Ike, is.

Apart from sporting a mullet and leather wristbands, Ike looks fairly normal—he's wearing a black suit and tie. To be honest I was half-expecting him to be wearing leather pants and no shirt.

Ike introduces himself and then gives me a quick rundown on the proceedings. Then, I'm introduced to our other witness, Nigel, the Jon Bon Jovi impersonator. And he looks nothing like Jon Bon Jovi.

I've got to say that I never thought I'd be getting married with a Jon Bon Jovi impersonator standing beside me. But, honestly, I don't care. All I care about is that Evie's here, and she's about to become mine for real.

"Ready?" Trixie ask me.

I press my hand to the ring box in my pocket. Then, I give her a nod.

She lifts a remote in her hand, and the humming sounds of the intro to "Livin' on a Prayer" begins.

Evie appears and begins walking up the aisle.

She has never looked more beautiful to me. Seeing her like this, walking toward me, about to become my wife, literally takes my breath away. I know it sounds cliché, but I don't care.

Her eyes meet mine, and she smiles.

And the world narrows down to the beautiful girl coming toward me. For some crazy reason, she sees something in me. She loves me and wants me forever.

And, God, do I want her.

I've never wanted anything more. And I know as long as I have Evie, my life will be as perfect as she is.

A dam kept everything, everything that was me…that was *us*.

Now, he's caught me in here, like I'm some sneaky person, and he's stormed off, angry. I feel like I've intruded in on his private thoughts, a secret I was never meant to see.

I only came in here because nostalgia pulled me here. I just wanted to remember for a while.

Then, I opened the door and saw everything. So many of my sketches that I gave to him are framed and hanging on the wall, including the first one I ever drew of him, which is hanging in the center.

My easel is set up by the window, like it never left. My sketchpad that I left behind is on the table. Beside it are unfinished sketches. My pencils, the ones he bought me, are in their holder.

Our wedding rings are on the dresser. Our wedding picture is in the frame that Max bought us as a gift. The pendant I bought Adam for his birthday is hanging over the corner of the frame.

And my wedding dress has been hanging in the closet, the only thing in there.

The room is filled with him and me, our past, and I need to know what this means.

*Why did he keep these things? Why does he still have them after all these years? And why keep them in this room of all places? In his old bedroom where so many of our memories were made?*

*I have to talk to him.*

I put my wedding dress back where I found it and leave the room.

His bedroom door is open, but he's not in there.

I head down the stairs. Turning into the living room, I see him standing at the glass doors, his back to me, as he is staring out at the twilight sky.

"Adam…"

His whole body stiffens at the sound of my voice. On quiet feet, I move across the wood floor toward him.

When I reach him, I stop just a step away. "I'm sorry. I wasn't prying, I swear. I only went in there because…memories, you know. I just wanted to remember the good times. I had no idea…all those things…our things…were in there."

I tentatively lift my hand. Carefully, I touch his back with the tips of my fingers. "You kept…everything. Why?"

He spins around. Grabbing my wrist, he yanks me to him, so my chest slams into his, forcing the air out of me. He stares down at me, a mixture of hurt and anger and frustration in his eyes. "I don't want to talk. I just…" He squeezes his eyes shut. Then, they flash back open, and without another word, he slams his lips down on mine.

Even though kissing him is probably the wrong thing to do right now, I don't stop him. If anything, I encourage it.

Just the feel of his mouth on mine…it's like I'm finally breathing again after being underwater for too long.

Adam's an addiction I could never give up.

I wrap my arms around his neck, parting my lips, letting his tongue have the entry it's seeking.

He kisses me rough, frantic. His hands are everywhere, like he can't touch enough of me.

Spinning me around, he pushes me against the wall. "I need to be inside you." He breathes heavily against my mouth. "I just fucking…need…you, Evie."

His words are my undoing.

His fingers skim my thighs. He takes hold of the hem of my dress. Bunching it up in his hands, he pulls it up and over my head.

I rip his shirt off, sending buttons scattering everywhere.

That's when things get a little crazy.

Literally tearing off my bra, he slips his fingers into the cups, curling his hands into fists around it, and rips my bra in half. He shoves it off my shoulders, and I shake it the rest of the way to the floor.

I can't even bring myself to care that he's just shredded my new bra, the one I bought with the matching panties, which also just lost their life to his hands.

The silky material floats to the floor, landing on my bare feet, and I kick it away.

We both go for the button on his jeans at the same time. He lets me undo it.

I yank the zipper down, loving the sound it makes. It gives me chills, knowing that I'm that much closer to having him inside me. His eyes watch me the whole time.

When I have his jeans open, Adam shoves them down over his hips. That's when I see he's commando underneath them.

*Holy fuck.*

There's just something about knowing he was naked underneath there the whole time that drives me wild, turning me on beyond reason.

I stare down at the beautiful sight of his thick cock straining upward, wanting me. My mouth waters.

*That's what I do to him.*

It gives me a feeling of immense power, something that I rarely feel around Adam.

I want to drop to my knees, take him in my mouth, and taste him, but I don't get a chance.

His hands go to my ass, and he lifts me, shoving me back against the wall.

Then, his mouth is on mine again, devouring me, as his cock thrusts up inside me.

I scream his name into his mouth.

But there's no respite, no time to adjust to his size. He just starts fucking me, hard and thorough, and it's so damn fucking good. He's relentless, like a machine, and I love it.

I love him.

"Mine." He slams home, his eyes pinned on mine. "Right now, you belong to me," he growls.

"Yes," I cry out.

My fingers slide into his hair, gripping it. I pull his mouth back to mine, and I kiss him hard and deep. I give all I can, and he takes it.

Then, suddenly, he pulls away from the wall, taking me with him, causing me to squeal out in surprise. I lock my ankles together around his back, my arms tight around his neck. We're moving through the living room, him carrying me, still inside me.

"Where are we going?" I ask, clinging to him like a spider monkey.

I've always loved how strong Adam is. He carries me like there's no effort at all, like I weigh nothing. And I definitely weigh something. The tubs of Chunky Monkey I eat regularly have made sure of that. But he makes me feel sexy and feminine in only that way he can.

"Bed. I need to fuck you on a flat surface."

I don't bother pointing out that he's just passed a few flat surfaces on his route through the living room because I want to be in his bed.

He moves quickly up the stairs. Reaching his bedroom he walks in, and lays me down on the bed.

He comes down with me, but he pulls back, slipping out of me.

I hate the empty feeling left inside me.

But I'm quickly distracted when he starts kissing a path down my body, starting at my collarbone. He kisses my breast, licking and sucking. His teeth tug on my nipple, driving me wild.

He continues his descent, and then he slides off the bed. On his feet, he leans over me. Grabbing hold of my thighs, he yanks me down the bed until my ass is right on the edge. He drops to his knees before me.

There's just something about seeing Adam kneeling down there, staring up at me, that does crazy things to my insides.

He pushes my thighs apart with his hands. Then, he runs a finger down my center, making my toes curl.

"Always so wet for me." His voice is almost a groan.

He places his finger in his mouth, sucking me from it, and he closes his eyes.

My body shudders with need.

I've always loved how he does that, like he gets off on the taste of me.

When he opens his eyes, I see they're dark with need.

He spreads me open with his fingers and puts his mouth on me.

A sound of pure unadulterated ecstasy leaves me. My head presses back into the bed as my hands grab for his hair. It's hard to get a good grip on his short hair. I really miss his long hair.

He licks me with gusto. Skilled in the knowledge of how I like it, he brings me to the edge with perfection. In next to no time, my muscles are locking up tight, and I'm screaming out his name.

I can feel him pressing tender, soft kisses to my pussy. His tongue is still tasting me as his fingers knead my thighs.

I push up onto my elbows, looking down at him.

He lifts his head, staring up at me. His mouth is glistening with me. He rubs his thumb over his lips and then puts it in his mouth.

I shiver all over.

Adam gets to his feet. But before he can do anything else, I slide off the bed, dropping to my knees in front of him. I take his cock into my mouth.

"Jesus, Evie." He shudders. "Your mouth feels so fucking good."

His praise tugs low in my belly.

I haven't had a chance to do this to him since we started sleeping together again. Adam is always so in control, so dominant in the bedroom. He was sexually dominant when we were younger, but he's definitely stepped up his game since then. I'm just trying not to think about how he's achieved that.

I can taste myself on him, and the reminder that he was just inside me and that he'll soon be back there brings me back, turning me on even more. My pussy throbs between my legs, which is surprising, considering he just gave me an epic orgasm less than a minute ago.

Wanting to please him, I take more of him into my mouth, but I can't take him all. My gag reflex has never been amazing, and Adam's cock is big. I circle the base with my hand, gripping firmly. Then, I suck him hard and jack him off in tandem, just how I know he likes it.

*Or used to like.*

"Fuck yeah. That's it, Evie. You suck me so fucking good."

*Still likes. Yay me!*

His hips shift forward as he grabs my head, his fingers tangling in my hair, and he starts fucking my mouth. But he's careful never to push back too far. He always was.

It makes me love him all the more.

He fucks my mouth while my hand jacks him off. Then, all too soon, he's pulling away, his cock slipping from my mouth.

"I need to fuck you. Now." Hands under my arms, he picks me up and tosses me onto the bed.

I hit the mattress with a gentle *oomph*.

Adam is on me in seconds.

Hands pinning mine above my head, he thrusts inside me.

"God, Adam!" I close my eyes against the sensation, my fingers squeezing around his hands, my nails biting his skin.

I expect him to start fucking me like a madman, but he stays still inside me.

I open my eyes, and he's just staring down at me.

Releasing my hands, he rests his forearm on the bed by my head, his fingers brushing the hair from my face before stroking my cheek. His gaze is almost tender, a look I haven't seen on him in a very long time.

He runs his other hand down my side and along my thigh. Then, he curls his hand around my leg, lifting it, and he hooks it over his hip.

Lowering his mouth to mine, he softly kisses me.

Then, he starts to slowly move inside me. It's so very different from all the other times we've had sex recently.

This feels like it used to all those years ago, back when he still loved me.

And I can almost make myself believe that, in this moment, that's what's happening—that he's making love to me.

So, that's what I do.

I close my eyes as I wrap my arms around him, and I let myself believe.

Our lips are still pressed together, not kissing, just breathing into each other.

He makes love to me, until I start to feel that familiar pull in my lower belly, my clit tingling from each firm stroke from the base of his cock.

"Adam…" I whisper his name.

"Come for me, Evie."

My body shatters around his, and I know he's done. The feel of me tightening around him always sets him off.

He lets out a long moan, my name mixed in with it, his body shuddering. He comes inside me, coating my insides with his release.

We stay here, him inside me, as we kiss soft, gentle kisses, making out like we used to when we were kids. It's been a long time since we've done this.

I try not to think what it could mean for us.

But I am hoping against hope that something has changed here. I know I'm a fool to think this, but I can't help myself.

I wish for more, not what we had because I know I can never get that back, but something new with him.

I'd just be happy to have anything of Adam, anything he's willing to give me.

I run my fingers down his side, causing him to laugh against my mouth. I love the sound. He always was ticklish there.

"I should clean up. I just don't want to move."

"So, don't." I stroke my fingers down his back.

He lifts his head and stares into my eyes.

I see something change in them, something that leaves me feeling cold. It's almost like he's switching off on me.

Desperate to keep him with me, I press my lips to his, kissing him. He kisses me back, but it doesn't feel the same.

*I've lost him.*

Shutting my eyes, I draw back from him.

He pulls out of me and sits on the edge of the bed. His back is rigid.

"Talk to me," I say softly.

He glances back at me, his expression closed off. "There's nothing to talk about."

"What about what I saw…the things in your old room?"

His face darkens, his brows pulling together. "I told you downstairs that I didn't want to talk about it. That hasn't changed." He gets up from the bed and walks over to the chest of drawers. He pulls open a drawer and gets out a pair of running shorts.

"Why won't you talk about it?" I ask, sitting up, pulling the sheet up and around me.

"Because what's the fucking point?" He pulls the shorts on with tense, jerky movements.

"The point is, we can't keep avoiding stuff all the time, like those things in there." I point to the wall. "And about what's going on here, between us."

He slams the drawer shut. Then, he grips the top of the dresser with his hands, his head bowed forward. "Nothing is going on between us." The words come out gritted.

And they hurt like a bitch. But I don't show it.

"That's bullshit, and you know it." I shift onto my knees, facing him. "Just talk to me. Tell me why you kept my things all these years."

"Why do you fucking think?" He spins around to face me, his eyes wide with anger. "For the same reason I keep coming back and having sex with you all the damn time.

257

Because I never got over you! I've spent the last ten years of my life pining away over you like an idiot while you moved on to a brand-new life, doing God knows what, fucking God knows who!"

I don't why, but instead of feeling guilt, his words incense me.

Maybe it's because of an article I read a few days ago. It was an old article, but I regretted reading it the moment I did. It talked about the upturn in Gunner Entertainment's success since Adam took over the helm. I was proud of him while reading it until I got to the part where it said he was as successful in business as he was with women.

"You've hardly been pining." I sound bitter and jealous. Maybe it's because I am. "I know there have been other women over the years, Adam. *A lot* of other women." The second I say it, I know that it was the wrong thing to say.

"Don't you fucking dare." His voice is low but as deadly as a striking cobra. "You don't get to comment on how I've been living my life while you've been gone. You left me, remember? And so what if I fucked other women? I was free to do so. Yeah, I fucked them, hundreds of them, and I loved every minute. And you know what, Evie? Every single one of them was better than you, even the bad fucks."

A sob breaks from me. I press my hand to my mouth, as tears start to run down my cheeks.

"Does that hurt, Evie? Does it feel like your chest is cracking wide open, and you're bleeding out? Because if it does, then you're getting a little taste of how I've felt every single day for the last ten years!" he roars at me. "Only difference here is, you knew where I was. You could have come back anytime. And you know what? I would have taken you back in a second, like the dumb fuck I am. But me?" He slams a hand against his chest. "I was left with nothing! No fucking clue where you were, what you were doing, or who you were doing it with!"

"I wasn't doing anything with anyone!" I yell, fighting back. "There hasn't been anyone since you! There has only ever been you!"

He stills, his eyes boring into mine.

"There's—" His voice cracks. "There's been no one…else?"

I look away. "No."

"Why not?" His voice is almost a whisper.

Gathering my courage, I force my eyes back to him. The look on his face has softened a little, and it gives me the nerve to say the truth. "Because I never got over you. I didn't want to let you go, so I could never move on."

"Jesus, Evie," he breathes out. He roughly rubs his eyes with the palms of his hands. Then, he pushes his fingers into his hair. "None of this makes sense. Why did you leave me in the first place?"

That's the question I can never answer.

Shaking my head, I stare down at my hands.

I hear him sigh. He's frustrated because he knows I won't answer.

"I'm sorry…for what I said before," I speak quietly. "I should never have said what I did about you and other women." I nearly choke on the words that have been burning me from the inside out since he first spoke them. "You were right when you said I had no right to pass comment on the way you lived your life."

*And I'm sorry for everything. For hurting you all those years ago. For hurting you now.*

"Evie." He takes a step toward the bed, bringing him closer to me.

I lift my eyes to him. He looks tired, weary. But he's still beautiful, so very beautiful that it hurts sometimes. And one of those times is now.

"What I said about those…women…I shouldn't have said it because it's not true. I was just angry. And…I wanted to hurt you."

*You did.*

"All those women…" Dragging his hand through his hair, he lets out a solemn-sounding breath. "They were all just temporary replacements for you. It was all I could do to cope with losing you. I might have been sleeping with them, but it was always your face I saw, your…void I was trying to fill." He looks past me, his eyes on the wall behind me.

I'm trying to process what he just told me. Emotions hang heavy between us.

Hearing him say that about those women, that they were replacements for me, doesn't make it hurt any less. The thought of him with anyone else kills me.

But I made the choice to leave him, so I only have myself to blame.

"I don't know what to say," I utter softly, my fingers gripping the bedsheet surrounding me.

He blows out a breath, a solemn laugh escaping him. "Me neither. I just…I don't know what to do anymore, Evie."

He slowly brings his eyes back to mine, and the look in them terrifies me.

He looks lost and desolate, but most of all, he looks like he's given up.

*Please don't give up on me…on us.*

"I don't want to lose you," I whisper, my eyes filling with tears again.

He closes his eyes, letting out a long breath, before opening them again. "You don't really have me—not in the way that matters, not in the way that you used to."

I know he's not saying it to hurt me or to be cruel. He's saying it because it's the truth.

And fuck does the truth hurt.

A tear runs down my cheek, onto my lip, and into my mouth. I rub my face with my hand. Adam's eyes track the movement.

"I'm not over you, Evie. I don't think I ever will be. But I can't be with you because I don't trust you, and I don't forgive you for leaving me the way you did."

"I'm so sorry for leaving you. You have to know that by now."

"I do know. I believe you when you say it. But how can I be with you, when I'll just be waiting for the day you walk out the door? I can't put myself through that again. I just can't." He takes a step away from me as his arms wrap around his chest, like he's shielding himself from me.

"I'm not going anywhere, Adam. I'm here to stay. Forever."

"Nothing's forever. You taught me that."

"That's not true. And I'm not leaving again. I promise. I won't leave you ever again."

"I don't believe you."

"I swear to you." I'm pleading. *What else can I do?*

"You swore those exact words to me once before, in front of a minister, so to me, Evie, right now, your words mean shit."

I feel frustrated and lost. I don't know how to make him believe me, so I decide to just go for broke and tell him exactly how I feel.

"I love you," I say. "I never stopped, not for one second."

His eyes close, like he's in pain. "Don't…"

I climb off the bed, taking the sheet with me. I stand before him. "It's the truth. I love you. I love you so much."

"You don't get to say that to me!" His eyes flick open, lit with anger again, and he steps back from me. "You have no fucking right to do this!" He turns away, his head in his hands, breathing heavy.

I want to touch him, hold him, but I know without a doubt that he'll push me away, and I can't handle any more rejection from him right now. I already feel like I'm falling to pieces.

261

Adam pulls in a shuddering deep breath. Lowering his hands from his face, he turns back to me.

"You're killing me, Evie." His voice is agonized. "You're like a bullet lodged in my chest, and I can't get you out. And you're killing me. Slowly. So, I'm begging you…either tell me the truth—tell me why you left, and I'll see if it's something I can get past, see if we can move forward together, so I can try to learn to trust you again—or just…just fucking let me go. *Please.* Because I can't keep doing this with you."

My chest closes up, taking all my air with it.

I start to panic.

I feel trapped.

Because when you've held something in for as long as I have, keeping it a secret, it's hard to let it out, to finally tell the truth.

Fear of the unknown keeps those words locked up tight inside of me.

I fear his reaction. I fear that he won't see the rational side of what I did, that he'll only see the betrayal.

*I did what I had to back then, but will he see it that way?*

My fear is that he won't. And I don't want to lose him.

*But aren't I going to lose him anyway?*

Sinking down on the edge of the bed, I curl my fingers around the mattress, and I close my eyes, pushing more tears down my face. My lips are sealed tightly together as I contemplate.

But my silence is too long.

And he takes that as my answer.

Because when I open my eyes back up, he's gone, and the bedroom door is swinging shut in his wake.

And this time, I don't follow him.

"What about surfing?" I say, propping my feet up on the dashboard.

We're driving back home from Vegas, in the final stretch of our journey, and we're talking about Adam's options now that he's staying in Malibu because he's, you know, my husband.

I stop the squeal of delight from slipping out.

"What about it?" Adam glances momentarily from the road to me.

"Well, you said before that, when you were younger, you wanted to be a pro surfer. And you're good, Adam, really good. I know Grady would help you get started, get you talking to the right people. You could begin entering local competitions, start building up your name."

I see his mind working as he stares at the road ahead.

"You really think I could do it?"

"I think you can do anything you put your mind to."

"I'd have to work another job while I'm doing it 'cause the winnings would be small, if any at all."

"I'm working full-time now, and I'll be able to pick up extra shifts if I need to, so you don't need to worry too much."

Now school is over, I'm full-time at Grady's, and I know if I ask Grady for extra shifts, he'll work something out for me.

"My woman is not keeping me," he says in a silly caveman voice. "I keep my woman."

"You're a tool!" I laugh.

"Yeah, but I'm your tool."

"Yeah, you are," I say softly, looking down at my ring.

I've spent a lot of time staring at my wedding ring since Adam put it on my finger two days ago.

After we got married, we stayed in Vegas the next day, a mini-honeymoon kind of thing. Adam wanted to spend the whole day in our hotel room, having sex, but I managed to get some clothes on him for a few hours, so we could do something. There's not much to do in Vegas when you're too young to gamble and drink, so we ended up going to Adventuredome, which was really fun. Then, after Adventuredome, we came back to the hotel. We ordered room service for dinner and spent the rest of the night in bed, having sex, lots of it—not that I'm complaining. I've also learned that calling Adam my husband gets him hard, like instantly. Got to say though, hearing him call me his wife turns me on just the same.

I glance up, seeing the sign for Malibu.

*Almost home.*

*Almost time to tell Dad that I'm married.*

My stomach twists into one big knot. I'm nervous as hell to tell Dad.

"What are you thinking about?" Adam asks me.

"Me, you, us. Telling Dad we got married." I move my eyes to him.

"Does your dad have a gun?" He glances at me.

"No," I answer, laughing.

"Good. I can take an ass-kicking, but there's no coming back from a bullet wound."

"He won't kick your ass. He only has one good working arm, remember?"

He gives me a serious look. "You only need one arm to throw a punch, babe."

"True." I laugh again. "But I know my dad. He's more of a lover than a fighter. I think he'll probably be shocked. Then, he'll be mad that I lied to him about where I was going. But I think once we get past the all of that, it'll be okay." I'm not sure who I'm trying to convince here, Adam or myself. "When were you thinking of telling your parents?" I ask him.

His lips twist, a frown appearing over his brows. "I'll call Ava once we've told your dad."

"You don't want to go see her and your dad? Tell them face-to-face?"

"No. I have no desire to see either of them. Honestly, I have no clue where they are. But wherever it is, you can bet your ass, they definitely aren't together. I'll call Ava, tell her that we're married and that I'm staying in Malibu with you. I'll let her relay the message to Eric."

"How do you think she'll take it that you're not going to Harvard?"

"Honestly, I don't think she'll give a shit about me not going to Harvard. That's Eric's thing. Always has been. All Gunners have to go to Harvard," he says in a harder, deeper voice, mimicking his father. "Me not going to work at the studio? Ava won't like that one bit. She and Eric both. But like I give a shit. I have you, and the rest can just go to hell." He reaches for my hand, threading his fingers through mine.

We drive the rest of the way home, our fingers entwined together.

We pull up outside my apartment building and get out of the truck.

I meet Adam around the back as he's getting my travel bag from the trunk. I catch sight of the garment bag containing my wedding dress and get butterflies in my stomach. The dress is going back to the beach house. I didn't think showing up at home with it would be a good idea.

Then, I'm reminded that I have to tell my dad that we're married, and those butterflies turn to a sick feeling.

"I think we should just go to the beach house now, and I'll tell Dad tomorrow."

Adam laughs softly. "It's going to be fine, babe." He puts my travel bag down and takes me in his arms. "We're gonna go in there and tell your dad. He's probably going to yell. But I'll tell him how much I love you and that I'm going to spend the rest of my life loving you and taking care of you. And he'll see that I mean it and that we're meant to be together. Then, he'll calm down, and everything will be okay."

"You make it sound easy."

"It will be. In a few hours, you'll look back at this moment and say, 'God, Adam, you were so right. You're such a genius.'"

"More like cocky, I'd say."

"Oh, I'm definitely cocky." He pushes his hips into mine.

I slap his ass with my hand, and he chuckles deeply.

"Fuck, babe, that felt good."

"You're incorrigible." I laugh as I pull away from him.

"It's your fault," he says, picking up my overnight bag. "Because you're so damn hot."

As I walk toward my building, I throw him a sexy look over my shoulder. My feet hit the stairs, and the nerves come back with a vengeance.

"Go on," Adam urges with a push on my ass.

Taking a deep breath, I walk up the steps.

I feel like I'm walking the green mile as I walk toward my front door. My dad's not a bad guy. He's the best dad a girl could ask for. But I've never lied to him before—at least not a big lie and especially not a whopper like this.

The reality of what I've done is sinking in now.

Before, I was too high on the thought of marrying Adam. I was floating on a cloud.

But now, that cloud has bumped me straight back to earth.

"Ready?" Adam says when I stop outside the door.

I glance back at him. "No." I give a weak smile. "But I have to tell him. Let's get this over with."

I unlock the door, letting us in. The minute I step inside the apartment, I just know something's wrong. I can feel it, like a chill on my skin seeping to my bones. The air feels solemn. I can taste its acridity in my mouth.

I can only remember two times when I felt like this before.

The first was when I was taken into a room at school and told that my parents had been in a car accident and that my mother hadn't made it. The second was the first day we found out that Casey had a brain tumor.

Turning into the living room, I put my handbag down, and I'm met with my dad, who is sitting on the sofa. He lifts his eyes to mine, and I just know.

"Where's Casey?" My voice shakes a little, as my eyes work the room for a sign of her.

"She's in her room, lying down."

I exhale, but I don't relax. "Dad…what's wrong?"

Adam stands behind me, putting his hands on my arms.

267

Dad lets out a breath and presses his hand on his knee. Then, he looks up at me. "The appointment we had scheduled for next week for Casey's scan results…well, the doctor's office called first thing this morning and asked us to come in today instead." He blows out another breath. "We just got back from there."

"What did the doctor say, Daddy?" My eyes start to sting with tears.

He bows his head, taking in a deep breath. Then, his head starts to shake from side to side as he lifts it, looking back at me. "I didn't call you 'cause I knew you were already on your way back, and I didn't want to worry you in case it was nothing."

"But it's something."

He nods a solemn movement. "The chemo hasn't worked, Evie. The tumor's grown. They're…they're stopping Casey's treatment."

*Oh God, no.*

"No." I gasp. Tears start to run down my face.

Adam's hands grip me tighter, pulling me back to him.

"No, there has to be something they can do. Wh-what about more chemo or a new drug they could try, or a clinical trial? There has to be something!"

Dad shakes his head again. "Dr. Hemmings told me he would check again on the national database for a clinical trial. But he told us not to pin too many of our hopes on it." Dad blows out a breath. "You know how much Dr. Hemmings loves Casey. If there were something he could do for her, he would."

*Everyone loves Casey. No one more than Dad and me though.*

"Daddy…"

"I'm sorry, baby." He gets to his feet. "It's not the doctor's fault. He's done everything he can for her. He'll keep her on the drugs to make her as comfortable as possible until…"

*She dies.*

"No." I turn in Adam's arms, and he wraps them around me. I sob in his shirt.

Adam holds me tight, not saying a word. What could he say that would make this right?

*Casey is going to die.*

*I'm going to lose my sister.*

I curl my fingers into Adam's shirt, clinging to him.

*How can I go from being so happy to feeling the worst I have ever felt in my life?*

This is worse than when Mom died because Casey is still here. She's so young, and we're going to have to watch her die.

I feel my dad's presence behind me.

His hand touches my back. "Evie."

Adam releases me, and I turn to my dad. He's not crying. He's being strong. But I can see in his eyes that it's killing him.

I fall into his arms. "We can't just let her die." I cry. "We have to do something."

"If I could do something, baby, I would. I swear to you."

I blink up at him. "How…long?"

"Maybe four months at the most." Tears fill his eyes this time.

"Then, there's still time. We can find someway to save her. Maybe a new drug will come on the market." I can feel hope trying to fight in me.

Dad's eyes flicker to Adam behind me. Then, his hand comes to the back of my head, tilting my eyes to his. "It might. Hold on to that hope, and so will I. We'll keep praying that something happens to save her."

I stay in Dad's arms for a long time. Adam goes to the kitchen and starts to make coffee.

I just want to be with my sister right now, so I leave my dad and Adam.

I walk down the hall to Casey's room and quietly open her door.

She's lying on her bed, facing the window. She looks so tiny there.

She is tiny and so young.

She deserves to have a life, a long life.

We lost Mom. *Haven't we lost enough without losing Casey, too?*

Kicking off my shoes, I climb onto the bed behind her and put my arm around her.

She turns her head, looking back at me. "Hey," she says.

I bite my lip to stop from crying, blinking the tears away. I need to be strong for her. "Hey."

"Dad talked to you?"

"He did."

She lets out a slow breath and blinks up at the ceiling. "I…don't feel ready to die yet, Evie. I know Mom's up in heaven, and I want to see her, but I don't want to leave you and Dad."

My heart cracks wide open.

I rub the tears from my eyes. "You're not going to die," I tell her. "Mom won't let it happen. She loves you, but she doesn't want you up in heaven with her. That'll mean she has to start picking up after you again." I smile at her, trying ease things a little.

Casey laughs softly. Her little giggle reminds me of when she was a baby, and I used to sit for hours with her, making her laugh. The memory hurts. It hurts so badly.

She curls her hand around mine, and I feel her tiny fingers hook onto my ring.

I freeze.

She lifts my hand and examines it. Then, she looks at me, her eyes wide. "You got married?"

I feel sick. *I'm the worst person in the world.*

Casey shouldn't have found this out right now. I should have taken my ring off. Adam and I left our rings on because the plan was to come in and tell Dad and Casey straight away. But, of course, that didn't happen.

"Yes," I answer slowly.

"Holy cannoli!" She turns over to face me. "I can't believe you got married!"

I give an uneasy smile.

"Was it in a church?"

I shake my head. "Vegas."

"Vegas! Oh my God!" She giggles. "Does Dad know?"

"No, and we don't need to talk about this right now. You're more important."

"No freaking way. We are so talking about this. And you say Dad doesn't know? Is Adam out there right now with Dad?"

"Yes…"

"And does he have his wedding ring on?"

*Shit.*

"Mmhmm."

"Then, Dad knows. He might not have spotted it right away, but I'm guessing he had other things on his mind then. Give him another five minutes, and he'll know."

*Fuck.*

But as I stare at Casey's face, my worry evaporates. I touch my hand to her face. "You're smiling," I say.

"Sure I am. Dad is going to blow a gasket when he finds out that you and Adam just got married in Vegas. And that means, for a short while, we don't have to think or talk about what's happening with me."

"Oh, Case." My eyes instantly fill with tears, and I wrap my arms around her, pulling her to me.

"Just so you know, I'm a little annoyed that I didn't get to be a bridesmaid," she says muffled against my shoulder. "But I am happy for you."

I hug her tighter. "We'll have another service, maybe on the beach, and then you can be a bridesmaid. How does that sound?"

She tilts her head back, resting it on the pillow, she smiles at me. "It sounds perfect."

As I lie here with my arms around Casey, staring into her beautiful face, I tell myself that I will make that a reality. She will be my bridesmaid. Because there isn't anything I wouldn't do to save her. I will find a way to save my sister.

# FIVE DAYS LATER

I'm losing hope.

I thought I would find some way to save Casey or that some miracle would happen or that the doctor would call and tell us he got her on a clinical trial for a new wonder drug. I convinced myself of it.

But nothing's happened.

No miracles. No calls.

Casey is still dying.

I'm still going to lose her.

Casey was right when she said Dad would spot Adam's ring. We had another ten minutes together before Dad knocked on the door, asking me to come out and see him.

He didn't blow a gasket though, like Casey had hoped. He was calm, rational. He told me he was sad that I'd lied to him. I felt sick at that one.

But then he asked me if I was happy.

I didn't feel happy at that moment. But I was happy with Adam, and I told Dad that and that I loved Adam.

Dad's eyes got all watery again. He wrapped his arms around me and told me that was all he ever wanted for me.

Then, he kissed me on the cheek and told me he was going to sit with Casey for a bit.

Adam called Ava later that day and told her that we'd gotten married. He said it didn't go exactly as he'd expected. She didn't yell when he told her that he wasn't going to go to Harvard or going to work at the studio, that he was staying here. He said she told him that he'd made that choice, so he would be cut off. He told her that was what he wanted.

And that was the end of that.

She made good on her promise.

His credit cards no longer work, and his car was taken away. At least he still has the truck for a bit longer. He'd paid in advance for that, and the beach house is paid up until the end of the summer.

He has some money that he'd put into a separate bank account of his own to tide him over until he can get work. So, technically, he's still living off his parents' money, but it's all he can do at the moment. And he's been talking to Grady about the pro-surfing thing.

Life is still going on. I'm still working.

But at the same time, it feels like everything is standing still.

I feel like I'm walking with sludge most days.

Right now, I'm just getting ready to go back to the apartment to spend the night with Casey.

I'm living between the beach house and the apartment at the moment. But, for obvious reasons, I've been spending more time at the apartment with Casey.

I came to the beach house from Grady's to spend some time with Adam before he goes out with Max. With me working all the hours I can and spending every spare moment with Casey, Adam and I haven't seen much of each other these last five days since we got back.

But tonight is Adam's bachelor party. Max insisted on it, considering he'd missed out on throwing Adam one before we got married, and he talked Adam into it with a kind reminder that he was pissed that he couldn't be there when Adam and I got married.

That worked. So, Max has organized a night out with Grady and the guys from the Shack. They're going to hit up some bars, and because Adam and Max are too young to drink, my husband and his best friend will be making good use of their fake IDs tonight.

Casey and my night together is going to be a mini bachelorette party, consisting of Disney movies and eating candy. And I couldn't think of a better way to spend it.

"I don't have to go out." Adam comes up behind me, wrapping his arms around my waist. He smells freshly showered with aftershave.

Shoving the last of my dirty clothes into the laundry basket, I turn to him. I'm starting laundry before I leave because I've run out of clean work clothes, and I need some for tomorrow. On top of everything else, the washer at the apartment is broken.

He looks so handsome in his black shirt and blue jeans with his hair tied back from his face.

"No, go out, and have fun," I tell him, lifting my hand to his face. I run my fingertips over his scruff.

"Well, at least let me drive you to the apartment before I go." He turns his face into my hand, kissing my palm.

I glance at the clock on the wall, seeing the time. "You can't. You're going out soon. I need to put this laundry in the wash. Then, I'm gonna wait for it to finish, so I can throw it in the dryer. That way, it'll be ready for me in the morning."

"I can wait with you until it's done."

I let out a laugh. "There is no way that Max will wait an hour for my wash cycle to finish." I press my hand to his chest. "It's fine. I'll get the bus."

"I don't like you getting the bus, and it'll be dark out by then."

"I know, but I'll be fine. The stop is right outside. And Dad is going to meet me at the other end."

He stares at me for a long moment. "Okay. But you're gonna need these clothes in the morning?"

"Yeah, I'll stop by before work, so I can get changed."

"No, I'll come to the apartment in the morning and bring your clothes to you. Then, I'll drive you to work. Okay, wife?" He brushes his nose over mine, shifting closer.

"Yes, husband." I grin, knowing the reaction I'll get.

He groans, pushing his hips against mine. I can feel him getting hard already.

"God, hearing you say that…"

"I know." I slip my hands around his back.

"Hey, fucker!" We hear Max's voice yell up the stairs. "Taxi's here!"

Adam lets out a sigh and then releases me.

I pick up the laundry bag, but he takes it from me, and I follow him downstairs.

Max is already outside, heading for the taxi, and the front door is open.

"Where are you meeting Grady and the guys?" I ask Adam.

"Duke's," he tells me. "Gonna grab something to eat first and then hit up some bars."

"Well, have fun."

"I'll try." He puts the laundry bag down and wraps his arms around me. "But it'll be hard without you there."

He presses his lips to mine, kissing me deep. I wrap my arms around his neck.

Breaking off, breathing heavily, he presses his forehead to mine. "Change of plans tomorrow. I'll come pick you up earlier. You can get changed here—after I've finished making love to you. How does that sound?"

"Sounds perfect."

"Put her down, and hurry the fuck up, Gunner!" Max shouts from the taxi. "I have some serious drinking to do and you're wasting precious time! You're gonna see her again in a few hours, for fuck's sake!"

Adam glances out the door at Max. He lifts a finger, signaling a minute.

He looks back to me. "So, I'll see you in the morning."

"You will."

He kisses me one last time. Then, he lets me go.

"Tomorrow morning. You and me, naked." He grins, stepping back through the open door.

I hold on to the edge of the door, leaning against it. "It's a date."

"Love you, Mrs. Gunner."

"Love you, too, *husband*." I smile as I enunciate the word, knowing what it does to him.

He lets out a groan before he turns away and gets into the taxi.

I watch them go, waving at them, before shutting the door.

I grab my bag of laundry and lug it to the laundry room.

Laundry is on, and I'm sitting out on the patio, sketching on a piece of paper I grabbed from Adam's printer and a pencil I found lying next to it because I'm too lazy to go upstairs and grab my sketchpad from his bedroom. I'm catching the last of the day's light before night draws in.

I hardly get a chance to draw anymore, so this is a nice change.

I'm doing a sketch of Adam. It's of him looking back at me, right before he got into the taxi.

I have Adam all drawn, and I'm working on the back outline when I hear the doorbell ring.

Putting the paper down, I make my way through the house to the front door.

Reaching up on my tiptoes, I check the peephole, and my breath catches.

I take a step back.

*What is she doing here?* With everything I have going on at the moment, I could really do without having to deal with her.

Preparing myself I take a fortifying breath, then, I unlock the door and pull it open to the sight of Ava Gunner.

"Evie." She smiles, but it's as fake as every part of her.

"Adam isn't here." My tone is cool. I can't help it. I hate the way she's treated Adam, and I'm not going to pretend it's okay, or that I like her.

"I know. I came to see you."

I freeze. "Why?"

"We have things to discuss."

I give a confused look. "I don't think you and I have anything to discuss."

"Oh, we do."

Tired of this already, I say, "Seriously, we don't. Now, if you don't mind." I go to close the door, but she presses a hand to it, stopping me.

That pisses me off. My eyes flicker to the large man standing by the limousine, who is watching our interaction with hawk-like eyes.

I bring my stare back to Ava. "Look"—I lower my voice—"I know you're a big Hollywood star, and you're used to having people do as you say, but I'm not one of them."

"Really?" She tsks. "Is that any way to speak to your new mother?"

I scoff. "You're not my mother. You're barely Adam's mother."

"Evie, I'm not here to pick a fight with you. I'm here because I have a proposition for you."

"And I'm positive that whatever you have to say, I definitely do not want to hear it."

I'm just about to slam the door in her face when she says, "Not even if it could save your sister's life?"

I stop the door and blankly stare back at her. "Is that a threat?"

"No. On the contrary, I'm offering a way to help save Casey. I know she's dying. The chemotherapy didn't work, and the doctor has stopped her treatment."

Pain starts to crawl up my throat. "How do you know all of this?" My words are quiet, sore.

"I make it my business to know everything, especially when it comes to my son."

"You don't know everything." I fold my arms, defiant. "You didn't know we were married until he told you a few days ago, *days* after we had gotten married." My words are petty, but I'm not exactly feeling mature right now.

She smiles. It's a winner's smile, and it sends unease crawling up my spine. "Oh, Evie, I knew the second that you got married because Adam used his credit card to pay for your little wedding, the credit card I have control of. I know everything. And I know your sister has months to live, if she's lucky, and that the doctor has tried everything over the years to save her—surgery, radiation therapy, more surgery, chemo. Drug after drug, and nothing is working. The tumor just keeps coming back. I also know her doctor tried his hardest to get her into a clinical trial, but none were available to her."

I'm standing here—my heart pumping in my chest, my stomach churning—because I just know that whatever it is she's going to say is going to leave me with a choice to make.

And if it's the choice I think it is…then I've already made it.

"But what if I told you that I know people? Powerful people. And they told me about this new secret clinical trial for brain cancer that's about to start in San Francisco. It's not known to the wider market. It's a brand-new drug that is showing advanced results already. Life-saving results. A drug that could potentially save your sister's life. And what if I told you that I have a place for Casey on that trial?"

*Casey. A place for her on a clinical trial. That could save her life. I won't have to lose my sister.*

I look Ava in the eyes and say, "Then, I would ask what you want in return."

She smiles a sick, twisted kind of smile. "You're smarter than I first had you down for, Evie. Why don't I come inside? You can pour me a whiskey, and we'll discuss the details."

I stare at her for a long moment, my heart pounding, knowing I'm about to make a deal with the devil. And I know, in that deal, I'm going to lose something...*someone* important, really important.

*But Casey...*

I take a deep breath.

Then, I pull the door open wider and stand aside, letting the devil in.

## Evie
## CULVER CITY · AUGUST 2015

*I* step out of the car and then thank the driver as he hands me my overnight bag.

It's Sunday morning, and I've just gotten back home from Malibu.

When Adam walked out of his bedroom, leaving me there, I went back to the guest room and stayed there. I'm ashamed to say I hid in that room all night. I spent a lot of time staring at the wall, longing for him, with the smell of him still on my skin.

Finally, I forced myself into the shower and went to bed early.

I lay awake for a long time, listening for any sound of movement in the house, but there was nothing. I didn't know if he was still there or not, and I was too afraid to go check. I must've dozed off at some point because I awoke to the sound of an engine revving early in the morning.

My first thought was that it was Adam, that he was leaving, and my stomach sank.

I quickly left my room and went downstairs. There was a note waiting for me on the coffee table.

It said that he had to leave early, a problem at work, and a car would be here to pick me up to take me home at ten a.m.

I knew the work thing was a lie. He just didn't want to be stuck in a car with me for an hour, and I couldn't blame him for that, no matter how much it hurt and how sick it made me feel.

He had told me that I could either tell him the truth or let him go.

My silence was my decision.

*Why would he want to be around me after that?*

Honestly, I don't want to be around me sometimes.

So, I got dressed and went for a walk on the beach because I didn't know what else to do until it was time for my ride home.

I unlock the front door to our apartment, letting myself inside. Dad's sitting at our little dining table, newspaper spread out on it with his coffee to the left, his hand curled around the mug.

The sight brings a small smile to my lips.

Everyone reads the newspaper online nowadays, but my dad still likes to go and buy his morning paper and read it with a coffee.

"Hey," I say. "Where's Casey?"

"Still sleeping. She was out last night." He looks up from his paper. "Uh-oh. What's wrong?"

"Nothing." I put my bag down.

"That's not your nothing face. That's your something-has-happened face. The same face you had a few weeks ago after you'd seen Adam for the first time in ten years. Only, this time, you look worse."

"So, basically, you're saying I look like crap. Gee, thanks, Dad."

I sit down, reach over, and take his coffee mug from his hand. I take a sip and then give it back to him.

"You went to Malibu with Adam, didn't you?"

I told Dad that I was going. I just didn't say it was with Adam. That was why I had Adam pick me up outside the building, so Dad wouldn't see.

"Mmhmm," I answer noncommittally.

"And you've been seeing him all this time, haven't you?"

"Mmhmm."

"And you haven't told him the truth about why you left, and now, it's all come to a head—hence, the face."

"You got me bugged or something?" I open my jacket up, examining it.

"Funny. But, no, I'm just know a dad who knows his daughter." He folds his paper up and puts it aside. "It's time to tell Adam the truth, Evie."

I give him a look. "I can't."

"Can't isn't a reason."

"Fine. I don't know how to tell him."

"It's simple."

"No, it's not. I made a deal with Ava. I can't go back on that. What if I do, and Karma bites me in the ass for it?" I know Dad doesn't believe in that stuff, but I do. I believe every action has a consequence. Every wrong will be righted, one way or another.

"I'm pretty sure Karma has Ava on its list—high on its list—with this very reason right by her name. I think you'll get a free pass with Karma on this one, Evie."

"Yeah, but…" I blow out a breath. "In a twisted way, I owe Ava, Dad. She saved Casey's life."

"She didn't save Casey's life. She gave us the opportunity to be able to. And it's not like she did it out of the goodness of her heart. She took from you as much as she gave."

*He's right. I know he is, but…*

"How do I tell Adam? How do I even start?"

"You start at the beginning."

"I just…" I drag a hand through my hair. "I don't want to hurt him any more than I already have."

"You're hurting him right now."

"Dad…" I wince.

"No. I'm sorry, Evie, but you need to hear this. If Adam is the same kid I knew ten years ago, then you're hurting him. That kid loved you. He loved you like I loved your mom. It's that once-in-a-lifetime kind of love."

"He doesn't feel like that anymore." I shake my head, my eyes starting to fill with tears.

"That kind of love doesn't die because of time or distance, Evie. Believe me, I know." There's an ache in his voice, which makes me hurt more. "It's always there, burning away. And Adam's might be hidden and buried under a lot of anger and pain at the moment, but it is still there. He just needs to find his way back to it. But that can only happen with you being honest with him."

"But what if—"

"There are no what-ifs, Evie. You should have told him at the time. I should have made you and stopped what was happening. Maybe we could have done things differently. Got Casey that treatment some other way. If I'd—"

"No. There was nothing you could have done. You had already done everything you could. Bending to what Ava wanted was all I could do. She held all the cards."

"But it meant that you lost everything."

"I didn't lose everything. I still had you and Casey. That was the most important thing."

"You had to make a sacrifice, one you shouldn't have had to make. Not at your age. Not at any age."

"I'd do it again in a heartbeat. I would never choose differently." No matter how much it hurt. It would have hurt more to lose Casey.

At least I knew Adam was out there, living and breathing, even if it was without me.

Dad lets out a hard sigh because he knows I'm right. He would have made the same choice if he were in the same position. He'd have done it without a thought.

I might have made the choice, but I did think about it, just for a second. I paused because of how much I loved Adam.

"Just…tell him the truth, Evie. He has a right to know." My dad picks his coffee mug up and gets up from the table. "I'm going to make some pancakes. Casey will be up soon, and she'll be hungry. You want some?"

"No, I'm good. Dad?"

He stops by the kitchen door.

"What if I tell him, and he doesn't understand why I did what I did? What if he doesn't forgive me?"

"How could he not? You chose to save a life over having one with him. He would have done the same."

"I know, but…I should have told him sooner."

"Yeah, you should have. But we all make mistakes, Evie. Just stop looking for reasons not to tell him and start looking at all the reasons you should."

I sit there, tracing patterns on the tablecloth. Left with Dad's words in my ears, I think about Adam, think about what I should do.

Then, I think about what I saw at the beach house in his old bedroom.

Getting up, I go to my bedroom. I open my closet door and reach up, getting the shoebox I keep on the shelf.

I open it up, looking down at the mementos I kept. There are old ticket stubs from movies Adam and I saw together, the receipt from the meal he took me to on my birthday—that night was the first time we had sex—and the pencil I used to sketch that first picture I did of him, the one that hangs on his old bedroom wall with the others. Then, there's our wedding photo. We got two copies—one for us and an extra for Dad to have.

I pick up my old diary, which I never did write in, and open it to the center page. A pressed rose is there, the one Adam bought me on our first date. I pick up the folded piece of paper in there, close the book, and open the paper up. It's the last picture I ever drew of him, the one I started the night I left but never got the chance to finish. I could never bring myself to finish it.

I don't even realize I'm crying until a tear hits the paper.

Carefully drying it away, I fold the paper up and put it back into the box.

I kept our memories for all these years because I never stopped loving him. Maybe he kept his memories for the same reason. Maybe Dad's right. Maybe Adam's love for me isn't gone. Maybe it is just buried under all his anger and my lies.

His words from last night come back to me…

*"Tell me the truth—tell me why you left, and I'll see if it's something I can get past, see if we can move forward together, so I can try to learn to trust you again."*

The only way I stand a chance of ever getting Adam back for real, of having a future with him, is if I tell him the truth.

I could tell him and still lose him, but it's a chance I have to take.

Getting to my feet, I make my way through the apartment. I poke my head into the kitchen, the scent of pancakes filling my nose.

"I'm going out," I say to Dad.

He looks over his shoulder at me. "To see Adam?"

I blow out a breath. "Yeah."

"'Bout time." He smiles. "And, Evie? It's gonna be okay."

I leave the house, praying that Dad is right, that everything is going to be okay, that Adam will be able to forgive me.

## Evie
### BEVERLY HILLS · AUGUST 2015

*I* park my car just a little down the street from the studio and turn off the engine.

Nerves suddenly get the better of me, and my body starts to tremble, my heart beating faster.

*Come on, Evie, you can do this.*

Taking a deep breath, I get out of my car, hands still trembling, and I walk to the main doors.

As I'm walking, it dawns on me that he might not actually be here. I know his note said he left early because of a work emergency, but I thought that was a lie. And it is a Sunday. I figure the office would be closed. So, he could actually be at the hotel or anywhere else.

*Crap.*

*Well, I'm here now. Might as well check it out.*

When I get there, the main door is locked. But I can see a huge-looking guy with a bald head, wearing a security uniform, sitting in the reception area. His eyes are looking down at the desk, probably reading a magazine. Well, that's what I would do if I were stuck in an empty office building on a Sunday afternoon.

I tap on the glass door, catching his attention.

He looks at me, so I wave my hand.

He gets up from his chair, not looking particular happy about the fact, and walks over to the doors.

He stops by the door and gives me a look that screams, *What the fuck do you want?*

"I, um…is Mr. Gunner here?" I say through the glass.

"Who's asking?"

"Evie. Evie Taylor." I won't pull the wife card again.

"Well, Evie-Evie Taylor, you are out of luck. Mr. Gunner isn't here."

*Fuck. Fuckity fuck!*

*Fine, I'll just ring him and find out where he is.*

I turn to leave, then, I realize that I don't have my cell with me. It's in my bag, which I left at home.

*Triple fuck!*

*Fine, I'll just go to the hotel, and if he's not there, then I'll go home and get my cell—*

*Hang on.*

I turn back to the glass door and rap on it again, louder this time.

Huge guy had almost made it back to the reception desk.

He stops and lets out what looks like a massive sigh. Then, he turns back to me and marches over again.

"What?" he says loudly.

"You said Mr. Gunner isn't here."

"He isn't." His expression practically growls at me.

"But that's his car right there." I point to the black Range Rover Sport, which took me to Malibu yesterday. I recognize the license plate.

His eyes narrow on me. "Look, girlie, I get that you think that you're something special and that Mr. Gunner will take one look at you and cast you as the lead in his next movie. Maybe he will. Who knows? But that day will not be today. I am under strict instructions to not bother him, and you, girlie, are not worth my job."

"But that's just it, I'm not an actress. I'm not here to see him about a movie. I'm actually…well, I'm a friend of his."

He lets out a laugh that sounds like he's heard this a thousand times before. "If you were his friend, then you would be standing on this side of the door, and not out there, wouldn't you?" He gives me a knowing look, folding his arms over his huge chest.

I let out an awkward sounding laugh. "Well, that's the thing you see…Adam—Mr. Gunner, he doesn't like me very much right now and with good reason. So, that's why I'm out here, and not in there. And that's why I need to see him. So, I can explain."

"No can do, girlie."

*Ahh!*

"*Please.*" I press my palms to the window. "All I'm asking is, you call him and let him know I'm here. I'd call myself, but I left my cell at home."

He stares at me for a long moment. So, I put my best pleading face on.

All I seem to do is plead with Adam's staff to let me through to see him.

"Fine!" he huffs, reaching for his cell. He dials and puts it to his ear.

"I'm sorry to bother you, sir, but I have an Evie Taylor here—um-hum. Okay." He hangs his cell up, putting it back into his pocket. "He doesn't want to see you."

"He said that?"

"Those exact words."

*Jesus.* If he had smacked me in the face it would have hurt less, than Adam's blatant rejection.

I watch as his expression changes to one of pity. I'm guessing it's because of the look on mine.

I'm *really* close to bursting into tears.

*Come on, Evie, pull yourself together.*

I suck in a breath, blinking the tears away. "Well…thank you for trying. I really appreciate it."

I turn from the door and stand there, not sure what to do.

Then, from nowhere, I feel a sudden rush of anger.

*Well, fine, Adam doesn't want to see me, but I want to see him.*

He asked me last night for the truth, and that's what I'm here to give him.

I've come this far, and I'm not going anywhere until I see it through to the end.

With determination in my stride, I march over to the bench across the street, facing the studio, and I sit down on it.

Okay, it might not be a massive declaration. And I'm actually starting to feel a little deflated, and stupid, now my ass is on this bench.

But this is all I've got. So, I'm staying put.

I mean, if I wanted to go all out, I could have tried to ninja kick open the door to the building—not that I know ninja, or how that would have even worked out—and if I had by some miracle made it through the door and made a dash for Adam's office, I'm pretty sure huge guy in there would have taken me down in seconds and then called the cops. And I really don't feel like spending the night in a prison cell.

So, I'm waiting here until Adam leaves the building.

Then, I'll make him talk to me. Well, I don't need him to talk. I just need him to listen.

# TWO HOURS LATER

Bench seats are not made for long periods of sitting. Both my ass cheeks are numb, and my back hurts.

Two hours is a really long time to sit. I mean, one hour is a long time, but two? This second hour feels longer than the first. I never realized how long an hour was until I had to sit here for two of them with absolutely nothing to do but stare across the street at Adam's building. And God knows how much longer I'm going to be here.

But I'm not moving. I'll sit here all night if I have to.

I know I look like a complete dick, but I don't care.

I came here to tell Adam the truth, and that's what I'm going to do. I'm going to wait here until he leaves his building, and then I'm going to force him to hear me out.

I can't remember the last time I sat for this long. Sure, I sit and watch TV for long periods of time, but I'm watching TV.

The last time I just sat like this and did nothing…was ten years ago—with Adam. We would sit up on my rock or just on the beach, and I would sketch for a while. Then, when I was done sketching, we'd just watch the sun fade into the ocean together, just being together.

Now, I'm sitting here alone, outside his building, and he doesn't want to see me.

I tilt my head back and stare up at the sky. The clouds are slowly drifting over.

I let myself remember good times, happier times.

There was a time when I wouldn't allow myself to remember the good times because it hurt too much to do so.

It hurts now, but it's a pain I'm familiar with.

A shadow falls over me. I drop my gaze, and my eyes meet with Adam's.

My breath catches. My heart stills.

"You suck at stakeouts," he says in a low voice that sends chills over my skin. "I could have left the building and walked straight past you, and you wouldn't have noticed."

He sits down beside me on the bench. My eyes follow him. My mouth is open.

*He's here.*

"Wh-why didn't you?"

"Well, after two hours of waiting, I figured you must really want to talk to me."

He was watching me from his building. I don't know what to make of that. I want to think he hasn't given up on me completely. But he might after I tell him what I'm here to say.

"I did—do. I do want to talk to you." I swallow nervously, my mouth as dry as the desert. "And I would have waited for as long as necessary to make that happen." I need him to know that.

"Well, I'm here now, so talk."

I take a calming breath, trying to gather my thoughts. I've got so many things to say to him, and I want to make sure I get this out right and say everything I need to.

I blow that breath out and start talking, "I lied to you." I look at him and hold his stare. "That first day in your bungalow at the hotel, you asked me if Ava had anything to do with my leaving, and I said no. That was a lie."

His expression doesn't change, but I see the anger flickering to life in his eyes.

He doesn't say anything. He just continues to steadily stare back at me.

I look ahead, my hands pressed together in my lap, as I keep talking, "That night of your bachelor party, after you left, Ava turned up at the beach house. I didn't let her in at first. I told her that you'd gone out. She said she wasn't there to see you. She was there to see me. She told me that she had a proposition for me. I told her that whatever it was she had to say, I definitely wasn't interested."

I meet his eyes. I want him to see the truth in mine while I say this, "I was ready to shut the door in her face. Then, she started telling me things. She knew stuff about me, my family…about Casey. She knew that Casey was dying. And she told me there was a way she could help with that.

"There was a medical trial with a new drug, a potentially life-saving drug. It wasn't available to the general population. It was invitation only. But she told me that she knew people, powerful people, and that she had gotten Casey a place in the trial. What she wanted in return for that place was…" A sudden tear drips from my eye. I quickly catch it. "I had to give you up. She brought annulment papers with her. She'd had them drawn up the day after we'd gotten married."

I already have his attention, but that garners me more of it. I know what he's thinking. He didn't tell her until days later that we were married.

"She knew the moment we got married. Your credit card payment…" I explain.

Dawning settles on his face, but he still doesn't say anything.

I drag my fingers through my hair, my eyes looking straight ahead again. "Ava told me she would let Casey have that place on the medical trial, and she would pay for any medical aftercare that she needed. In return, I had to leave you." I look at him again. "It was you or Casey. I didn't have a choice, Adam."

Tears start to flow freely, and I let them. I don't care that we're out in the open.

"I had to sign the annulment papers. She made me leave my wedding ring behind. I didn't want to. I wanted to keep something, so I would have…something. But she said I had to hurt you. Apparently, the annulment papers wouldn't be enough. Then, I had to leave the papers there and go with her. I wasn't allowed to ever contact you again. I said you would look for me—because I knew I would have looked for you. I guess part of me wanted you to find me…and the other part was scared that, if you did, she would pull the plug on Casey's treatment. But she said she would make sure that you wouldn't find me ever. I guess she made good on that promise.

"She had travel already arranged to take me, Casey, and Dad straight to San Francisco. I guess…I guess I was a sure thing. I had to go home and tell Dad while she waited outside. It…wasn't easy." I brush away some tears.

"We never told Casey…how we got her on the trial. We just told her that her doctor had gotten her on it. We quickly packed what we needed, and then Ava put us on a private jet at LAX to San Francisco. We were met by someone at the other end. We were put in an apartment near the treatment facility, and Casey started treatment the next day."

I turn to face him. "You have to know, I never took any of Ava's money. If she spent any money on Casey's treatment, I didn't know about it. And as soon as Casey was given the all-clear, we left the apartment and got our own place. Any follow-up treatment Casey needed was paid for by me and Dad. By that point, I had a full-time job working in a coffee shop."

"Why didn't you come back after Casey's treatment was over?" His voice is even, detached…cold.

My heart stills. "The treatment took a long time. She was on the drugs for six months. It was a year before we got the all-clear. Then, we had to wait for follow-ups. And there was always that fear that it might return. Back then, Ava was my only option to getting Casey the treatment she would have needed if the tumor came back, like it had before. And…when we finally realized it wasn't coming back…so much time had passed." Biting down on my lip, I dry my face with my hands and stare down at the pavement beneath my feet. "I wanted to come back…so badly. But I didn't know how to. I was…scared."

"Of what?"

"That you wouldn't be waiting when I came back. That…you'd have moved on."

He lets out a humorless laugh. "I never did. That was your mistake, Evie."

"I know that now. But back then, I didn't. And I know this will sound screwed up, and you might not want to hear this…but part of what kept me away was Ava. It wasn't fear—well, maybe a little fear." I laugh a sound much akin to his. "But no matter how I felt about Ava, no matter how much I despised how she'd treated you all your life or what she did to us—how she used my sister dying for her own gain—I…well, I owed her. I still have my sister, living and breathing and healthy, because of Ava. I made a deal with her. I made a deal that I would never tell you the truth…a deal that I'm breaking right now."

"You make it sound like you're doing me a fucking favor," he snaps.

It's the first real sign of emotion I've gotten from him. Even though he's snapping at me, I cling on to that as hope.

"That's not what I'm trying to do. I'm just…I'm trying to make you understand why I couldn't tell you back then."

"You could have told me the instant you got back."

"You're right. But when you've held something in for so long, kept a secret…it's hard to get the words out. It's hard to say them. And even still, I felt like I owed Ava. And…I know your relationship with her was difficult, but she's your mother. I didn't want to be the reason your relationship with her ended. I know what it's like to lose a mother, Adam. I didn't want that for you, no matter how she is. I couldn't be responsible for that."

"But you could be responsible for obliterating my heart?" He stands abruptly.

My eyes follow him. Then, the rest of me does until I'm standing in front of him. "Adam—"

"I don't know what to do with this, Evie. It's too fucking much. Too fucked up. I want to be angry with you. I am angry with you. So very fucking angry." He turns his face away.

When he brings it back to me, my heart splits in two. I see it there in his eyes. I've lost him again, and this time, it's for good.

"Last night, I asked you for the truth. I told you, if you gave it to me, I would see if I could get past it. Today, you've given me that truth. Now, I'm telling you...I can't get past it. And I don't mean what you did—choosing Casey and saving her life. Hell, I would have told you to go, had I known. I would have told you to leave me, if it meant saving Casey's life.

"But the moment you knew Casey was better, whether it was one year or five or ten, you had the chance. Countless times, you had the chance to tell me throughout those years and all these weeks since you've been back. But you've chosen not to because"—he lets out a disbelieving, painful-sounding laugh—"you *owed* my cunt of a mother. You left me here in the dark all of that time, knowing what she'd done to me, what she was still doing, what she's always done to me—controlled my fucking life! That"—he points a finger at me, taking a step back—"I can't forgive.

"So, now, I'm telling you, Evie, leave me the fuck alone. I don't want to see you. I don't want to hear from you. I don't want to breathe the same fucking air as you. I want you gone from my life. I want you to disappear just like you did ten years ago. But this time, I want you to stay gone."

Then, he turns and walks away down the street.

All I can do is watch him go, my arms wrapping tightly around my stomach.

Whoever said the truth would set you free was a fucking liar.

I don't feel free. I don't feel better. I feel like I've just put a gun to my own heart and pulled the trigger, and now, I'm bleeding out, slowly and painfully.

## Adam
### BEVERLY HILLS · AUGUST 2015

*I* walk for a long time, just wandering around Beverly Hills, because I don't know what else to do. There's too much in my head, too many thoughts, and I don't know what to do with them.

And when I finally do know, I find myself standing outside the place I once called home.

Only, it was never a home. It was just a house I lived in.

It might be a big, beautiful glamorous house that most people would give their right arm to live in, but I hate this house. It reminds me of the loneliness I felt growing up. It was the place where I learned I was never wanted. I was needed for the studio and nothing else.

This house represents the emptiness inside of me, the emptiness that Evie used to fill—before Ava stole that from me, too.

Using the key I have, I let myself in through the main gate.

Millie, my mother's longtime housekeeper, is waiting at the open door for me.

"Adam, so good to see you. It's been so long. Your mother never said you were coming. I would have prepared some food for you." Millie always has the need to feed me. Maybe it was her way of trying to make me feel better while I was growing up, trying to fill the lonely empty void she could see in me.

Maybe she still sees that now.

"She didn't know I was coming." I force myself to smile at her.

"Well, she's out back, on the terrace. I'll let her know that you're here."

"No, it's fine." I stop her with my hand. "I'll surprise her."

"As you wish." She smiles. "Can I get you anything to drink? Your mother's having her afternoon cocktail. You know how she likes them."

"No, I'm fine, Millie. I won't be staying for long."

I walk through the vast empty house. The house that is void of family photos. The only pictures hanging on the walls are of Ava—portraits, photos of her movies, pictures of her with other celebrities.

But none of me—no baby pictures, no school pictures.

No family photos of me, her, and Eric.

*But why would there be? We were never a family.*

Neither of them ever gave a fuck about me. I was a means to an end for both Ava and Eric.

I step out onto the terrace. Ava is sitting on a chair at the table, sipping on a cocktail. Her cell is in her hand, and she's reading something on it, like she doesn't have a care in the world. Maybe she doesn't.

"Hello, Ava."

She jumps at the sound of my voice, nearly spilling her cocktail.

"Jesus, Adam. You startled me. What are you doing here?" She shoots me a cool look as she puts her glass and cell down.

I stand for a long moment, just staring at her, trying to understand. I know why she did what she did. I just can't understand how, how she's done any of the things she's done to me.

She might not have beaten or abused me, but she has broken and hurt me over the years. Left me alone as a child. Starved me of love. Tore me down. Had me do her bidding. Take care of things no kid should have to take care of. Had me see things no kid should see.

She might not be an abuser in the physical sense, but she's an abuser of the heart and mind. Yeah, she's definitely one of those. A fucking expert at it.

"I know, Ava."

"You know what?" she snaps. "You're going to have to be a little more specific than that, Adam."

And that's because there are probably so many things that she's done to me, taken from me, that I don't know about. Probably never will know about.

But this is the big one, the one that mattered.

The only thing that ever mattered to me, Ava stole from me.

I take the seat on the other side of the table from her, so I can look her directly in the eyes when I say what I have to say.

"I know about Evie and what you did."

She freezes. And even though I knew it was the truth, seeing her reaction slides that knife in a little deeper.

I don't love Ava, but she is my mother.

To a small child, a mother is a god. No matter how awful that mother is to the child, no matter the shitty, wretched things she does, the connection that child has to his mother just can't be severed. It can be broken but never severed.

And that's where her power lies.

It's the power that Ava has always had over me.

She has always had the ability to cut me hard, and there is fuck all I can do about it. I can hate her, loathe her, but at the end of the day, buried deep down in there, I'm still that little kid who just wants his mother to love him. And I'm the one who gets cut each time he remembers she doesn't love him and never has.

I know that. And I'll live with that.

Because living my life without Ava in it will make things a whole lot easier.

"I don't know what you're talking about." She frowns.

Denial—Ava's first line of defense. And it's not because she's worried about hurting me. It's because she's worried about losing something—the part in her latest film...or more, losing the studio.

Everything always comes back to the fucking studio.

I lean forward, putting my arms on the table, linking my fingers together. "I'm not here to play games. Admit it or don't—I really don't care. I know the truth because I know you. I should have figured it out years ago. *That* was my mistake, a mistake I won't make again.

"Ten years ago, you stole from me the most precious thing in the world. You used the love Evie had for her dying sister to get what you wanted from me. I knew you were evil, Ava. I just didn't know *how* evil.

"So, now, I'm here to return the favor, eye for an eye and all that. Your career is over. The film is gone. And all future films with Gunner Entertainment are gone. The studio is gone. I had already planned on giving it to Richard, but being the stupid fuck that I am, I was going to give Richard the studio with the terms that he keep you on with a full-time contract. That's gone now. And you know, without me, you won't get a foot in the door there. Or anywhere. Because you're old and washed up, Ava. And I will personally ensure that you never work in this town again." I push my chair out, standing.

She still hasn't said a word. She's just staring at me, expressionless.

"Taking Evie from me bought you ten more years at the studio. I hope they were worth it. Goodbye, Ava." I turn and start to walk away.

I hear the scrape of her chair against the ground.

"I will fight you on this, Adam, and you know I'll win," she says from behind me. "You can't just take my studio from me."

Stopping, I turn back. "I can do whatever the fuck I want because the studio isn't yours. It never was."

"It was always mine."

"Then, you should have done a better fucking job at ensuring that you got your name on the deed!" I yell.

She lets out a shallow laugh and sits back down on her chair, casually tossing her arm around the back of it. "Have your little show, Adam. Stomp your feet. Give your little speech. I'm not worried. You know why? Because you'll be back. You *always* come back. And I always get what I want."

I look at her, releasing a tired breath. "You're right. I always say I'm going to leave. Always say no to that favor you want. No to that part in a film you desire. No to that problem you need me to sort. But then I always come back. Always do that favor. Always give you that part in the film. Sort that problem for you. But the thing is, Ava"—I take several steps toward her until I'm looming over her— "people have a fucking limit, and I reached mine when I found out that you stole my wife from me! Now, if I can't make it any clearer that you and I are done, then you can take my extended silence as my answer."

Then, I walk out of that house with the sounds of her yelling behind me, and I feel truly free for the first time in my life.

# Adam
## BEVERLY HILLS · AUGUST 2015

*I*'ve tried not to care, tried to pretend that I'm okay.

I know the truth now, so I can move on.

But thing is…I can't.

The more I've sat and thought about what Ava did, the angrier I've gotten. The more I think about Evie keeping the truth from me while climbing into my bed and making me want her again, the more the anger manifesting inside me grows like a fucking tornado, and I feel ready to blow.

But worst of all, I miss Evie. I miss her more than I did in all those ten years combined. Even now, after all of this, I still love her.

Can you believe it?

I'm seriously fucked in the head.

But then Evie's absence has always been the hole in my life that I could never fill.

Maybe I deserve this shit because I'm such a stupid fucker.

The bartender has just poured me another drink when the door to Reilly's opens.

Max slides onto the stool beside me. "Good to see you're spending your time off work effectively."

"What are you doing here?" I pick up my glass and take a drink.

"Well, I haven't heard from you in five days, which is a long time in our world and weird for you 'cause you always have been such a needy bitch when it comes to me. So, I called your office, and Mark told me that you weren't in today and that you haven't been in all week, which is odd for you because you never take a day off, not even when you're sick. You know, I've never been able to wrap my head around that because you fucking hate that studio."

"And your point is?" I take another drink before placing the glass on the bar. I curl my hand around it.

"My point is, the studio is where you hide. You hide in that place, burying your shit in your work. You're not there, so something is severely wrong. I called your cell." He points to it on the bar. "And you're clearly ignoring that, so I stopped by the hotel."

"You stalking me?"

"Always. You know I can't get enough of your hot body."

That almost gets a smile out of me.

"I'm your friend, Adam. I wanted to check on you and make sure you were okay." Max tells the approaching barman, "Couple of fingers of whiskey and another of whatever this asshat is nursing." He squints at my glass. "What the fuck is that anyway? Water?"

"Vodka, neat, assface."

"If you're looking to get shitfaced, that's the way to do it."

That's exactly what I'm aiming to do, what I've been doing these past few days.

I take another sip of vodka, enjoying the burn down my throat. It's the only thing currently reminding me that I'm still alive.

"I saw Evie." Max drops the words into the air like a dirty bomb.

My eyes flash to his, and I slam my glass back down on the bar, nearly breaking it.

"You, what?"

"I saw Evie."

"When?" I grit my teeth so hard that my jaw might shatter.

"When I stopped by the hotel, looking for you, and of course, you weren't there. So, I went to the coffee shop."

The barman puts our drinks down on the bar.

"Thanks," Max says to him. He picks his glass up and takes a sip. "Fuck, that's good."

"Evie?" I growl. *Jesus, it hurts to even say her name.*

He puts the glass down, lifting a brow at me. "By the way, thanks for telling me that you were still married, fuckface. Gotta say, I didn't see that coming."

I don't even have the energy to be sorry for not telling him. "I told you that she was back. You didn't need to know any more than that."

Ignoring me, he says, "I'm going to take it that you were severely embarrassed by the fact that you never filed those annulment papers, and that's why you hid it from me. For future reference, I already know what a loser you are, so you don't need to hide anything from me. And I'll also forgive you for not telling me that you were fucking her again because I already figured that one out. You don't need to be a genius to know that—even though I am a genius. You and Evie never could be in the same room without mauling each other."

"I don't want a fucking history lesson," I say through gritted teeth. "What I want to know is why you were talking to Evie."

"Because you were in hiding, and she clearly had the answer as to why."

"And?"

"And we talked. She told me everything, including what happened the other day. She told me why she…left you."

I look away.

"I'm so sorry, man." His hand comes down on my shoulder, squeezing before letting go. "Ava hit a new all-time low with that one."

I drop my head, running my hand into my hair. I don't want him to see the hurt on my face.

"I knew you had to be in a fucked-up place right now, and as you weren't at your office or the hotel, I thought I'd check Reilly's before driving to Malibu. Glad you were here though 'cause I don't enjoy driving in traffic. But I didn't want you to be alone. Thought you might need to talk."

"I don't need to talk. And I really fucking want to be alone."

"Yeah, you might think that, but I know you, and you being alone right now isn't the best idea. You definitely need to talk because I know exactly how you're spinning this shit in your head. So, let's talk." He turns in his seat to face me.

Moving my hand from my head, I flick a look at him. Then, I pick my vodka up and drain the glass. Pushing the glass down the bar, I get the fresh vodka Max ordered for me, and I down that as well. I lift a hand to the barman, signaling for another.

"There's nothing to talk about, Max," I say when I realize he's not going anywhere.

"Sure there isn't. You find out that your mother fucked you over in the worst possible way, and now, it's just plain sailing and daisies."

I ignore him, staring straight ahead.

"Evie's hurting, Adam, just as badly as you are."

"I don't care if she's hurting," I snap.

I don't mean that. It kills me. It's all killing me.

"She should have told me the truth." My fingers curl around the empty glass.

"Come on, you're not being fair."

"Not being fair? Are you fucking kidding me?"

"Just hear me out." He holds his hands up. "How could she tell you? If she told you, then she'd lose that chance to save her sister's life. She was eighteen years old and faced with an impossible choice. If that were me and you needed a treatment that could possibly save your life, I would have chosen you without a second thought. Nothing would have been more important than saving the life of my brother—because that's what you are to me, Adam. You're my brother.

"And Casey was just a kid, a kid who was dying. You know how much Evie loves her. She was working her fingers to the bone to help pay for her medical bills. If Casey had died, Evie would have blamed herself. And Ava clearly knew that, and she used it to her advantage. We know the kind of people Ava is. Evie doesn't. She didn't stand a chance against Ava. Neither of you did really. The instant Ava decided she wanted Evie gone, there was only ever one outcome, and it was the one that happened The only good thing that came out of Ava's fucked-up-ness, doing this to you and Evie, was saving that kid's life.

"You're laying the blame for this at the feet of two people when it should be only one. Evie was just as innocent as you were in this. You need to stop punishing her. Either forgive and take her back, or let her go once and for all."

"I have let her go."

"No, you haven't." He shakes his head at me. "You don't know how to. You haven't been able to for the last ten years, and you sure as shit can't now. So, you either stay here and mope like a little bitch, or you go find Evie and talk to her."

I stare at him, a pain in my chest so severe, it feels like my heart is failing. "I can't forgive her." I shake my head. "She should have told me the truth the second she came back. She didn't. And I can't forgive her for that."

"Yeah, she should have. But put yourself in her place. She was a kid when it happened. She's held on to that shit for ten years. Then, she gets back, and you're here. She was afraid to lose you again. She might have left, but she lost you as well."

"That you talking or her?"

"Me."

"You on her side or something?" I snap.

I snap because I hear the truth in his words, but I don't want to accept them.

I want to feel angry. If I don't have my anger, then I have nothing.

"Stop being a dick, Adam. You know I'm on your side. I'm always on your side. That's why I'm saying these things. I want you to be happy. And Evie's your happy." He finishes his drink and stands.

"You leaving?" I ask in a low voice.

"Yep. Things to do, pussy to see." He winks.

I watch him walk toward the exit.

My mind races through the words he just said. But I keep looping back to one thing.

*Evie's my happy.*

He's right. I've never been happier than when I was with her.

And I've spent a really long time being miserable.

I don't want to be miserable anymore.

"Max?"

He stops opening the door, and looks across at me.

I move my eyes from him, staring straight ahead, unable to look at him while I say, "Evie…is she still at the coffee shop?"

I don't have to see his face to know the smug bastard is smiling.

"No. She said she was heading home right after I left." Pause. "You need a ride to her place?"

Swiveling my stool around to face him, I let my feet hit the floor. "Yeah," I say, finally meeting his smirking eyes. "A ride would be good."

"Guess my pussy can wait." He grins. "Come on then, loser. Let's go get your wife back."

# Adam
## CULVER CITY · AUGUST 2015

"So, I'm driving you to Evie's, but you don't actually know where she lives." Max sighs.

"I know which apartment building she lives in, assface. I just don't know which fucking apartment it is."

"Well, I guess you could try knocking on every door in her building. Or you could do a John Cusack and stand outside her apartment building with a boom box, playing your song to get her attention. Only problem with that is you don't have a boom box, so you'd have to play it from your iTunes app on your phone, which isn't anywhere near as cool, or romantic. And can you even get Bon Jovi on iTunes?" Max grins at me.

"You're a dick." I chuckle, shaking my head.

I could do what Max said, play her our song, but I have a much simpler, although less romantic, way of finding out which one is her apartment.

Getting my cell, I dial the number of my divorce lawyer.

"Adam, you must be a mind reader. I was going to call you today," Harrison says.

That makes me pause. "Why?"

"I got signed divorce papers back from Evie's lawyer with new terms and a letter from Evie personally. Do you want me to send it over to you?"

"No. Read the letter to me now," I say, my heart climbing into my throat.

"Okay. One sec. Just let me grab it."

I hear rustling and then the tearing of paper.

"Right, I got it. Okay, so it says, *'Adam, I know you said you didn't want to see me or hear from me again, and I'm not writing this letter to go against that, but with the divorce still in process and how the terms stood with the money, I couldn't not write to you. I don't want the money, of course. So, I'm rejecting the terms. I'm not doing that to piss you off or to hang on to you in some vain hope that you'll find a way to forgive me because I know you won't. And I understand why. But I also know you want me gone, so I know you'll accept my terms. My lawyer has redrafted the papers, and I've signed them on the terms I originally set—abandonment on my part. I will leave our marriage as I entered it—well, in the financial sense anyway. All you have to do is sign, and then your lawyer will file them. And then I guess that's it.*

*"I just want to say I'm sorry one last time. I'm sorry I lied to you. I'm sorry I let you down. I know my apologies don't count for anything anymore, but I just needed one more chance to say it.*

*"And just…be happy, Adam. You, more than anyone, deserve happiness. I'm just sorry it couldn't be with me. Yours always, Evie.'"*

My whole body hurts, like every single one of Evie's words have cut into me, and I'm bleeding out from the wounds.

"Adam, are you okay?" Harrison's voice comes down the line.

I take a breath, forcing words to come. "Harrison, do you have Evie's address? All I need is her apartment number."

"Sure."

I hear some keys tapping.

"She's in apartment ten."

"Thank you."

"What do you want me to do with these papers?" he asks. "Should I send them to you to sign?"

"No. The only thing I want you to do with those papers is burn them."

I hang my cell up, shoving it in my pocket.

"Everything okay?" Max asks me, concern in his voice.

I shake my head. "I just need to see Evie. Now."

I feel Max's foot press down on the gas.

Five minutes later, he's pulling up outside of her building.

"You want me to wait?" he asks as I'm getting out of the car.

"No, it's fine. You go."

I sprint to her building. Catching the door as someone's leaving, I go straight in and run up the flight of stairs, heading for her apartment.

Reaching apartment ten, I bang on the door.

The door opens, revealing Evie's dad. He looks the same, just a little older and a little grayer.

"Mr. Taylor," I say slightly out of breath, having a déjà vu moment. I remember doing this exact thing after the first time Evie met Ava.

"It's still Mick, Adam." He gives me a slight smile. "I'm guessing you're here to see Evie. She's not home, I'm afraid."

"Oh." Disappointment lines my insides. "Do you know where she is?"

"Why do you need to see her?" His tone is fatherly, protective.

"I just need to talk to her."

"Look, Adam, I know you were the injured party in this whole thing, but Evie hasn't had it easy these last ten years. I don't want her getting hurt any more than she already has been."

"We were both the injured party in this," I tell him.

"I'm glad you see it that way now. And while you're here, I'm going to tell you that I am sorry for everything that happened back then."

His apology surprises me. "You don't have anything to be sorry for."

"I didn't stop it. I could have stopped it."

"No, you couldn't have. None of us could have. Your daughter was dying. You had a chance to save her. No father in his right mind would turn that down, no matter the cost."

Mick's eyes sweep the floor. "Saving Casey's life cost me Evie. It wasn't in the same way it would have cost me Casey, but I did lose Evie that night." His aging eyes meet with mine. "After she left you, she was never the same. I'd just gotten her back after she'd lost her mother. Then, when she left you...she never got over losing you.

"I've watched her these past few weeks since you've come back into her life, and I saw her on Sunday after she talked to you. She's hurting, badly. Evie has experienced more hurt and loss than a girl her age ever should have to. You have the power to hurt her unlike anyone else, Adam. So, I'm asking you, as her father, if you're here to hurt her any more, please don't. Just leave her be. *Please.*"

His words are imploring, and they cut me.

I knew Evie was hurting. I knew I hurt her. But hearing it come from Mick...makes it more real.

It was hard for me to see Evie's pain because all I could see was my own. But hearing from him how bad things have been for her, how badly my words and actions have affected her…I just need to see her and fix this.

"I'm not here to hurt her, sir. I swear to you. I just…I need to see her."

I'm not going to stand here and tell him the words I need to say to Evie. That I'm beyond sorry for what I said the other day. That I forgive her for waiting so long to tell me the truth. That I don't care about any of that anymore. All that matters is her. Having her with me. That I need her in my life. That I love her.

The only person who is going to hear those words is Evie.

Mick blows out a breath. "Look, I don't know where she is. All I do know is, she's been coming home late from work every day this week. Usually, with sand all over her shoes."

He gives me a look, and I instantly know where she is.

"Thank you," I tell him in earnest.

Then, I'm running through the building to the exit. My cell pressed to my ear, I call Max. "Where are you?"

"Still outside. Figured I'd wait for ten in case she kicked your ass out."

"You're the best fucking friend ever. I ever tell you that?" I say as I burst out the exit, seeing his car still parked there.

"You have but not enough. I could do with hearing it a little more often."

"Needy bastard." I laugh before hanging up my cell.

I open the car door and climb inside.

"Where are we going?" Max asks, putting the car in drive.

"Malibu."

# Adam
## MALIBU · AUGUST 2015

This is corny as fuck, and I'll probably get hassle from the neighbors for the noise, but Max was onto something with the song thing.

From the moment we got together, Evie and I were always living on a prayer. It was the right song for us back then, and it's the right song for us now. Only, we aren't living on a prayer anymore. And we will make it this time.

Okay, that was weak as shit. But it's the best I've got right now.

I can see Evie sitting up on her rock, her arms wrapped around her legs, her chin resting on her knees, as she stares out at the ocean.

I knew she'd be here. This was our place. It's *still* our place.

I set my docking station up, sitting it on the patio railing. I skip through to our song, turn the speakers up loud, and press Play.

The intro starts quietly, and then it's quickly blasting out.

I see the moment she hears the song because her whole body stiffens. Then, very slowly, she looks over her shoulder in my direction.

I'm already moving across the sand, toward her, my heart beating like a motherfucker.

Her eyes are locked on me as I close the gap between us, but she doesn't move.

When I reach Evie, her eyes finally leave me, flickering to the beach house and then coming straight back to me. She looks unsure. And she's been crying. I can see the red around her eyes now.

And in this moment, I promise myself that she will never look this way again, not because of me.

"I'm sorry," she says softly. "I thought you came to the beach house only on weekends. I'll go."

She starts to get up, but I stop her.

"No. Stay there." I climb up the rock until I'm sitting in front of her.

She's so fucking beautiful. Even sad, she's beautiful.

"You haven't come up here to push me off, have you?" She gives a half-smile.

I know she's trying to make light of the situation, but I can hear the nerves in her voice. I know she's scared. I am too. I'm fucking terrified.

"No. I talked to my divorce lawyer. But that's not why I came. I was already on my way to see you."

"Okay. But let me say something first, Adam. Well, give you something. I was going to send it with the papers, but I changed my mind, decided to leave it at the beach house for you. Well, put it in the mailbox for you." She reaches into her bag and pulls out a sheet of paper. It's folded, frayed on the edges. "The night I left, I was working on this. I never had a chance to finish it because Ava turned up…but I've kept it all these years. I've been coming here the last few days to finish it off. I always draw better here. And I've finished it now, and I wanted to give it to you."

I take the paper from her hand and open it up.

It's a drawing of me, standing by a car.

"It was from that night, the night I left. I was always sketching pictures of you. You know that. And I don't know why…just that night, the image of you standing by that taxi stuck in my head, and I wanted to capture it. Almost like…like I knew I would never see you again." She blows out a breath, her lip trembling. "And I just…I want you to know, that night I left, I *was* thinking about you. I was always thinking about you. For the last ten years, you are all I've thought about."

Tears sting my eyes and burn down the back of my throat. Swallowing, I rest the drawing safely in my lap and then look up, meeting her eyes with determination in my own.

"I'm not signing the divorce papers that you sent to my lawyer, Evie. I'm not signing them because I still love you. I've loved you from the first moment I saw you sitting up here, and I've loved you all the time in between. Every second of every minute of every day for the last eleven years, I have loved you. And I forgive you for not telling me the truth. I understand why you didn't. Now, I need you to forgive me, too."

"You've done nothing wrong," she whispers.

A tear runs down her cheek. I catch it falling, taking her face in my hand. I feel her body tremble under my touch.

"Ten years ago I failed you. I didn't protect you from Ava. I should have. I know how fucking sick and twisted she is. I should have seen it coming, that she wouldn't just roll over and accept me leaving the studio after we got married. That she would go after you. In the back of my mind, I always thought that maybe she had something to do with you leaving, but I didn't push hard enough to find out the truth. I'm sorry for that. And…" I hang my head in shame, and my hand drops from her face, feeling like I don't deserve to touch her in this moment. "I'm so sorry that I was cruel to you the other day when you told me the truth. The things I said…the harsh, horrible things…I didn't even mean them."

I feel her hand touch my hair, her fingers running through the strands. It soothes me. Mends the broken parts in me.

Then, her hand moves down my face as I lift my eyes back to hers.

I see her eyes shining with tears. But they don't look like tears of sadness. I see only happiness in them.

"I love you," she says. "I don't care about anything else. The past, the things we've said or done to hurt one another—none of it matters now because you're here. And I love you so very much."

"God, I love you." I grab her face in my hands, and I kiss her.

Then, she's kissing me back.

Our song is still playing in the background, and nothing has ever felt sweeter.

Breaking away from her lips, panting, I press my forehead to hers. "Just promise me one thing."

"Anything."

"Don't ever fucking leave me again."

"Never," she promises. "I will never leave you again."

# Epilogue

## Evie
## MALIBU · JULY 2016

Today is what would have been our eleventh wedding anniversary. I say *would have been* because Adam and I are divorced.

Don't panic. It's not a bad thing. It's a good thing, a really good thing.

Getting divorced was our beginning again. And we needed a new beginning.

We were apart for so long that we needed to go back to the start.

Our marriage, in a lot of ways, was the end for us.

We needed new.

Getting divorced and finding us again were new—but Adam has told me in no uncertain terms that I will be Mrs. Gunner again one day.

And honestly, I can't wait for that day.

But for now, I'm happy. We're happy.

In the beginning of us starting again, we just dated. We got to know each other again, and it was fun. It's still fun.

We deserved fun after everything we'd been through.

But this is Adam and me, and just like twelve years ago, when we first met, we were pretty much inseparable from the get-go.

Two months after we got back together, I moved into the beach house with him. If Adam had had his way, it would have been two days. I just hadn't wanted to rush things even though I really did want to rush things. My restraint deserves an award.

Dad and Casey moved to Malibu with me. It's only around a thirty-minute drive into UCLA from Malibu, and Casey and Dad were ready to get back to the beach. I didn't want to be too far away from them, so it's worked out perfectly. I'd wanted them to move into the beach house with us, and Adam had been fine with that. But Dad had said that Adam and I needed our own space to just be together. He was right. Crazy as it sounds, even though we were married, Adam and I haven't ever lived together properly.

We had that one week after we got married, but I was bouncing between the beach house and our old apartment.

Now, we're actually living together, and it's amazing.

Adam left the studio. He wanted to sign it all over to his Uncle Richard, but Richard wouldn't let him. He said Adam might not want any part of it now, but that could change in the future.

Richard proposed a fifty-fifty split of the studio with Adam as a silent partner. Adam reluctantly accepted, but I think a part of him still likes having a reason to be in contact with his uncle.

Richard runs the studio day to day, but he brings over things for Adam to sign when necessary, which is often. I'm glad that Adam still has a connection to someone in his family.

Ava, on the other hand…well, she's no longer a part of the studio, of course. Adam had it in his head to ruin her career. In the beginning, he was hell bent on revenge.

I told him that the best form of revenge is no revenge at all.

Ruining Ava's career wouldn't change the things she had done to him. It wouldn't make him feel better.

I told him that he needed to let Karma have at her.

Surprisingly, he listened. And he just let go of all the anger and bitterness he felt.

I know he's freer for it.

Me? Well, I'm still waiting for Karma to do her thing. She sure is taking her sweet time.

Ava has stepped away from Hollywood. But only to New York to star in some big prime-time show. Last I heard, there was talk about an Emmy nomination for her performance.

I guess some people really are the kind who fall in the ocean and come up with a gold watch.

But what Ava doesn't have is love.

She can star in as many films or TV shows as she wants, win as many awards as she can, but one thing Ava will always be is alone.

Adam never will be alone. He has so people who love him—me, Max, Richard, Dad, Casey, and Grady. And that is what counts above anything else.

Speaking of Grady, he and Adam opened a surf school together. It's called Off The Hook Surf School.

Adam got the qualifications needed to be able to coach surfing. I've never seen him happier than when he is working there with Grady.

Grady still has the Shack, and since I've been drawing again, he's started letting me sell some of my drawings there.

I also help out with admin stuff at the Off The Hook. Dad is working there, too. He's been doing the accounts. He actually started doing them for the Shack, too. It's good to see him getting back to doing what he enjoys. He can't do anything too taxing, and it takes him longer to do the accounts than the average person would, but it's not like there's a rush, as they're the only the accounts he does.

And Casey is doing well in school. She's happy.

Life now is as it should have been ten years ago.

I'm not bitter about losing those ten years. Do I wish that Adam and I had had all that time together? Of course I do. But we didn't, and it meant Casey was able to get well. It was how it had to be. Both Adam and I have accepted it because we have each other now, and that's all that matters.

My cell starts to vibrate on the table beside me, pulling my eyes from the view of the ocean.

I see the name on the display, and I instantly feel sick.

I knew this call was coming. I just didn't expect it to be today.

Knowing I can't hide from this, I take a deep breath and answer, "Hello?"

"Evie Taylor?"

"Speaking."

"I'm calling with the test results."

Another deep breath. "Okay. Go ahead."

"Positive."

My breath rushes out of me.

"Miss Taylor?"

"Thank you for letting me know." I hang my cell up, curling my fingers around it.

My stomach clenches. My mouth dries.

Adam and I are in a good place. We're settled and happy. We've found our happy.

This…I just don't know. This could change everything, and not for the better.

My fingers immediately go to the necklace hanging around my neck. The necklace that holds my wedding ring. Adam has the same, his wedding ring on a chain around his neck. He wanted us to wear them close to our hearts until the day we're ready to put them back on our fingers.

But this, now…I just don't know—

"Hey, babe."

I turn at the sound of Adam's voice. He must have just gotten home from the surf school. I didn't realize the time.

He's smiling. I guess I'm not because he takes one look at my face, and his smile drops.

"What's wrong?" He steps through the door, coming out onto the patio, toward me.

"Nothing." I clear my expression, forcing a smile.

*No more lies, Evie. Tell him.*

"You're sure?"

I'm nodding my head before I realize I'm doing it.

*Tell him.*

His expression clears. "Good, because we need to go."

"Go?" Then, I immediately remember. "Oh God, yeah, the surprise."

Adam told me this morning right before he left for work that he had a surprise for me.

"It's not *the* surprise. It's *your* surprise. And you seriously forgot?" A smile tips up the corner of his lips. "Because I remember you trying to persuade it out of me this morning."

"I didn't forget. I just misplaced it for a second. And yes, I'm ready to go." I get to my feet.

I'm trying not to think of what surprise he's gotten for me on what would have been our wedding anniversary. He hasn't mentioned the fact of what today is, and neither have I.

I figure he hasn't mentioned it because he's leaving our past behind and focusing on the future.

Adam wraps his arms around my waist and brushes his lips over mine. "Tell me you're happy."

He asks me to say this all the time. It's the reassurance he needs from me. And I will give Adam anything he needs.

But right now, I feel deceitful.

I press my lips together and smile. "I'm happy."

And I am. I really am. I just don't know if he's going to be happy when I tell him what I have to tell him.

*I have to tell him.*

"Me, too, babe. Now, let's go 'cause I'm dying to show you your surprise."

*I will tell him. I'll just do this surprise thing, and then I'll tell him.*

# Adam
## MALIBU · JULY 2016

Evie is distracted. She thinks I can't tell, but I can tell. And it's making me nervous because I have no clue what's bothering her.

I want to ask her, but I don't want to spoil things before I get to give her the surprise I've been working on all week.

I've bought her a space to sell her drawings in. It's right by the surf school and just recently became available. Evie can turn it into a gallery and won't have to sell her drawings out of the Shack anymore.

I know she'll be pissed that I'm spending money on her, but since she wouldn't let me give her any in the divorce that she pushed for—yeah, I'll be rectifying that little issue soon enough because I want her to be my wife again—I've taken to buying things for her.

I've also taken to doing good things with my money, which equates to mostly giving it away.

I just kept enough to keep Evie and me comfortable. She's struggled financially all her life, and I don't want that for her anymore.

And I still get a lot of earnings from the studio, which helps to facilitate the surf school. It's still in its early days, so it's not making a lot of money right now.

But aside from setting up the surf school, I've given almost all my money away to charity. I gave the money to people who needed it a lot more than I do. Mostly kids who got the shit end of the stick in life.

I know money doesn't fix everything. I grew up with it in abundance, and my life was still shit.

Love is what kids need. But I can't love every kid in the world.

I can, however, give them a roof over their heads, clothes on their backs, and food in their bellies. So, that's what I've done.

And I feel fucking good about it.

Doing things for others makes me feel great, especially doing things for Evie.

I pull up outside the shop and turn off the engine.

I feel her looking at me. Giving her a big smile, I climb out of the car, meeting her on the other side.

Taking her hand, I walk her to the door.

"What's this?" she asks.

"It's yours." I open the door, walking inside. "You need somewhere to sell your drawings. This came up a week ago, so I bought it. It needs a bit of a cleanup, and some paint on the walls, but I think it's a great spot for you to sell your work, and the bonus is you'll be close by me all day long. I know we're not married in the technical sense anymore, but to me, Evie, you will always be my wife, so it's also an anniversary present."

She's staring at me, her eyes look a little glassy. Then, she glances around the store. Her eyes come back to me, and then out of nowhere, she bursts into tears.

"Hey." I go straight over to her, taking her in my arms. "What's wrong? Is this too much?"

"No. It's amazing. It's all amazing. Perfect. You're perfect." She pulls back, wiping her face with her hands. "Everything is just so perfect. And I didn't get you anything because I didn't know you were going to buy me something so huge. And I have something to tell you, and I'm scared that I'm going to ruin everything."

My heart pauses. "Ruin everything? How?" My voice is tight. I can't help it. After everything I've been through with Evie, it would be strange if I wasn't tense right now.

She stares at my face. Her lips tremble, and she presses them together.

I know she does that when she's holding something in, something she's afraid to tell me.

My heart starts back up, beating in double time. "Evie, just fucking tell me because you're really scaring me right now."

"I'm pregnant."

Everything stops for me. I can't breathe. I can't think. All I can hear are those words.

Her words.

*"I'm pregnant."*

*Evie's pregnant. She is carrying my baby inside of her.*

"I missed my period," she starts to babble. "I was too afraid to take a home test, so I went to the doctor yesterday, and they took blood to do a test. I didn't expect to hear for a few days, so I was forcing myself not to think about it, but they just called right before you got home, and they confirmed it. You had this surprise, and I didn't want to spoil it for you. Fuck, I'm spoiling it." Her voice shaking, she pushes her hands through her hair, stepping back. "We're divorced, and we've only been back together for a year, so I understand if this is too much too soon, and I can—"

"Don't finish that sentence." I take her face in my hands.

Tears are swimming in her eyes, and I can feel tears filling my own. I know that might make me a pussy, but right now, I don't care.

"Nothing has ever been too much too soon with you." I brush my thumbs over her cheeks, tracing her tears. "You're really pregnant?" My voice is suddenly hoarse.

Blinking, she gives a tentative, watery smile. "Yes, I'm really pregnant."

I kiss her, hard. Then, I pull her into my arms, hugging her tight.

"Can't breathe." She laughs, softly.

I release my hold on her. Stepping back a touch, I press my hand to her stomach.

"My baby is really in there?" I can hardly believe it.

She nods her head, gently. "Yeah, it's really in there."

I drop to my knees in front of her. My face level with her stomach, I hold my hands on her hips, speaking to her belly…speaking to our baby…my baby, "Hey, if you can hear me in there, I'm making you a promise right now. I promise to be the best daddy ever. I promise to be there for every single moment in your life. Your first word. First step. I will be at every school play, every baseball game—"

"What if it's a girl?" Evie brushes her hand through my hair.

I glance up at her. "Then, I'll drive her to every ballet class and be there for every single show she does." Looking back to her stomach, I press my lips to it. "Whatever you are, whoever you choose to be, whatever you want to do…just know that I'll be there. And there will never be one second of your life that you don't know that I love you."

I hear a sob come from Evie, causing me to look up at her again.

She comes down to her knees, facing me. Tears are soaking her cheeks. "God, I love you, Adam Gunner."

"And I love you, Evie Taylor. I've loved you since I was eighteen years old, I will love you till the day I die, and I'll keep on loving you after that."

Sliding my hands around her neck, I undo the clasp on her necklace and hold her wedding ring between my thumb and finger. "I think it's time for me to put this back on your finger. What do you say?"

She reaches out and removes my own chain from around my neck, holding my wedding ring in the palm of her hand. She looks at me, smiles and says, "I say, yes."

# Acknowledgments

I'm half-asleep while writing this. This is what I get for doing it at the deadline, so I'm going to keep this really brief and just say a big thank you to all the usual suspects—my husband, Craig, and my children, Riley and Isabella.

Trishy, Sali, Christine, Jovana, and Naj—You are all amazing in your own unique, beautiful ways. I heart you all to the moon and back.

Of course, thank you to my agent, Lauren, who continues to put up with me constantly changing my mind without a word of complaint.

Also, a huge thank you goes to all the bloggers who tirelessly help to promote and get the word out about my books.

And lastly, my readers—Thank you for continuing on this amazing journey with me.

See? I told you it would be brief. ;)

Until next time…

# About the Author

SAMANTHA TOWLE is a *New York Times*, *USA Today*, and *Wall Street Journal* bestselling author. She began her first novel in 2008 while on maternity leave. She completed the manuscript five months later and hasn't stopped writing since.

She is the author of contemporary romances *The Mighty Storm*, *Wethering the Storm*, *Taming the Storm*, *Trouble*, *Revved*, and *Revived*. She has also written paranormal romances, *The Bringer* and The Alexandra Jones Series. All have been penned to the tunes of The Killers, Kings of Leon, Adele, The Doors, Oasis, Fleetwood Mac, Lana Del Rey, and more of her favorite musicians.

A native of Hull and a graduate of Salford University, she lives with her husband, Craig, in East Yorkshire with their son and daughter.

Printed in Great Britain
by Amazon